WORTH THE RISK

THE RISKS WE TAKE DUET 1

BELLA MATTHEWS

Editor: Jessica Snyder, Jessica Snyder Edits

Copy Editor: Dena Mastrogiovanni, Red Pen Editing

Cover Designer: Shannon Passmore, Shanoff Designs

Photographer: Wander Aguiar, Wander Aguiar Photography

Formatting: Savannah Richey, Peachy Keen Author Services

Dena ~ Thank you for taking such incredible care of my words.
Each book shines brighter because of you.

The course of true love never did run smooth.

— WILLIAM SHAKESPEARE

PROLOGUE

Not all love stories have happy endings.

Romeo and Juliet died for love. I wanted to live for it.

I wanted a love that would set the world on fire.

But I never thought I'd strike the match and watch it burn.

CARYS

"ARE YOU SURE I LOOK OKAY?" I EYE MYSELF IN THE BROKEN mirror hanging crooked on the wall inside the Rathskeller's ladies' room. The bar is about fifteen minutes from campus and lucky for me, pretty lax about looking too closely at fake IDs. "Honestly, Emerson. I don't know how I let you and your brother talk me into this. I sing show tunes, not rock. The guys would be better off with you out there, rather than me."

I tug down the black leather skirt I borrowed from Em, then turn and look at myself from another angle.

Seriously, how does this cover her ass when it barely fits over mine?

I paired it with a strappy, bright-pink lace corset I had sewn over spring break. Em convinced me this was a killer pairing, then tossed me her black knee-high boots to finish it off. I barely recognize my own reflection tonight. It's a far cry from my jeans and Chuck Taylors, but I definitely don't hate what I see.

My entire body vibrates with nervous energy as I glare at her through the hazy reflection in the filthy mirror. "Swear to God, if the stage is too high, I'm going to be showing everyone my panties." At least I didn't wear the G-string panties that match the corset. Then I'd really be in trouble.

Emerson smacks my hands away and turns me to look at her. "It's a two-foot platform, Carys. And it's not like you're doing a burlesque routine out there." Her eyes run over me from head to toe before stopping on my boobs. "Besides, nobody is going to be looking up your skirt. They'll be too busy trying to look down your top." She runs her fingers over the lace. "Can you make me one of these? I love it."

I nod my head and try to resist glaring at my roommate. "Your rationale is sometimes a scary thing, Em." Last July, we were notified that we'd been paired up as roommates for our freshman year at San Diego University of the Arts. By the time we moved in a month later, I knew she was meant to be in my life.

The two of us were thrilled.

My family, not so much.

They hated that I was moving to the opposite side of the country for college while they were all together in Kroydon Hills, Pennsylvania. Not in an unsupportive way, more like a *you're the baby, and we don't want to stop interfering in every possible, increasingly boring aspect of your life* way. They'd never understand.

I guess it makes sense when all I've ever told them is that I needed to figure out what I want to do with my life. Being away from their expectations is supposed to be helping with that.

So far, so good.

"Jack and Theo wouldn't have asked you to sing with them tonight if they didn't think you could do it." She fluffs my dark hair over my shoulders, then hands me her red lipstick. Always red for Em.

Her brother, Jack, and his fraternity brother Theo are two years older than us, and formed their band, Six Day War, last year. They've been the Friday night house band here at the Rat for a few months, but their original lead singer/bass guitarist quit abruptly. He bailed when he got an offer to sing backup for some top-forty pop band, leaving them without a singer days before their next show. I think they're trying to find another guy to replace him, but Emerson offered my somewhat willing vocals for tonight, while Lucas, one of their younger fraternity brothers, is filling in on the bass, so they didn't have to cancel tonight.

What sounds like a fist slams against the wooden door, and I jump a mile. "Come on, Carys. It's time."

My eyes fly to Emerson's, the nerves ratcheting up. "I don't know how I let you talk me into this."

"Suck it up, buttercup. You've sung in front of an audience before. Hell, you sang the National Anthem at the Philadelphia Kings football games in front of thousands. You can handle a little rock music in front of a bunch of drunk college kids at a hole-in-the-wall bar." She smacks my ass. "Now get moving."

One more deep breath and I raise my head to look at her. "I'm going to get you back for this. When you least expect it, I'm coming for you."

Em laughs in my face. "Ooh. I'm terrified. Now get out there and get this shit done."

I barely manage a single step through the door of the bathroom before Jack, Theo, and Lucas converge on us. Theo's twirling his drumstick through his fingers until he sees me and stops. He whistles and motions for me to spin. "Hell-o, Miss Murphy."

Theo is a goofball.

He never takes anything seriously, but he's pretty to look at, so most people with a pulse give him a pass.

Okay, and *maybe* we also hooked up after one too many games of beer pong at the beginning of last semester. "Looking good, Carys."

"Of course, she looks good. But how're you feeling? You

good to go?" Jack hands me a bottle of water and then gets smacked by his sister.

"She's better than good. She's great. Knock 'em dead, guys." Em squeezes my hand and throws a smile Lucas's way before she disappears down the hall.

"I hate to sound like an idiot." Lucas blushes—actually blushes. "But is it 'Carrie' or 'Caress'? Half the people I know call you CC, and I have no clue how to pronounce your name."

"Don't worry about it." I turn to look at the bassist, and my nerves subside for a minute. "No one does. It's *Care-is*. It's Welsh, meaning *loved one*."

I spent my life on a stage. I've sung anything from Gershwin to Lin-Manuel Miranda and everything in between, but musical theater is a very different beast, and there's a slight tremble in my voice, betraying my nerves tonight.

Jack rubs my shoulders for a second until I inch away. He's always very handsy, although not in a creepy way. But I have no interest in flirting with my roomie's brother. "You've got to relax and have fun, Carys. This is going to be awesome. You've got this."

Theo laughs, then taps Jack's chest with his drumstick. "Dude, did you look up inspirational phrases on your phone or something?" He looks at me, his dark brown eyes full of excitement. "Just have fun, C. Enjoy the rush. Now let's go."

Fun. Right.

Theo and Jack walk ahead, but Lucas holds back. "Hey, Carys . . ." Lucas is the classic all-American guy. Blond hair. Blue eyes. Broad shoulders. He almost reminds me of someone else who checks those boxes. But Lucas could never compare to that guy. "Is Emerson seeing anyone?"

"Nope." I cringe internally because I know Em is not

going to date a musician. She'll flirt with him, but she'll never give him a real chance. She's told me that more than once. Emerson and Jack's dad is a rock-star drummer, and, according to her, the industry breeds an unhealthy dose of insecurity, raging narcissism, and instability. She wants no part of this world. Never has.

But I don't tell Lucas any of that.

He'll find out, one way or another.

The four of us take to the makeshift stage, the bright lighting making it difficult to see anything beyond a few feet in front of the platform. I run my hands lovingly over the microphone as the guys set up. The familiarity from years of performing soothes my heightened nerves as Jack introduces the band.

"How ya feeling, San Diego? I'm Jack, and we're Six Day War." A roar comes from the crowd. The guys' audience has been steadily growing since they started playing here, and the loud applause makes me happy for my friends. "We've got a few guest performers with us tonight, so how about you show 'em how we do it at the Rathskeller? Let me hear you!" Jack nods once at Theo, who taps his sticks together as he counts us off. He looks over at me from across the stage, his lips kicking up on one side, and my body hums with excitement as I sing the first haunting lines of "Voodoo" by Godsmack.

The first few lines of the song are all me, and I slip right into them like I fucking own them. These people might not have known they were getting me instead of the former lead singer tonight, but as soon as I open my mouth, they shut up and take notice. My nerves evaporate as I realize singing for a band doesn't have to be any different from what I'm used to doing on stage. I can still hide behind a character like I would in a musical. This time, I'm playing the lead singer in a band.

The chaos of the loud voices in the bar fades away, and we all fall into perfect sync like I've done this a million times before. Jack roams the stage with his guitar, playing into the sultry beat of one of my favorite songs as he shows off for the crowd.

It's always been easy for me to get lost in the music.

And this song makes me feel like a sexy rock goddess who can own the stage right along with Jack.

Before long, I'm dipping into the lower range of my voice, emphasizing the rasp I can use with ease after years of voice lessons, and bringing the crowd with us.

By the middle of the song, all my earlier nerves are forgotten, and I've slipped into a space I know well. Emerson was right. Performing is performing, no matter the audience or the music. I'm actually having fun on stage, moving around comfortably and playing it up with each of the guys.

Owning it the way Jack does.

Well . . . at least I'm trying to.

COOPER

"How long do you think we've got before we're spun again?" I ask as I look around at my teammates. The adrenaline from the last thirty-six hours is still thrumming through my veins. My SEAL unit, Charlie Team, just finished what was originally supposed to be a six-month deployment.

It ended up being closer to seven months.

And we had to go silent for the last two weeks while we were off base. We had everything under control, but no calls were happening. Those of us with people waiting back home had no choice but to leave them to worry alone.

Everything came together quickly at the end, and Charlie Team was on a plane home a few hours later.

My teammate Axel looks at me with waning patience.

Like I'm a puppy who just peed on the floor.

Sidenote, he's usually a dick.

Axe is a few years older than me. He likes to play the part of the clown who just follows commands. But he's a great guy most of the time.

"We got back ten hours ago, Sinclair. Take a breath. It should be a few weeks."

"Leave him alone, Axe. I remember when *you* were the new guy. I'd never seen such an ugly fucking shade of green before." Rook, our team's number two, taps his bottle of beer to mine as the bartender pours a round of shots. He's a lot more reserved than Axel. Not much of a talker.

The old wooden door to the Rathskeller opens with a loud crack as the wind catches it and our team leader, Ford, walks through with his arm around his wife, Jessie. Master Chief Ford Walker has been a member of Charlie Team for the better part of the last fifteen years, and the team leader for the last seven. According to him, this bar has always been home to our team. Even if tonight there seems to be an abundance of college kids filling the tables.

Ford looks around to see who's here as he guides Jessie to a barstool next to Axel and nods at the bartender. "Hey, Brenda. You leave that husband of yours yet?"

"Oh, Brenda, we could be sister wives." Jessie claps her hands together animatedly.

Brenda snaps her bar towel at Ford and smiles. She's maybe five feet tall and at least sixty-five, but she's a tough broad who I wouldn't want to cross. Ford loves to make her blush, and then she turns into a high-school, shy girl. "Oh hush, you." She slides two bottles of beer in front of them. "I'm just glad my boys are all home safe."

She claimed Charlie Team as hers long before I joined the teams. Her son was a SEAL who died in Iraq after 9/11. His framed picture hangs on the wall of the bar, along with a few other fallen brothers. She looks over each of us with watery eyes, then turns quickly and heads to the other end of the bar to help some douche in a pink polo with a popped collar.

Never a good look.

Ford eyes me, Axel, Linc, and Rook. "Where's Trick?"

"He's putting Wanda to bed, then meeting us here." Wanda's a Belgian Malinois fur missile, who also happens to be the best damn military working dog there is.

"One of these days, he's going to get in trouble for keeping that dog at the house instead of on base with the other military dogs." Jessie may be Ford's wife, but she tends to try to mother the rest of us.

"Come on now, Jessie. Don't try to act like a hard ass. You love Wanda." Ford pulls Jessie against him and whispers something in her ear, eliciting a giggle.

"I just want him to be careful. I know his dad pulled a few strings, but former SEAL or not, it makes me nervous. And before you say it, I know he's also the top MWD trainer in the country and Wanda was one of his pups. But I grew up military, and they don't bend rules. I just don't want to see any of you get in trouble." She sips her beer, ignoring the chatter happening around us.

Axe downs his shot of whiskey, then wraps his arm around Linc's shoulder. "You gonna be my wingman tonight, kid?"

Jessie laughs into her beer. "You need a whole wing team, Axel."

"You're just pissed you settled for the old man next to you before you met me, Jess." Axe grins like he thinks he's being smooth, then elbows Linc.

Linc cups the brim of his University of Georgia baseball cap and looks away, distracted. When the teams were drafting from my BUD/S class, Charlie Team picked Linc and me. That was two years ago. But we'll both be the two new kids on the team until somebody else comes along, and the guys take every chance to remind us.

"Come on, man." Axe leans down and adds, "I'll even teach you how to pick up a woman."

Linc shoves Axel away. "Nah, brother. You're on your own." He tracks a beautiful brunette who's walking toward the bar, then stands to make room for her. "Ma'am." He lays his Georgia accent on thicker around the ladies.

"Hiya, handsome." She leans against the bar between

Linc and Axel. "Geez, is there a *Magic Mike* convention in town?"

"No, ma'am." He offers her his hand. "I'm Linc."

Her dark blue eyes are nearly purple as they drag over the length of him before settling on his face. The rest of us watch in amusement as she answers, "Emerson."

"Can I buy you a drink, Emerson?" He steps in closer to her and waves down Brenda. "Brenda, can we get . . ."

"A hard cider, please," Emerson answers as an appreciative smile spreads across her red painted lips.

Axel adds, "And another round of shots too, Brenda."

The static of a microphone hums through the sound system. "How ya feeling, San Diego? I'm Jack, and we're Six Day War. We've got a few guest performers with us tonight, so how about you show 'em how we do it at the Rathskeller? Let me hear you!" None of us are paying close attention to the dude on the mic. We're too busy watching Linc, the eternally shy member of the team, kicking some pretty impressive game with the even prettier girl.

But then the song starts, and the voice that's singing . . .

That voice.

I turn around to take in the stage and stop dead in my tracks.

Because on stage is my Carys Murphy.

My best friend's little sister.

My new stepsister. Well, not completely new. But thanks to my dad marrying her mom a few years ago, she and her brother, Aiden Murphy, are now family. Never did feel like it though.

Only she doesn't look like Carys. She looks like a fucking wet dream come to life.

Linc must see it, too, because he elbows me. "Holy shit, man. Isn't that Murphy's little sister?"

"That's my roommate," Emerson announces proudly. "She's singing with my brother's band tonight."

Linc's the only one of my teammates who's met my friends and family from back home.

The other guys have no idea why I can't take my eyes off the woman on that stage.

They have no fucking clue how hard I've tried to look at her like a little sister for the last three years. It was a lot easier before that. She was two years younger than me in high school, and she didn't hang out with us. But she's grown up, and she's not looking so damn little tonight.

"Wait—what?" Emerson screeches as the song switches to an upbeat rock song. Carys's voice morphs from haunting to powerful as she smiles and leans back against the dude playing the guitar. Linc turns so Emerson can hear him better and whispers something before she turns around and raises a hand to slap my chest.

Her mistake.

I catch her wrist, blocking the attempt before she can come close to landing a blow. I've only been in the Navy for a few years, but it's been long enough to learn I don't like someone I don't know touching me. And I don't like being fucking hit.

She stares at me. "Umm. You can let go now."

"Ready to keep your hands to yourself?" I quickly glance her way, and she glares at me until I release her wrist.

"Sorry. I wasn't going to hit you. Just a little shove. I feel like I know you already." When I give Emerson a *what the actual fuck* look, she cocks her head to the side. "Seriously. If he's right, and she's your stepsister, that makes you Cooper, right? I mean, one of her stepbrothers is old and married and playing for the Philly Kings. That means you're the Navy SEAL." Realization crosses her face, and she looks at the group of us with a new interest. "Oh. Now that makes sense." Her excitement grows, and Linc and I groan. "That makes you all—"

Ford steps in. "That makes us all military, ma'am. And we'd like to leave it at that, since this fine establishment is full of people."

Emerson lets that sink in for a minute. She probably has no idea that SEALs don't publicize what we do for a living, even if the movies like to portray it differently. We don't have to hide it, but it certainly makes it easier to keep our covers intact later if we don't brag about it now. "Does Carys know you're back?" Her eyes are sharp. Scrutinizing. She eyes me carefully and pops a perfectly arched eyebrow. "She didn't mention anything."

Before I get the chance to answer or even comment on the fact that this woman knows who I am, Axel jumps in. "You know the babe up there with the fuck-me shoes and suck-me lips?"

I grab the front of his shirt and shove him back against the bar so quickly, the rest of the team doesn't even realize what's happening. "Not another fucking word comes out of your mouth about her. Got it?" The words rip from somewhere deep in my chest.

He smiles a shit-eating grin right back at me but places both hands in the air. "I'll take that as a yes." Then he looks back at the stage. "Ooh, this is going to be fun."

"Leave her alone, Axe man. Carys is a good girl." Linc shoves Axe back a step.

Emerson's head swivels like it's going to pop right off her body, and she rolls her eyes toward Linc. "Umm, pretty sure she'd hate being described as a good girl."

Axe licks his lips, looking like Emerson just handed him the Christmas present he'd been begging Santa for. "Even better. A good girl who wants to do bad things. This is gonna be so much fun." Yup, and there's the dick. But it's not like he'll actually do anything. At least I don't think he will. Not once I lay it down.

"Not a chance, brother. Carys is off-limits. Pass it around. Nobody touches her. Nobody thinks about her. Nobody disrespects her. Got it?" The venom in my tone leaves no doubt about the significance of that statement.

He nods his head while he watches me with unreadable eyes. "Yeah, man. I got it." Then Axel grabs Trick as he walks through the door to go play a round of darts in the back.

"I'm guessing Carys didn't know you were home. She hasn't mentioned anything." Emerson sips her cider as she stands between Linc and me. "That's definitely something she'd have mentioned."

I bring my eyes back to the front of the room.

She's in her element, completely at ease and having fun.

It's a really good look on her.

She works the audience and owns the stage, commanding the attention of every person in the room.

Including me.

Fuck me.

She turns, and the lights hit her just right, illuminating soft curves a man would kill to memorize. A bead of sweat slides between the valley of her full breasts, and my mouth waters. I shouldn't notice, but it's impossible not to. My cock stirs in my jeans, and I try to discreetly adjust myself in the middle of the bar.

This could be a problem.

CARYS

"Holy hell. That was *insane*." My entire body is alive with excitement as we finish our set and move into the hall behind the makeshift stage.

"Heads up," Jack calls to me as he tosses a bottle of water my way.

A bottle I watch sail past my head in slow-mo.

I was never the athlete in the family.

"Talk about an adrenaline high. I mean, I've sung in front of a crowd before, but that . . . That was intense."

Theo wraps his sweaty arms around me and drags me in close. "Carys, that was crazy. You were amazing." He plants a sloppy kiss on my cheek before he lets go. "You were good in practice, but that . . . *that* was unreal."

"Thanks." I step back as I wipe my damp face. There was never any real chemistry between Theo and me. It was a onetime thing after a few too many beers when I was trying to convince myself I'd made the right decision in moving across the country. It was fun . . . Enough.

Not necessarily a mistake.

But not my shining moment either.

I've definitely gotten the feeling that Jack was disappointed to not have joined us that night, but there was no way that was happening, and he's never pushed it since.

Jack slings his arm around my shoulders. "Come on. We need to celebrate that performance." He looks back at Theo and Lucas. "I think we've found our sound."

I don't correct him, but as much fun as that was, I don't know if I want to do it again. Singing for fun is one thing. But these guys want to get picked up by a label, and that's not something I'm looking for.

The four of us break down the equipment and pack it up for the night before we walk out into the main bar and spot Em in the crowd. She's standing at the bar, laughing at something the guy on her right just said, and although he looks familiar, it's the guy on her left who has my every nerve ending firing like the Fourth of July.

It takes a second before my brain catches up to my heart.

But there he is.

The man I followed across the country.

Even if he'll never know it.

The man I've been in love with since I was fifteen years old.

A fact I'll never tell him.

The clueless man who'll never look at me as anything more than his best friend's little sister or, *lucky me*, his somewhat newly minted stepsister. Even if it's been three years since his dad married my mom, it still seems brand new when I look at him, and my traitorous heart skips a beat.

"Oh my God. Coop?" I take a tentative step forward, then stop, hesitating, my eyes locked on Cooper Sinclair. It's been almost a year since the last time we saw each other.

Since the last time our entire family was together.

There's no hesitation in Cooper's movement when he closes the distance between us and wraps his strong arms around me, lifting me off my feet. He even buries his face in my hair when he whispers, "God, it's good to see you, Carys." His warm breath tickles my skin and sends my hormones into overdrive with awfully un-sibling like thoughts racing through my mind before I'm placed back on solid, albeit slightly shaky ground.

And damn . . . he's never hugged me like that before.

I look over every inch of the man in front of me, from the well-worn jeans hanging from his lean hips to the broad shoulders stretching a black Kings t-shirt covered by a gray-and-black flannel—shoulders that are definitely more muscular today than they were when I saw him last summer. And those impressive muscles that make your neck look big and strangely strong while also making girls like me think stupid thoughts.

His sandy-blond locks are longer than I've seen on him in a while, which matches the scruff growing on his gorgeous face. And damn, he wears it well. Then again, I can't think of a single thing this man doesn't wear well.

Finally, I manage to get myself together and out of my lust-fueled haze enough to ask, "Do Mom and Coach know you're home yet? Everyone started freaking out when you went radio-silent a few weeks ago. Nattie's been blowing up the group text for days. I don't know who she thought would be stupid enough to hold out information on her."

"I haven't had the chance yet." He has the good graces to look ashamed as he answers. "We just got back today."

I shove a hand at his chest. "You need to at least text and let everyone know you're safe and home." A round of snickers come from the group of guys standing behind him.

Big guys. Sexy guys. All of them overly interested in our conversation, and I have no problem glaring at each and every one of them.

I recognize his friend Linc from the few times I've met him before, but I guess the rest of the guys are members of his team.

A guy with shaggy auburn hair and a barrel chest covered in a *Texas Forever* t-shirt steps forward. "Ain't ya gonna introduce us, Sinclair?"

Cooper throws his elbow back into the guy's gut. "Nope."

"That's not very nice, Cooper." I reach my hand out to the dude with the Texas twang. "Hi. I'm Carys. Great shirt. Classic show."

"Marry me?" he asks as he brings my hand to his lips. "Wait . . . don't answer that yet. Movie or show?"

Cooper groans, but I play along.

"Hmm." I put my finger to my lips and pretend to think about it for a minute. "Show all the way. Tim Riggins was my first love."

"Sinclair, man. Where you been hiding her?" he taunts Coop with a smile on his gorgeous face.

Cooper gives the dude a glare that would scare the shit out of most men, but not this one.

"Well, future wife, I'm Axel. But you can just call me 'future baby daddy.'"

A very unladylike snort creeps up my throat. Mom would be ashamed of me. "Wow. Does that usually work for you, Axel?" My playfulness comes easily with the comfort that comes from being around Cooper.

Axel's lips tip up in a crooked, cocky grin as he smiles, and I move down the line and offer Linc a big hug before I'm introduced to the rest of the guys. Standing in the middle of this group should be intimidating, but the smile on Cooper's face puts me at ease.

Emerson pats the stool next to her for me to sit down as I catch Cooper out of the corner of my eye, taking his phone from his pocket. His fingers fly over the screen, and the cellphone in my pocket vibrates. My eyes connect with his, and he flashes me his panty-melting smile as he holds the phone in front of his face.

My cell vibrates again. Then again and again.

Guess he just activated the family phone tree. When my mom married Cooper's dad a few years ago, they started a group text. It includes the two of them, my older brother, Aiden, Cooper's twin sister, Nattie, and their older brother, Declan, his wife, Belle, and me. We're a bit of a motley crew.

Well, truth be told, *they* mainly are.

I was always the younger one.

A little on the outside, looking in, I guess.

Envious of the friendships they had.

Wishing I was included.

I tug my phone from the pocket of my skirt, and sure enough, the text notifications are lighting up my screen.

Coop: Finally got back to Cali today.
Aiden: What? Like we missed your ugly face or something?
Nattie: You seriously couldn't text one damn time in the last three weeks, Cooper Sinclair?
Declan: Don't give him shit, Nat. He's texting now.
Nattie: Bite me, Dec. You try sharing a womb with someone for nine months and then be expected to go without talking to them for weeks at a time. It blows.
Coach: I don't want to hear about what blows or who bites, Natalie Grace. Give your brother a second to breathe.
Coach: Glad you're home safe, son. FaceTime tomorrow?
Coop: Yeah, Dad. I'll call tomorrow. Love you guys.
Nattie: Fuck that.

Cooper's phone rings a second later, and I can't help but giggle. "Nattie, right?"

"Yeah." He looks at the screen, then back at me. "Don't leave before I come back inside, okay?"

"Okay." He turns around, and my insides somersault as I watch him walk around to the other side of the bar, wishing I could follow.

Emerson grabs my arm and squeezes. "Oh my God. That man is even finer in person than he is in pictures. Damn, Carys. Now I know why you've spent the last five years lusting after him."

"Be quiet, Emerson." I yank my arm away and cover her mouth with my hand. "We're *not* talking about this here." My eyes scan our immediate area to see if anyone heard her. But I think we're safe.

She licks my palm, and I jerk my hand back and wipe it on her jeans. "Fine," she pouts. "But we're definitely talking about it later."

"Yeah," I agree, knowing I'm going to need to figure out how I feel before I can talk to her about it. "Later."

This man has always been forbidden.

Before he was my stepbrother, he was already one of my overprotective big brother's best friends. He was older. He was cooler. And he was not interested in a theater geek like me. But he was all I saw back then and for so many years since.

When his sky-blue eyes connect with mine from across the bar, logic tells me that he'll never look at me the way I've always wished he would.

But logic has nothing on what my heart wants.

COOPER

ONCE I'M DONE GETTING MY ASS CHEWED OUT BY MY TWIN sister for not calling her as soon as I got home, she lets me go with a promise to talk more tomorrow, so we can figure out the next time we'll see each other. The guys have moved to the back of the bar near the dartboard, but Carys isn't with them. I try to convince myself I'm just looking because I know what every guy in this bar is thinking after the performance she just gave. But even I know I'm lying to myself when I can't find her or her roommate anywhere.

"Hey, man." I move next to Linc, who's waiting for Jim, one of the guys from Echo Team, to miss a ball on the pool table so he can take his turn. "Where did Carys go?"

"Emerson's brother came over and told the girls there was a party back at his frat house. Since he was their ride, they left too."

Jim misses his shot, and Linc moves to line his up.

"The hot little brunettes?" He turns to a few of his own teammates. "We were sad to see them go, weren't we, boys?" His team agrees, and I clench my teeth, knowing they were looking at Carys.

She didn't even say goodbye because she'd rather be surrounded by a bunch of drunk and horny college assholes.

What the fuck?

I jerk my phone out to see if she messaged, but there's nothing there.

Not sure why I expected anything else.

Trick sits down on the barstool next to Rook and Ford. "Don't look so heartbroken, Sinclair. According to Linc, the lover boy over there, we're having a party at the house tomorrow night."

Linc sinks the eight ball, then turns around, his face as red as the three ball. "Whatever, asshole. I needed an excuse to see Emerson again." If it's possible, his blush deepens, and I'm strangely relieved to know I'll be seeing Carys again.

Ford laughs at the utter embarrassment on Linc's face. "Yeah well, your girl's roommate sure jumped at the chance for the two of them to come." Ford throws me a shit-eating grin. "I wonder why the little singer would do that?"

"You owe her one, Linc. Emerson wasn't sure till Carys said yes." Trick grins smugly.

Jim pipes up, "We'll crash your party, kid. I'd be happy to take Emerson off your hands when you can't figure out what to say."

Ford shoves him back with one hand to his chest, closing ranks. "Who you calling kid?"

You can be as big of an ass as you want to one of your teammates, but not to one of ours.

Only we get to do that.

My older brother and I were complete assholes to each other growing up, but we never let anyone else get away with that shit. The team is the same way. A brotherhood.

Jim nods at Ford, then grabs his boys and heads to the dartboard, and I let out a breath I didn't realize I was holding now that I know I'll get the chance to see Carys again tomorrow.

Her perky little ass is going to pay for leaving without saying goodbye.

"Don't worry, Linc. Nobody's gonna cock-block your

girl. But you could have just asked her out. It's called 'a date.' You don't need to throw a damn party." Trick's not what you would call a people person. He gets along with Wanda much better than he does with most humans.

Linc hangs his stick back up on the wall. "Yeah. I got nothing. Party sounded like a good idea at the time. Less stress." He looks around at the guys. "You're all gonna come, right?"

Everyone laughs as we exchange knowing looks. The poor bastard gets so nervous around women.

Ford grins, then finishes his beer and grabs his keys from his pocket as Jessie hugs Linc. "Call me tomorrow if you need help. I love throwing parties."

"Thanks, Jessie." Ford's wife often takes pity on us.

Not only is he our team leader, but he's the only married guy in the unit. And he really out-kicked his coverage with her. She's everybody's big sister. She already tried shooing away the girls hanging on Trick and Axe. She doesn't like it when we hook up with women she doesn't deem worthy.

Ford nuzzles his nose in her hair, and she giggles. "We're outta here, boys."

"Lucky fucker," Linc says what we're all thinking as Axe orders us another round.

The truth is SEAL marriages don't usually last. We're gone more days a year than we're home, and our partners are expected to hold everything together on their own. They give birth alone, more times than not. Birthdays, holidays, bad days . . . You handle them all alone, while we're off kicking down doors. You've got to be a really strong person to marry someone on a team.

Hell, I had a girlfriend in high school break up with me because she saw what this life did to her brother. We hadn't even graduated yet, and we ended. As much as I want the wife and the white picket fence, this is the life I chose. No turning back.

Linc, Trick, and I walked through the door sometime around one a.m., wide-awake and a little buzzed but far from drunk. Fortunately, one of the good things the Navy beats into you early on is to sleep when you can, where you can. We can fall asleep so fast it borders on narcolepsy, and I know the second my head hits the pillow, I'll be out.

As I lie down on my own bed in a room I'm not sharing with Linc for the first time in months, I'm grateful I can stretch out without my feet hanging off the foot of the bed. At six foot four, I'm one of the taller guys on the team, and the ability to stretch out on a bed in a room that doesn't smell like Linc's dirty fucking socks makes me happy.

Just as my eyes close, the phone on my nightstand vibrates with an incoming text. I roll over to grab it, and my chest does a funny kind of squeeze when I see who it is.

Carys: You awake?
Cooper: I am now.
Carys: Sorry. I shouldn't have texted this late.
Cooper: No. Don't worry about it. You OK?
Carys: I never got to say goodbye earlier.
Coop: I noticed.
Carys: Sorry I bailed.
Cooper: Why did you?

It bugs the hell out of me that I care and have never been able to control it. Once I saw her, I wanted to spend time with her. The dots stop and start a few times before she answers.

Carys: Your roommate invited us over tomorrow night.
Carys: Well . . . I guess technically it's tonight now.
Cooper: Yeah. Pretty sure he's interested in Emerson. You gonna come?
Carys: Why Cooper Sinclair . . . If you wanna know what makes me come, you're gonna have to work harder than that.

My heart pounds against my chest as I reread Carys's answer again, and I have to adjust my cock in my boxer briefs at the realization that I'd very much like to know what makes this woman come.

Cooper: You drunk, Carys?
Carys: Maybe a little.
Cooper: You shouldn't say things like that to me.
Carys: Why not?
Cooper: Because I'm your brother.
Carys: Stepbrother.
Carys: Ask me what I'm thinking about, Coop.

I'm not ready to ask the question sitting on the tip of my tongue, let alone know the answer. Fuck me, I'm even less ready to figure out why I'm thinking about my stepsister this way.

Cooper: Maybe when you're sober. Night, Carys.
Carys: Chicken

I toss and turn, trying to get to sleep, but thoughts of what Carys Murphy looks like when she comes haunt me.

I try thinking about someone else. Hell, anyone other than her. It's not like I've been celibate out here for years, but after an hour of this shit, I get up to take a cold shower. Apparently, some things—more specifically, *someone*—can still keep me awake.

Standing under the cold spray of water, I give in and stroke my cock, thinking about the last girl I was with during our deployment. Her pale skin under my fingers. Her pink lips stretched around my dick. It doesn't take long to come. And when I do, I drop my head against the cool tile. Water pelting my shoulders and my eyes closed.

"Fuck," I groan.

Because when I come, the face I see isn't the girl from deployment.

It's Carys Murphy, my best friend's little sister.

My fucking stepsister.

Nothing can happen with her.

Nothing is going to happen with her.

Nothing.

And maybe if I tell myself that enough times, I can shut down all thoughts of what she looks like when she comes.

CARYS

I'VE NEVER BEEN WHAT I WOULD CONSIDER AN *ATHLETE*. My brother is an all-American football player at Kroydon University. As if that wasn't enough, when Mom married Coach, we became one big happy family full of athletes. One of my stepbrothers is a pro quarterback, and my stepfather is a former all-pro football player turned professional football coach. Hell, my stepsister-in-law is a former professional ballerina. Even my little brother, Callen, who's just shy of two years old, throws a football better than I can during our family's Thanksgiving Day games. Those genes didn't just skip me. They ran away screaming.

But I love to run.

The solitude of distance running has become an escape for me over the past few years.

It helps me de-stress, whatever the stress is. School. Family. Expectations.

After working up to it, I ran my first marathon a year ago, and I was hooked. So, I guess I'm officially an athlete now. But truthfully, I just like the way it makes me feel. The endorphins are addictive, and I always feel better about myself afterward.

As I stretch after today's seven miles, the song playing in my earbuds switches over to the ringtone of my cell phone and alerts me that my bestie, Daphne, is calling.

"Hey, D. What's up?" I ask as I cross the courtyard

behind my dorm and sit down on the soft grass under my favorite tree. Yes, I have a favorite tree. Outside is my happy place.

"Hey, Carys. Just checking in. I wanted to see how your rockstar debut went last night. Am I dropping out of school to follow you around the world on tour yet? Gotta make sure you don't forget the little people when you're playing the stadium crowds."

Daphne and I have been best friends since elementary school. She and our other friend, Chloe, were a year ahead of me in school, and both stayed in Philly for college.

Days like today, I wish they were both here with me now. They'd be brutally honest about my mixed emotions over seeing Cooper last night.

Who am I kidding? They're not mixed. They're lust. They're want. They're need. They're the giant mushy place in my heart where only he lives. But those feelings suck and shouldn't exist. *Hence*, needing brutal honesty.

"Last night was fine . . ."

"Fine? Seriously? You can do better than fine." A horn honking echoes through the connection, followed by D cursing someone out. "God, I hate people who have no clue how to drive in the city. Anyway . . . explain."

I lean my head back against the tree's trunk and close my eyes. And for a moment, I remember what it felt like to be held by Cooper last night.

"He's home, D." The vice around my heart tightens.

Silence stretches for a few moments before her quiet voice asks, "Have you seen him?"

"He was there last night. At the bar. And Em and I are going over to his place tonight."

"Oh, you need to give me more information than that. Come on. That's just messed up." Daphne sighs. "Start from the beginning and don't leave anything out."

"I didn't know he was in the bar until we got off the stage and found Emerson standing with Cooper and his team. And D . . . when he hugged me. My God. It was like that scene in the *Wizard of Oz* when everything goes from black-and-white to technicolor." I sigh and stretch my legs.

"And . . . ?"

"And there was this minute where I thought maybe he felt it too. But it was gone as quickly as it happened. Then I had a little too much to drink." I think back to that text and cringe. "We were texting later on after I left, and I was trying to flirt."

Daphne blows out an exasperated breath. "Well, what happened? Did he flirt back?"

"Maybe? I'm not sure. He shut me down, but there was something there." I bang my head against the tree. "What am I going to do, D?"

"Carys Catrina Murphy. You did not go to school on the other side of the damn country just for a fine arts degree. We've got one of those schools in Philly, if that was all you were looking for. I know you wanted to get away and figure out what you want to do with your life. But how many times did you tell me that maybe going to college in San Diego would give fate a little nudge? Hmm? I seem to remember hearing that more than once when you were making your decision."

I hate when she middle-names me.

"I know . . ." I mutter. I could have just as easily gone to the University of The Arts in Philadelphia if I'd have wanted to. But I wanted to get to live life away from home. I wanted to see what it was like to go to school with people I hadn't known since preschool. To interact with a world that didn't know everything about my family because four generations of us have lived in the same damn town for a hundred years. Or people who worship

31

my stepfather because he's a championship-winning football coach.

And yes, the fact that I got accepted to an art school in San Diego meant I'd be closer to Cooper . . . Just in case.

"I can't hear you."

Oh, the little bitch.

"You know I didn't." Damn it. She's the only person in Kroydon Hills who knows how I feel about him. She was there the day we met. She was there the day he left. And she was there the day after our parents got married. She knows everything.

"How did it feel seeing him last night? It's been almost a year, right?"

Cooper spent six months training in Virginia Beach last year before his deployment and came home for a weekend before I left for California. I haven't seen him since. I pull my knees up against my chest and rest my head on them. "It's him, D. It's always been him. Seeing him reaffirmed that. But it can also never be him."

A sound comes through the phone like she just smacked her steering wheel or maybe her dashboard. "I get it. I really do. I can't imagine that there's any way to wade into these waters without the ripple it causes reverberating across your whole family, Carys. But You've been half in love with Cooper for years. If you're ever going to take a chance—and I'm not talking a slightly drunk at your mom and stepdad's wedding chance—now's when you do it. When a whole country separates you and your family. When no one is physically there to get in the way. What's the worst thing that can happen?"

"He can shoot me down again." I don't know if I could handle that. Not when the pain of his words from two years ago still stings like a fresh wound and our lives are inextricably linked through our parents' marriage.

"But what if he doesn't?"

I guess that's the question . . . But what if he doesn't?

Two Years Ago

"Carys, you better knock it off. If Mom catches you drinking, she's gonna be pissed."

My big brother is the ultimate hypocrite. Aiden Murphy has been drinking at parties for years. But as soon as I walk through the door, he likes to act like he's a perfect angel and has always made sure everyone treats me the same way.

Do what I say and not what I do might as well be his motto.

Mom and Coach rented out a beautiful castle-esque resort in the mountains for their New Year's Eve wedding. The grounds outside are covered in snow, while the inside is decorated in fresh green garlands and red-velvet ribbons for the holidays. Golden glowing candles are scattered throughout the ballroom, nestled in red and white roses and vibrant greenery. It's everything my mother wanted and then some. A wedding fit for a queen who refused to surround herself with anyone except the people who matter most in their lives. And insisted, for privacy's sake, that they rent the entire resort. I think there's maybe a hundred of us in the entire hotel, and their staff is probably used to ten times that.

The entire weekend has looked like a Hallmark movie jumped off the screen to come to life. It's perfect. And yet, I'm miserable.

"Don't be an ass, Aiden. I've lost track of how many

beers you've had to drink tonight. And don't think I didn't notice you sneaking out of the ballroom with Sabrina twenty minutes ago and coming back in with your shirt wrinkled and your tie missing." His girlfriend, Sabrina, blushes and tucks her face against his chest with a laugh as Aiden's face turns red. I think it's red with anger, not embarrassment.

The band switches to a slow song. "Come on, Aiden." Sabrina tugs at his hand. "Dance with me."

He kisses the top of her head like a lovesick fool, then points two fingers at his eyes and back at me. *Whatever.* Like he's got his eyes on anyone besides Sabrina.

As he leads her to the dance floor, she turns and winks at me. At least he's in love with someone who can handle him for me.

The two of them join my new stepsister, Nattie, and her boyfriend, Brady, on the dance floor. Meanwhile, I catch my new stepbrother, Declan, and his wife, Annabelle, straightening their clothing as they come out of the bathroom . . . together. Guess we know what they were doing.

It seems like love is in the air tonight for everyone. Well . . . everyone but me.

Not that I'm the only single person here, but today was a glaring neon sign of a reminder that I can never be with the person I love.

Oh, screw this.

I grab the white faux-fur stole I wore for the bridal party pictures outside earlier and another glass of champagne from a passing waiter. Then I slip through the French doors to the patio for some fresh air, which preferably doesn't have so much love wafting around.

Bitter party of one in the house.

Hmm . . . drunk and bitter. What a great way to spend your mom's wedding day.

The small stone patio is surrounded by tall, green snow-covered shrubs, giving it a hidden feel. There's one lonely granite bench tucked away on the edge of the stones, covered in snow.

For one second, I consider cleaning it off and sitting down, but drunk or not, my ass is not willing to get that cold. My gown is a gorgeous strapless silk creation in cranberry-red with a slit up the thigh that I'm surprised Mom was okay with. Pretty. But not meant for snow. However, my shoes are pinching my toes, so standing here isn't the best option either.

Hmm. Maybe I could numb the pain in my feet with the snow on the ground.

Okay. Maybe I *have* had a little too much to drink tonight.

Fuck it.

I drop my stole onto the snowy bench and accidentally knock my hand against the granite in the process. *Shit.* That hurt.

"What did that bench ever do to *you?*"

My head spins, and it's entirely possible that the rotation of the Earth slows down.

Yeah, I've definitely had enough champagne tonight.

And there he is. The cause of my bitterness. The love of my life.

Can you find the love of your life at seventeen?

Well, I found him nearly two years ago, so I guess really, it would be at fifteen.

Of course, that was before today. Before he officially became my stepbrother.

Fuck love. She's a nasty bitch. Because only a woman could be this cruel.

"You okay, Carys?" His voice is rough, like he hasn't gotten enough sleep lately. And I can't help but wonder just how good it would feel to sleep in his arms. My entire body warms at the thought. What would it be like waking up to those eyes? Those baby blues, framed by long, light-brown lashes a shade darker than his dirty-blond hair. I love his eyes, and they're staring at me.

Wait, why are they staring at me? *Oh shit*. He asked me a question.

"Yeah. I'm good. Just needed a little air. That's all."

I shouldn't stare, but I can't stop. Coop's been away at bootcamp for months. And he looks good. He's gotten bigger. Broader. He was always muscular before. But he looks older now. Stronger. So fucking good.

And now, he's my stepbrother.

I'm going to have to keep reminding myself of that little fact. Because you are not supposed to want to kiss your stepbrother. Dreaming of the way his hands would feel against your skin is absolutely not allowed to happen. And any chance I may have ever had of us together has to be packed away.

Damn it. I hate packing.

Okay . . . no more champagne.

My eyes well up, and I look away.

"Carys, . . . you sure you're okay?" His voice softens. "You want my coat?" Coop doesn't wait for me to answer before his tux jacket is slipped around my shoulders, and his spicy scent envelops me. I force the tears away and straighten my spine.

"Thanks." I turn back around as music drifts through the doors and sway. "I love this song." It's an old Lifehouse song Mom used to play on repeat. "Everything." I guess it's fitting.

Cooper tugs on the lapels of the coat, bringing me in closer. "You should be inside dancing."

"With who? Everyone else is already paired up."

He places a hand on my waist. "Dance with *me*."

I stare at him, momentarily in shock. It's not a question, and I don't answer with words. I just hesitantly step closer and let him wrap his arms around me. I lay my head against his chest and breathe him in as my body presses to his, like this was always meant to happen, like this is where I was always meant to be. And all I can do is pray this never ends.

It's a beautifully haunting slow song that I'd sung around the house whenever Mom had it on.

Before I realize it, I'm singing along quietly, tucked against Coop's chest.

His chin is resting on my head, and even in my heels, I feel tiny in his arms.

And I realize this is it.

This is all I'm ever going to get with him.

He's all I want. All I need. He's everything to me . . . and he'll never know it.

One of Cooper's hands is resting just above my ass. So close . . . but not quite there.

His other hand is resting on my shoulder, drawing circles through the coat, and I desperately wish I could rip it off my body so I could feel his skin. He's got to know what he's doing . . . right?

I tip my head up to look at his face. "Coop . . ."

His hand slips from my shoulder to my neck. "I love listening to you sing, Carys. It reminds me of home."

His face is right there, and I swear he's staring at my lips.

Holy shit. He's going to kiss me.

His grip on my neck tightens as his thumb grazes my cheek, and I lean in.

Then nothing. What the hell?

"Hey, man," a sexy Georgia accent says.

Oh, holy shit. How did I not hear Cooper's buddy Lincoln come outside? He came home with Cooper for the holidays and fit in with the family like he'd always been there.

Coop drops his hands, and we each take a step back as Linc hands him a beer.

"Hey there, Carys." Linc smiles, and I kinda want to kick him in the balls for interrupting that moment but manage to control my ragey thoughts.

"Hey, Linc." My eyes dance between him and Cooper.

But Coop isn't looking at me anymore. Not like he was.

The moment is lost like it never existed.

Like I'm nothing.

I stand there, stuck in the moment. Waiting. Wanting desperately to go back. But Linc says something to Coop about Chloe, and I really don't want to hear about another freaking couple hooking up tonight. Instead, I slip out of Coop's coat and hand it back to him.

"Thanks, Cooper."

He tilts his chin toward me. What the fuck is that anyway? Why do guys do that? It's stupid. Words. Use words. But as I slip through the doors and lean against the wall, inside and out of sight, I overhear words I wish he'd never used.

Linc's voice carries through the closing doors. "Sorry, man. Didn't realize I was interrupting something out here."

"You weren't interrupting anything." Coop's voice is followed by a pause before he adds, "She's a little girl who's had too much to drink. That's all."

Ouch.

"She doesn't look like a little girl in that dress." Okay, maybe I don't completely hate Linc anymore.

"Whatever. She still looks like my seventeen-year-old stepsister."

Linc moves closer to the glass doors, so I take another step back and lean against the wall for support.

I don't think I've ever felt a door slam so tightly shut in my life.

CARYS

<small>Emerson decided we needed to be fashionably late to</small> the party.

According to her, thirty minutes was perfect. We wouldn't be the first ones there, but we also probably wouldn't be the last to arrive. My roomie put way too much thought into this, but since I don't have a car, she sets the schedule.

One less thing for me to stress out over, since I've been stressing about how tonight's going to go all day. I hate that it only took seeing Cooper Sinclair one time, and every feeling I've had for him for years has been magnified and taken up all the space in my mind today.

Em didn't even put the top down on her first love for our ride over to the party.

A baby-blue 1964 Mustang convertible.

Her car is always stocked with rubber bands, a brush, and there's usually a baseball cap or two floating somewhere in the backseat to keep the wind from whipping our hair everywhere. But tonight, the top stayed up, so there were no hair catastrophes.

I'm eternally grateful for that. My hair is my best asset. My ass is a little too flat, and my boobs are a little too small. But my hair is a shiny dark brown, with natural red highlights that flows in waves down past my shoulders. However, it doesn't hold a curl for shit, since it's also super thin. And I spent way too much time making sure it looked nice tonight for it to get messed up in the wind before we get there.

Once we park in front of the address, I run my hands over my hair to tame any last-minute fly-aways and check my makeup in the mirror one more time. I'm not a heavy makeup kinda girl. My lashes are long and black with a swipe of matching eyeliner to make my green eyes pop. And other than some pink lip gloss, that's it for my makeup routine.

I turn toward Em. "You ready?"

She adjusts the barely there top she paired with painted-on white skinny jeans. It's a beautiful soft black shirt with skinny straps that's held together by a few well-placed black ribbons connecting the back. I made it for her a few months ago, and it's pretty perfect, if I do say so myself. I love to design pieces with ribbons. There's just something I love about the idea of them being untied by someone special. And let's face it, you should be wearing lingerie to either make yourself feel confident and sexy or to make someone drop to their knees before they rip it off you.

The shirt Em's wearing tonight was one of the last pieces I made before I fell in love with designing lingerie instead of clothing. Sometimes you've got to try out every-thing before narrowing down what works for you. I like designing clothes, but I love creating lingerie.

Once we get out of the car, she turns toward me and tugs at her shirt. "Is everything where it needs to be?"

I make her spin so I can adjust her ribbons before giving her my stamp of approval.

Then she tugs my white boho shirt off my shoulders and down a little further in the front. "That's better. Nothing wrong with showing a little clavicle, CC."

I went with a tamer look than my roomie, with short

black shorts that make my vertically challenged legs appear a little longer and a flowy white boho shirt that slips off my shoulders in a very casual way. Sexy but comfy. At least, that's what I'm going for. Not in-your-face. Last night's look was as much in-your-face as I can take for one weekend.

As we walk up the short driveway, loud voices and laughter carry on the breeze, along with the heavenly smell of a charcoal grill, and my stomach growls in anticipation. We follow the red-stone path toward the sounds of the party, and Em knocks on the tall, wooden privacy gate, then pushes through it like she owns the place.

I want Em's confidence when I grow up.

We walk into the small backyard, and *damn*, that view is incredible.

And the ocean's not bad either.

The guys from the bar last night are scattered throughout the small space in board shorts and t-shirts. Two of them are shirtless, with droplets of water clinging to their golden skin, as they carry surfboards over to where a few are hanging from the fence. And holy hotness, Batman. I've never seen so many abs on one man before.

And my stepfather coaches pro football.

There are athletes around all the time.

Linc jumps up to welcome us, nearly tripping over his own feet to get to a giggling Emerson. No lie. She giggles like a little girl, and I look at her, wondering what happened to my badass roommate.

The door to the house clicks shut behind me, and I turn to see Cooper stepping out, stuffing something in the pocket of his dark-blue board shorts, water dripping from his damp blond hair, and a tight white, damp tee stretching across his firm chest and clinging to his muscles.

And I have to bite down on my bottom lip to stop my tongue from falling out of my mouth.

His eyes lock with mine as he smiles.

Just smiles that megawatt smile of his, and I'm done for. Damn him.

He throws an arm around my shoulders and squeezes. "Wasn't sure if you guys were coming."

I flush, thinking about our texts last night. I spent the day trying to forget most of it.

Out of the corner of my eye, I see Emerson and Linc slipping through the door Coop just vacated and roll my eyes.

Traitor left me alone already.

"Yeah. Em doesn't move super fast on the weekends. Sorry if you were waiting."

He drops his arm and presses his palm to the small of my back. "Come on. Let me introduce you to the rest of the guys." He guides me toward three guys lounging on a luxurious outdoor sectional with an equally expensive-looking firepit at their feet.

Actually, the more I look around, this place is way nicer than I was expecting.

He points to the two guys who hung up their boards before grabbing beers and sitting down. "You remember Ford and Rook."

I wave awkwardly.

"You met Axel last night too." Coop extends his arm toward the Texas twang guy from the bar, who stands and tips the straw hat he's wearing in my direction.

"Future baby momma." He snags my hand and drags me down next to him on the couch.

My eyes shoot to Coop's for help, but although he doesn't look thrilled, he doesn't say anything.

Well, okay then.

"Baby momma, did you meet the owner of this esteemed abode yet?" Okay, this guy is obviously the clown of the group. He kinda reminds me of a hyperactive puppy.

Cooper growls—actually growls. "Her name is Carys."

Hmm. *Interesting.*

Axel's eyes light up with mischief as his arm moves behind me on the couch in a very *first date at the movies* kind of way, and he plays with the ends of my hair.

"'Baby momma' just has such a nice ring to it though." He kicks his feet up on the firepit. This guy does absolutely nothing for me, and if Cooper wasn't here, Axel might actually creep me out a little. But I get the distinct impression he's doing this to rile Cooper up. And I'm all for it.

"Hey, Trick," Axel calls.

The tall brunette guy manning the grill turns to look at us. His golden skin glows against the bright orange Hawaiian-print board shorts hanging off his hips and the long-sleeved Salt Life t-shirt stretching across a broad chest. A big dog is sitting obediently at his feet. Watching.

"You met my future wife yet?" Axel's fingers skim my bare shoulder, then dip just under the elastic band at the top of my shirt.

I pull away while Cooper simultaneously kicks Axel's legs off the firepit.

Trick chuckles at Axe's annoyed huff. "You mean your future alimony payment?" He scratches behind the dog's ears and quietly says something that causes the big, scary, red furball to move faster than I've ever seen any dog move and promptly plant itself between Axel and me.

I look helplessly from the man next to me to the one manning the grill, and I hold as still as possible. "Um, am I . . ." I stutter and hold my hands up carefully in front of myself. "Am I allowed to touch him? Is he a military dog?"

Trick whistles and the dog goes from sitting up at

attention to dropping its head down on my leg, completely relaxed. "*Her* name is Wanda, and you can touch her now." He sips his beer and watches me tentatively run my hand over Wanda's soft red hair.

"Oh my God. She's a redhead." I look over at Cooper and can't hold back my smile. "Like Wanda Maximoff."

Coop's corresponding smile does insane things to my insides.

"Dude, Axe. You can fuck right off. Wanda likes her, and the girl knows her Marvel. She's way too good for you." Trick closes the lid of the grill and opens a cooler. "Want something to drink, Carys?" He reaches inside and grabs a beer, but Coop takes it from him before he can hand it to me.

"You driving, Carys?"

I look around the backyard to see if Emerson's come back out yet. "Em drove us here, but I might be driving home."

Coop digs back into the cooler and produces a bottle of sweet tea.

"You remembered." My heart does a crazy little flip that he knows what I like to drink.

"Like I could ever forget."

And there goes my heart.

The sun is setting by the time Emerson and Linc make their way back outside, slightly disheveled. The guys tease Linc until the tips of his ears turn red from embarrassment.

We're already eating around the firepit.

"So, Carys. Tell us about yourself." Trick turns the grill

off and finally makes himself a plate, before coming to sit down in one of the chairs across from me.

It's strange to think that these men, who remind me so much of my brother and his friends, are elite soldiers who've seen and done things I can't even imagine. They seem like goofballs. Mouth-watering, elite, deadly goofballs.

I wipe my mouth and take a sip of sweet tea. "Hmm." I look from Cooper to Trick, suddenly inexplicably nervous. "Well . . . I'm a student at SDU of A, studying fashion design and vocal performance."

"Bor-ing," Axel announces loudly. "So do you wanna be a rock star or pick out clothes for rock stars? Gotta say you sounded fucking killer last night. So my vote is rock star."

"You don't get a vote, asshole." Cooper stands across from me and grabs my empty plate, then dumps them both in the trash, grumbling.

"Why can't she do both?" Emerson asks from Linc's lap, nursing her third beer. Looks like I'm driving tonight.

I just shake my head. "I don't want to do both. Or either. My dreams of a career on the stage never included being a rock star. They included Broadway. And those days are long gone."

Em looks at me with surprised eyes. "But you're going to keep singing with Jack and Theo, right?"

Before I get a chance to answer, Axel stands, then lifts me from the couch, cradling me to him like he's about to carry me over the threshold. I wish this was the guy who made my heart beat faster. I laugh, but it's a little awkward the way he picks me up like he has a right.

"Future wife, do I need to beat someone down? Are you dating one of those guys?"

"Swear to God, Axe," Coop growls. "I'm gonna beat you if you don't put her down."

Axel nuzzles his nose against my hair as he whispers, "I'd think Sinclair had a claim to you if I didn't know better, future wife."

Damn, I wish I didn't desperately want Cooper to have a claim on me.

I don't tell Axel that though.

He jogs toward the back gate like I weigh nothing, and I lock my arms tighter around his neck, afraid he's going to drop me.

"Who feels like a little night swimming?" he yells over his shoulder.

I screech, and chairs scrape against the stones behind us. "No night swimming."

Axel runs down the beach with me in his arms, screaming.

No longer liking this game and silently wishing it was someone else carrying me.

COOPER

"Breathe, man."

I watch Axel disappearing down the sand and fight to contain my anger.

Trick's watching me with knowing eyes as everyone else clears out of the backyard and onto the beach. Everyone but Rook, him, and me. "I'm breathing."

"Are ya? Cause you look like you're about to kill Axel, brother." Rook stretches his arms along the back of the couch, wearing the same indifferent expression he always wears if we're not on an op. "He's pushing your buttons on purpose, you know?"

Of course, I fucking know. Telling Axel that Carys was off-limits was like waving a blood-red cape in front of an amped-up bull. I clench my jaw, fury simmering just below the surface like a pot boiling over. "She doesn't like the ocean at night."

"She's a big girl. She can tell him that." Trick drops into the chair across from me and runs his hand over Wanda's head when she comes to stand at his feet.

Rook raises his brow. "What's really pissing you off, Sinclair? Because you're fucking angry. Is it with him or yourself?"

"She's my stepsister. I'm just looking out for her. She doesn't need to get mixed up with Axe's shit." Even as I say the words, I know they're a fucking lie.

"You make it a habit of looking at all your sisters that

49

way?" Trick kicks his feet up on the table and leans back while Rook and he wait for an answer.

Fuckers.

This woman is not my sister. She never was. Our parents are married, but I've never been able to look at her the way I look at Nattie, no matter how hard I've tried.

Trick knows he's gotten to me when I don't say anything. "Yeah. I didn't think so. Be careful, man. You're swimming in dangerous waters."

It's a good thing I know how to swim. "I'm gonna go see what's going on down there. You coming with?"

Trick shrugs and lays his head back against the couch. "Nope."

Rook stands and grabs his keys from his pocket. "I'm out, but try not to kill Axe. It'd be a bitch to train someone else on comms. See you assholes later."

As I walk down the sand toward the dark ocean, Linc passes me with Emerson tossed over his shoulder, looking every bit a man on a mission to get back to the house. Her arms dangle down, and she squeezes his ass.

"Hey, Cooper . . ." she calls out on a laugh.

I turn around and watch her lift her head as she blows her thick, black hair out of her face. "I think our girl is gonna need a place to sleep or a ride home tonight." Linc smacks her ass, and she yelps. "Just saying."

Aw hell.

A little further down the beach, Carys sits in the sand, her arms tucked around her knees, and a white feather twisting in her hand. Her pale skin glows under the full moon, and her soft brown hair is blowing in the breeze. She's beautiful in a way I shouldn't notice. But there's no way to miss it.

When she tilts her chin up to look at me, there's something about her smile that seems forced. It doesn't reach her eyes. "I can see why you like these guys. The way they rib each other reminds me of home." The sadness in her voice pulls on a heartstring I didn't know I had. I want to fix it for her. But I can't.

Instead, I squat down next to the beauty beside me, balancing on the balls of my feet, not in the mood for a sandy ass. "Yeah. I can see that. Axel definitely reminds me of your brother when he's trying to be a dick." And maybe I want to put that thought in her brain, in case she ever gets the urge to think about Axe as more than a ridiculous flirt.

"Oh, ew. You had to go there?"

Mission accomplished.

"He's nothing like Aiden." She reaches out and tries to shove me off balance with a push to my shoulder, but it would take a hell of a lot more than that.

"If that's what you've got to tell yourself." I stand to my full height and offer her my hand. An electric current sparks between us when I tug her to her feet.

Carys's head barely reaches my chest.

She twists the feather between her fingers. "My grand-mother used to say feathers brought you luck. That they were a sign that someone was watching over you, keeping you safe." She places it in my hand. "For luck, Coop." Then she reaches down, grabs her discarded flip-flops, and walks ahead of me before peeking over her shoulder to see if I'm following. "Come on, Coop. Walk with me. I'm pretty sure I've got time to kill before Em's ready to go home."

"Yeah . . . about that." I look down, momentarily capti-vated by the sway of Carys's hips in her short shorts. She's tiny and delicate in a way that brings all my protective instincts roaring to life.

"Your girl sounds like she's planning on spending the night." In two strides, I catch up to the woman before me and try to stuff that thought back to the far edges of my mind. Keeping her locked in any kind of friend zone seems more difficult now than it does back home in Kroydon Hills.

"Great. She drove." Carys kicks the warm sand in front of her, seemingly annoyed. "I guess I'll grab an Uber when we get back to the house."

"I'll take you home." Dad would kill me if I let her Uber instead of offering her a ride.

She turns around to face me and walks backward. "You got a car in Cali, Coop? I thought you gave Nattie your Jeep."

"I did give Nat the Jeep. But I bought an older one about a year ago. I needed something out here when I wasn't deployed."

"Do you like it? Being out here, so far away from home? Is being a SEAL everything you wanted it to be?" She's still walking backward when she trips over something hidden in the sand.

I catch her, tugging her close before she goes down.

Carys's wild, emerald-green eyes dart to mine as I hold her against my chest.

She grabs my arms, steadying herself as her fingertips singe my skin.

Damn it. What is it about this girl?

She's everything I'm not allowed to want.

"You can let go, Coop." She presses up on her toes, leaning into me. Her warm breath skates over my skin as she whispers, "I'm okay."

"Yeah. Be careful. I don't need to call Dad and Katherine and tell them that you got hurt on my watch." I reach down and smooth her hair away from both sides of her face, trying to remind myself that she's my stepsister and this can't happen, but failing miserably.

"It's a good thing I'm not on your watch." She takes a step back, and I drop my arms.

Right. She's not my responsibility.

Then why does it feel like she should be?

Later, once Carys has accepted that Emerson and Linc aren't coming out of his room any time soon, she says her goodbyes, and I walk her to my Jeep. "You okay with the top off?"

Her eyes light up. "Can I blast the radio as loud as I want?"

I nod, and her responding smile could light up the whole damn street. Who knew control of the radio could make her so happy? Once we're in the Jeep, she starts playing with the buttons on the old unit until the first few notes of "Crash Into Me" by the Dave Matthews Band play through the speakers. Then, content with her find, she leans back in the seat and places her feet flat against the dashboard as she starts to hum, and I back out of the driveway.

She sings the song in a higher pitch than Dave does, and it changes its feel completely as her voice effortlessly harmonizes with his.

It's sexy as fuck.

And every time I look her way, her smile grows as she sings along, and her hair whips around both of us. She's swaying in her seat like she doesn't have a care in the world. Relaxed. It's the look of someone who's completely comfortable in her own skin. Which leaves me with more questions than answers.

I wait until the song she's clearly loving is over before

turning the radio down. "Why don't you want to sing anymore?"

"Umm . . . I was just singing." She throws her hair up into a bun on the top of her head.

"Earlier, you told Axel you didn't want to be a rock star. But you didn't say what you wanted to do. Why don't you want to sing anymore?"

The first time I ever saw Carys, she was next to a piano in the auditorium of our old high school. It was my first week of school, and I'd gotten lost looking for the chem lab. I walked into the room, thinking I was in the right place. Instead, I found this beautiful girl standing on stage, singing that song from *A Star Is Born* like a fucking angel. She had this huge voice that I couldn't believe was coming out of such a tiny body.

She leans her head back against the seat and turns to look at me. "I don't want to sing for a living. That doesn't mean I'll ever stop singing or writing music. I love it. But if I had to do it every day . . . if my career depended on it . . . I don't think I'd enjoy it anymore. I think that would ruin it for me."

"Okay, I can understand that. But where did the design part of your degree come from?" I slow for a yellow light and look at her quickly as her cheeks turn pink. "I don't remember you ever mentioning that before."

She grabs my forearm, and I warm at her touch. "Promise not to laugh?"

"Sure," I answer, desperate to know more, completely captivated by the woman next to me. "Now shoot."

"I've always been good at making things. Mom got me a sewing machine as a kid, and I used to make clothes for all my dolls. That eventually turned into me making my costumes for the plays. Doesn't exactly sound cool, so it wasn't something I ever really talked about." She brings her feet down from the dash and tucks them under her legs, like she's self-consciously curling into herself.

"But my junior year," she continues, "Chloe and I started hanging out more, once all you guys were gone, and I found out that she'd been sketching designs for years. We kinda started playing around, and it didn't take long to see how well we work together. Things have grown from there."

The pink blush covering Carys's face has spread down her neck and chest by the time she's done talking, and she stares out the windshield, avoiding my gaze. I want to kill whoever made her feel uncomfortable with this.

"Why do you look embarrassed? That sounds awesome. Do you like making clothes? Do you think it's something you'll do when you're done with school?"

"Well . . . we actually already started working on designs for our own line and just sold a few pieces from it to a boutique back home. We just haven't told many people yet." She tugs her hand off me as the light changes to green, and I miss the warmth of her skin on mine.

"Why not?" That's impressive as hell. I'd be telling the whole world if I could do something like that. "You should be proud of yourself. You found something you're good at that you want to turn into a career. Why keep it quiet?"

Carys takes a deep breath and then turns to watch the streets of San Diego pass us by. "We've been working on it for two years, and we've made all sorts of clothes. Some good and others, not so much. But we've figured out we've got a great eye for lingerie. So we've been focusing on that for the past few months. I haven't exactly decided how to tell my mother that after years and years of voice lessons, I don't want to sing. I want to design lingerie meant to make a woman feel beautiful and sexy. Lingerie that should be appreciated before it's ripped off a woman's body."

Holy fucking shit.

Carys wearing lingerie meant to be torn off her body might be the image that gets me through my next deployment.

And I'm officially going to hell.

CARYS

COOP STOPS IN FRONT OF MY DORM AND SHUTS THE Jeep off.

I'm sad our ride's over. Something was different about tonight. About this space. I'm not sure I've ever felt this level of comfort with Cooper before. And I'm a little scared I won't ever get to feel it again.

I cross my legs and turn my body to his, proud of myself that I'm ready to hug him goodbye without losing my nerve as he removes the keys from the ignition. "Thanks for the ride, Coop." Before I get a chance to lean in, he's out of the Jeep and rounding the front so he can open my door.

He offers me his hand, and my heart definitely doesn't skip a beat. "So chivalrous." I slip my hand into his much bigger one, and a part of me melts at the touch.

"Can I walk you in or is this a girls-only dorm?" He looks around like he's inspecting the building. "Where's the security guard? There's security, right?"

A laugh bubbles up at the sudden concern on his face. "No. Definitely not an all-girl dorm. And the campus is pretty safe. There aren't security guards for each building, but campus police monitor the entire area." I spin around and point out a police car moving slowly down the street. "See? Totally safe." Unlike my heart.

He grunts, then slides his big hand to the small of my

back in a move that makes every nerve in my body stand and take notice.

Coop and I don't usually touch.

We've never been like that. At least, not normally with each other.

I slide my keycard against the lock of the front door and turn to him. "Thanks for walking me home."

"Show me your room, Carys." His voice is rough and sexy, and it sends a shiver down my spine. His body crowds mine as the heat of it dances over my skin. "I need to know you're safe."

Damn him. He has no idea what his words do to my already swooning heart.

"Whatever you say, hot shot. But you do realize I've been living here for nine months, and nothing has happened. Right?" Cooper doesn't answer me, but something in his baby blues tells me to stop arguing because I'm not going to change his mind.

He stays close to me as I walk us both through the lobby and up the three flights of stairs to my floor.

Cooper's eyes are everywhere, taking everything in as if he's mapping out an emergency exit route. "Do you always take the stairs alone?"

"Oh my God, Cooper. Relax. It's perfectly safe." I'm not sure whether I should be annoyed that he's treating me like his baby sister or giddy that he cares about my safety.

I'm going with option number two.

I push through the door to my floor, and then we walk down the long, loud hall. A few doors are open as some people party between rooms. It's a Saturday night at the end of the semester, and everyone is blowing off steam. "See? Perfectly safe."

He looks less than convinced. "Just humor me, please."

My fingers tremble a little when I unlock my door,

suddenly nervous to have him here—in my space. It's a small room. Two twin beds sit on either wall with desks at each end, framing a large window that overlooks the quad courtyard behind the building. Em and I have made it as much our own space as we could, but I'm looking forward to moving off campus in a few weeks after the semester ends.

"Thanks for bringing me home, Coop. It was fun." This giant of a man is sucking all the oxygen from the room, and I move away to put some distance between us. "How long are you going to be home?" I scoop up some of the clothes that Emerson and I left on my bed earlier and throw them into the closet, then kick a bra under her bed.

She's lucky it's not one I made for her.

"Home, huh?" A smile tugs at his lips. "We never really know when we're getting spun up, but I actually got word this morning that I've been recommended for a training. I should be leaving in the next week or so." Thankfully, he's still taking stock of the room and seems completely unaware of how my lungs just stopped functioning.

I only got two nights. I'm not ready for him to leave yet, even if he's not mine.

"You're leaving again? You just got here."

He walks over to the window and pushes back our cute black-and-white curtains to check the lock before gently running his fingers over the sewing machine sitting on my desk. He picks up a swatch of crimson red lace and rubs it between his fingers. "Yeah. It was news to me too. But it's something I really want to do, so I can't complain. Being a Tier 1 operator is my ultimate goal. Sharpening your skills never stops. Laziness is the easiest way to get somebody killed."

"Oh." My heart drops to the floor. I never want to think about him being hurt. Or worse. "What's the training for?"

His shoulders tense, but he doesn't look at me.

Does he have to keep this kind of thing to himself?

"Is it hard?" The urge to reach out and soothe his tight muscles is strong, but I manage to resist. *Go me.* "Not being able to tell us what you're doing or where you are?" I leave off the part where I know it's hard on us. No need to add to whatever he's feeling already.

With the room a little more presentable, I sit down on my bed and scooch my butt back against the wall, then stretch my legs out in front of me and cross them at the ankles. I'm nearly twenty years old but still short enough that my legs barely touch the floor when they hang off the bed. *Gotta love it.*

Coop turns around, his blue eyes tight and tense. "It is what it is. It's part of the job. The less you all know, the better." He sits down next to me with his back against the wall, and a swarm of butterflies take flight in my stomach. Only a few inches separate us, but his long legs still manage to hang off the bed.

He stares at me for a long minute, and I wish I had some idea what he was thinking before he finally asks, "When does your semester end?"

His bare leg is next to mine, not touching but close enough to feel his body heat teasing me. Reminding me that awareness is equal parts arousing and frustrating.

"My last final's Wednesday. But I only have a week off before my first of two summer sessions starts. I'll be done with the first session in time to fly home for Callen and the twins' birthdays in July." Seven months after our parents got married, our little brother, Callen, was born. Two weeks later, Annabelle Sinclair, Coop's sister-in-law, gave birth to twin girls, Gracie and Everly.

Our family multiplies like bunnies.

He taps his head back against the wall. "I don't know if

I'm making it this year." Regret laces his tone. He made it for the celebration last year. "You think they'll even recognize me when it's not through an iPad?"

I give in to temptation and lean my head against his shoulder. I probably shouldn't, but I might not get the chance again. Closing my eyes, I whisper, "Are you really that clueless?"

Coop surprises me when he adjusts us and holds me tightly to him, squeezing my bare skin. This is nothing like what Axel did earlier. Cooper isn't handsy. His fingers aren't exploring my skin. They're firmly planted on top of my sleeve instead of skimming the edge of my shirt. But unlike earlier, need pools deep in my belly, and he has no idea how he's affecting me. I guess he really is that clueless. Or he's just not interested in me at all. Unfortunately, I think it's the latter, and I need to come to terms with it.

How many years can I carry an unrequited torch for Cooper Sinclair?

"We think about you and talk about you all the time, Coop. You might not physically be in Kroydon Hills with everyone, but you're still there. Those kids see you through their screens. They hear Cooper stories from all of us. The house is covered in pictures of all of us, you included. They're not forgetting about you. I promise."

"Thanks." His shoulders relax, but his voice is barely above a whisper. "I guess I needed to hear that."

He rests his head on top of mine for just a moment, and my entire body eases with the contact.

For months, I've been asking myself one question.

Were my feelings for him real, or were they just a high school crush that never went away because he left town? Were they based on a memory instead of reality?

Now I know for sure.

The memory of Cooper doesn't hold a candle to actually having him next to me. And now that he's here, I don't want to let go.

The new question I've got to ask myself is what am I going to do about it?

I spent Sunday studying for my last two finals. Well . . . trying to. If I fail the test I'm taking tomorrow, I wonder if the professor would take, *sorry, I'm obsessed with my step-brother*, as an excuse because trying to concentrate on World War II instead of deciding whether I should tell Cooper how I feel before he leaves again is not working out well for me. Probably not an acceptable reason, so I flip over the bright pink index card with the date of Franz Ferdinand's assassination written down and try to memorize it for the fiftieth time in the last ten minutes.

Judging by the fact my guess is still wrong, I probably should have started studying before today.

Oh well.

The girls across the hall asked me if I wanted to grab dinner with them, but I stayed in, trying to get through this. I hate tests. Always have. Studying for them sucks ass because I suck at studying.

Pity party, table for one, please.

When Emerson walks through the door sometime after nine that night, I've just put away my US history notes and opened my economics book. On to the next test.

Em, on the other hand, has been at Linc's all day and hasn't cracked open a single book. This bitch doesn't have to because she's a freaking genius, studying entertainment management, and her last name is Madden. Not to mention, she's glowing. Like, literally glowing. Damn. Life really isn't fair sometimes.

"Emerson Madden." I slam my book shut and roll off the bed less than gracefully. "What have you been doing all day?" I'm kidding, obviously. Because I have no doubt I know exactly what she's been doing all day. Or more precisely, who.

Her smile is a mile wide as she kicks off her shoes and flounces down on her bed. "Falling in love."

"What?" Em is not that girl. She doesn't believe in insta love and won't even let us read insta love books for our buddy reads. "Love?"

She reaches her hands into the air and measures something longer than a loaf of bread. "It's amazing, CC. His dick is utter perfection." She sits up and squeezes her pillow. "And. It. Curves." Then she squeals, "Curves," before she screams into the pillow. "And that man has stamina with a capital S." Her navy-blue eyes glitter as she turns her head toward me. "Oh. Oh. Oh. And his tongue . . . I've never met a guy who likes oral as much as Linc." She stands up as dramatically as she threw herself down and strips out of last night's clothes while she rummages through a drawer. "I legitimately lost track of how many orgasms I've had in the last twenty-four hours."

I have to force myself to close my mouth that's come completely unhinged at her declaration. "Is it okay if I hate you a little bit right now?"

"Yup," she sighs. "I'd hate me too. But seriously, C, the connection is insane. He's taking me out to dinner tomorrow night." She slips into her pajamas before turning back around. "Isn't it crazy?"

"Yeah. Crazy." I try to show as much enthusiasm as I can, when deep down inside, I'm so jealous, I kinda want to cry.

Maybe I'll just order a new vibrator instead.

My phone chimes about an hour after I finally go to bed with an incoming text. When I yank it off my desk, Theo's name is lighting up on my screen.

Theo: Hey Carys. You up for rehearsal tonight?
Carys: It's eleven o'clock, and I have a final at eight-thirty tomorrow morning. I'm already in bed.
Theo: Want some company? I could help you study. I'm really good with anatomy.
Carys: Unless you're going to give me all the answers to a history test, you're of no use to me.
Theo: You sure? Blowing off steam could help. And I'm happy to give you something to blow.
Carys: You've gotta get better lines, Theo. Seriously. That was just bad.
Theo: Can't blame a guy for trying. I'm available if you ever change your mind.

Do guys really think a line like that works?
Hey, want a dick to hop on if you're lonely?
Mine is a decent size and would be happy to oblige.

Theo: Can you rehearse tomorrow night?
Carys: Yeah. That works.

I turn my phone off, annoyed with the world.
Maybe I shouldn't have taken summer classes.
Maybe going back to Kroydon Hills for a few months instead of weeks would have been good for me. But I know

as soon as I'm back there, I'll fall back into being the youngest. The baby. It doesn't matter that I'm only two years younger than everyone else because they all treat me like I'm ten years younger. How are you supposed to figure out who you are and what you want when everyone around you thinks you need to be sheltered and protected like a porcelain doll?

Trying to figure out who you want to be sucks.

There. That's my adult fun fact for the day.

CARYS

Wednesday afternoon, I hand my professor my economics final, knowing I passed. That's all that matters. I don't give a second thought to whether it's by one point or one hundred points. That requirement has been fulfilled, and I don't have to take it again. Once I get outside, I grab my phone out of my bag and text Em.

Carys: Hey. I'm done with my test. Let me know when you want to go look at the apartment.

She and I have looked at a few places to live off campus, but none of them have been what we wanted. Thanks to her dad's overcompensation for always being out of the country, we have a much bigger budget than we anticipated. Apparently, rock stars are more generous with their money than their time. At least, according to Em.

Emerson: Stay where you are. We're coming to pick you up now.

I look around the parking lot for her Mustang but don't see it.

Carys: Who's we?

A horn honks as Jack's matte-black Dodge Charger

comes to a stop next to me. The window rolls down, and Emerson leans across her brother. "Get in, bitch. We've got a house to check out."

"What?" I look from her to Jack skeptically. It's just supposed to be Em and me today.

The back door opens, and Theo sticks his head out. "Come on, CC. Hop in."

"Umm . . . okay. But why are you guys going with us?" Maybe my brain is fried from finals, but I'm so confused.

Once I'm in the car, Jack whips out of the parking lot, and Em turns in her seat to face me. "So . . . Jack and I were on the phone with Dad this morning, and it turns out his new girlfriend is a producer on that show, *Selling SoCal.*" Em stops talking, and her wide eyes stare at me, waiting. Expecting a reaction, but I think I'm still confused. At least, I hope I am.

"Okay. So did your dad's girlfriend find the two of us an apartment to look at?"

Please say yes. Please say yes. Please say yes.

Theo throws his arm over the top of the back seat. "Not *just* the two of you."

"Emerson," I clap back, shocked. "My mom is not going to let me live with two guys."

She shakes her head. "Your brother lives with three guys and two girls. And . . . one of them is his girlfriend. What's she going to have to say about you living rent-free in a four-bedroom house with me, my brother, and his best friend?"

"Free? No way. I've got to pay rent." My mom may not be rock-star rich, but we've always been more than comfortable. Her grandfather started one of the oldest banks in Kroydon Hills years ago, and Mom has run it for as long as I can remember. Not to mention, Aiden and I both have trust funds our grandparents set up when we were born that Mom's invested over the years. I can definitely pay my own way.

"Just go with it, Carys." Jack's eyes meet mine through the rearview. "Dad's trying to impress his girlfriend of the week. And apparently, that means he's buying us a house. I'm pretty sure he doesn't give a shit if we even like it."

Emerson interrupts her brother. "I think he may have already bought it but doesn't want to tell us that. I think in his mind, if we like it, he's the hero when he buys it. But my money says it's a done deal."

I look over at Theo. "And you're okay with this?"

"I'm not like the rest of you. I'm here on a scholarship. If Stone Madden wants to buy a house and let me live in it rent-free, why would I say no?"

I guess Theo has a point. But I still feel ambushed.

Jack turns down a street with the ocean in the distance behind the houses, and my mouth drops open.

These are *really* nice houses.

Really nice.

When he turns into a long driveway leading up to a three-story, contemporary house full of windows, I get déjà vu. This house looks similar to—

"Ohmygod," Em yelps. "Linc's house is at the other end of the street." She's out of the door and walking to the end of the driveway to see just how close we are to Linc's before I even get my door open.

Once I'm out of the car, my annoyance ratchets up a notch. Because standing at the front door is a beautiful woman with a camera crew behind her, welcoming us.

I think I might kill Emerson.

69

Turns out, Em and Jack's dad, Stone, was already inside. He was sitting in the kitchen, waiting for them. He'd already bought the house, like Em thought. And okay, so maybe the place is perfect. It's only a ten-minute drive from campus. There are four bedrooms and five bathrooms with a finished basement that's already been equipped with a recording studio. And the backyard . . . well, the backyard is amazing. There's a deck, a hot tub, and a gorgeous stone firepit. And if that wasn't enough, it also has direct beach access.

Even I can't say no.

At least not to the house. I had no problem saying no to signing the waiver that would give them permission to use me on an episode of the TV show they're shooting.

Theo and I want to give Jack and Emerson some alone time with Stone and his girlfriend, so we head into the backyard. He follows me when I slip my sneakers off and push through the black wrought-iron gate to walk on the beach.

I've always loved the beach. The ocean, not so much.

"Hey, wait up." Theo catches up to me and bumps his shoulder against mine. "So, we're gonna be roommates."

"I guess we are." We walk down to the line of hard sand where the waves no longer reach.

"You know what that means, don't you?" Theo's dark hair shines in the sunlight, and his smile lights up his handsome face.

But he doesn't do it for me at all. When we hooked up months ago, I was trying to convince myself that I was available. That my heart didn't already belong to someone else. Because what's the point of someone owning your heart if they don't want it? Why can't we choose who we give it to?

Fate's a fickle bitch.

I stop just far enough that the water washes back out to sea before it reaches my toes, then turn toward Theo. "You know that there will be no roomies with bennies situation going on here, right?"

His hands skim up my arms, but there's not a goose-bump in sight.

Not even a teeny tiny one.

"Now, why would you go and ruin today by saying something so mean, CC? We just got a house with our very own recording studio in the basement and the beach in the backyard. This might be a normal thing for you, but this is not how I live when I'm in Ohio."

I plant my hands on my hips and glare at him. "Listen, it's a great house. Almost too good to be true. But—and this is a really big but—you and I make way better friends than anything else. And we're going to stay that way."

Theo's face twists, and I can't tell from the tight expression if he's really hurt or if he's kidding, so I soften my tone and stroke his ego a bit. "Besides, this time next year, you and Jack will graduate and move to LA. Before you know it, stadiums full of people will be singing your songs. You don't want a girl back in San Diego pining for you. You'll have groupies."

He's quiet for a minute before a mask slips across his face, and his goofy smile returns.

Theo does that.

Masks how he's feeling with humor.

But this time, he's quiet, and he's rarely quiet. "Some women are worth more than groupies, CC." He reaches for me, but a flying furball runs between us.

Wanda, Trick's military dog, quickly backs me up, so I'm a few steps away from Theo as Trick and a very shirt-less, very sweaty Coop jog over to Theo and me. Black basketball shorts hang from lean hips, showcasing a perfect V that I want to drop to my knees and lick.

Wow. Did it just get hotter out here?

I trace every indent of his muscular chest with my eyes. Take in every black line of his tattoos. And watch with rapt attention as a bead of sweat glides over his washboard abs.

Damn. He *has* gotten bigger since last summer.

Coop bends down and scratches behind Wanda's ears. "Good girl."

Seriously? Am I jealous of a dog now?

COOPER

"Hey, man. Isn't that Carys?" Trick points toward two people standing close together, just beyond the reach of the lapping ocean, as he and I finish up our run. The warm rays of the sun shine down, blanketing Carys in a golden glow. Tiny pale-blue cut-off shorts showcase her shapely legs, with a loose blue-and-white-striped V-neck t-shirt tucked in only at the front. Oversized white sunglasses are shoved up on top of her head, holding back chocolate-brown hair that's falling in waves over her shoulders.

She's the most effortlessly beautiful woman I've ever seen.

I'm not supposed to notice, and I hate that I do.

Almost as much as I hate knowing the dude she's with notices it too. How could he not? The difference is, he's allowed to notice her beauty and her playfulness. He's allowed to look at her in a way I shouldn't.

He's the drummer from the other night, and he looks awfully comfortable with her, which inexplicably pisses me off more.

Trick and I come to a stop fifty feet away, and I run my hand down the dog's dark fur. "Hey, Wanda," I say, then point down the beach. "Go save Carys."

Wanda takes off like the missile she is, and Trick groans. "Using a military weapon to interrupt her date? Doesn't seem fair."

"Fuck fair." I watch Wanda step between Carys and the dude as I jog over to them.

I've never been this guy.

The one who wants what he can't have.

If I want it, I earn it.

Then I claim what's mine.

Carys's wide green eyes meet mine, clearly surprised to see us.

"Hey, guys." She watches me scratch behind Wanda's ears before those fiery eyes trace every inch of my exposed skin.

Maybe I'm not the only one fighting this.

Whatever *this* is.

"Hey, Carys." I reach over without thought and kiss the top of her head, which is not how I'd typically greet her, then offer my hand to her friend. "I don't think we were introduced the other night. I'm Cooper."

Carys's cheeks flush. "Sorry." She turns to the guy, who's currently being cock-blocked by a sixty-pound military weapon still dutifully sitting between my girl and him. "Theo, this is Cooper and Trick. I don't think I got the chance to introduce you guys at the Rat last week."

Theo takes my hand, less than thrilled. "You're the stepbrother, right? Nice to meet ya."

I eye little drummer boy and force myself to remember he's right.

She's my stepsister. "What are you guys doing here?"

"We were just looking at our new place." Theo points behind me at the house covered in windows. "We're moving in this weekend."

What the hell? "You didn't mention that the other night."

When Carys Murphy gets pissed, she has this tiny tick in her left eye. It twitches. Just a bit, but I've always noticed it. And it's twitching now. Question is, is she pissed at me for asking or him for sharing?

"That's because I didn't know until today." The look she gives Theo is glacial. Good to know he's the cause of her twitch. "Emerson's dad just bought the place. So, everything sort of came together quickly." She stuffs her hands in the back pockets of her shorts, drawing my eyes momentarily toward her ass. "I'm not sure if it's this weekend or not. But the sooner, the better, I guess. Then I won't have to live on campus for the summer session. Do me a favor and don't mention it to anyone back home yet. I've got to let Mom know before Aiden finds out and tells her before me. I'm not sure how she'll take me moving in with two guys."

"Two?" I don't like the idea of her living with other guys, regardless of what her mom might say. And when did any guy who isn't me become other? When in the fucking hell did I start thinking of her as mine?

She glances at Theo, then back at me. "Yeah, Em's brother, Jack, and Theo."

Trick laughs like an asshole. "How many bedrooms?"

"Don't be a dick. There are four bedrooms. And a fully finished basement with a recording studio." She shakes her head toward Trick, and I kinda like that she called him out. It's nice seeing her hold her own. She never puts up much of a fight in Kroydon Hills, but I'm beginning to notice she's different here. More confident maybe?

"I'm hurt. You don't know me well enough to call me a dick yet. Give it time, and you'd probably come to that conclusion, eventually. But still, it's early for you to figure that out." Trick whistles, and Wanda moves eagerly to his side. "I'm heading back to the house. It was good seeing you again, Carys. Let us know if you need help moving."

"I'll catch up in a few minutes, man," I tell him before

bringing my attention back to the woman who's taken up what feels like a permanent place in my mind since I saw her on stage last week. "Show me your house."

"Was that supposed to be a question, Cooper?" Her voice is sharp, but her smile is soft.

"No." I slide my hand to her lower back. "Lead the way."

She silently laughs. "You gonna tell me I'm a good girl too?"

I lean in close. "You've got to earn it first, baby."

A small gasp escapes her pouty pink lips that I force myself to ignore while I think of all the ways she can earn it.

Theo doesn't say anything but follows us up the beach.

As we get closer to the house, I scan the façade and frown. The rear wall is made entirely of windows. You can see into the whole back of the house.

That's a problem.

"You guys are going to have to be careful. Those windows are a security nightmare. Anyone on the beach at night will be able to see right inside."

Carys ignores me and tugs me into the house, where her roommate and bandmate are talking to Stone Fucking Madden. Holy shit.

"Hey, Coop." Emerson pops up from the bar stool. "Is Linc with you?"

I look around at everyone in the room in shock.

Do they realize Stone Madden is standing in the kitchen?

He's been on the cover of *Rolling Stone*.

Twice.

Carys elbows me. "No. Linc's not with Coop. He and Trick were running on the beach and stopped to say hi."

Emerson's face falls. "Aww. Too bad. I could have introduced him to my dad."

"So introduce me to *this* guy, Emmie." Stone walks over to me and extends his hand, but I just stand there in shock like a complete asshole.

Carys stage whispers, "This is when you shake his hand, Cooper." She's making fun of me, but seriously . . . this is Stone Madden. "I'm sorry, Stone. I think Coop's had too much sun today."

I manage to get it together and take his hand. "Sorry. I'm a huge fan."

"Always nice to hear." He lets go of my hand and throws an arm possessively around a woman who looks a few years older than Carys and Emerson. "Well, guys. We're getting out of here for now. The keys are on the counter. Don't fuck the place up, okay?"

"Love you, Dad." Emerson kisses her father's cheek, then Jack thanks him too before Stone and his woman leave.

"Holy shit. Your dad's Stone Madden?"

Everyone in the room cracks up, but Carys takes pity on me and links her arm through mine. "Come on, Coop. Let me show you my room."

"Ooh," Emerson calls out.

Carys pushes me in front of her, shaking me out of my shock. "Shut up, Em."

The first floor is a mostly open concept with an eat-in kitchen and a family room. At the top of the stairs, there's an open loft looking over the first floor, then a long hall with bedrooms on either side. She opens the farthest door to a white bedroom with white curtains and white furniture.

"That's a lot of white."

"Yeah. But it all comes with the place, so I'll just add some color in. This way I don't have to buy furniture. Nothing in the dorm is mine except my papasan chair."

I can't help but open her curtains and check the locks on the sliding glass doors that lead to the balcony. "How did you get one of the rooms with a balcony?"

"Stone said ladies got the first choice, so Em and I picked the rooms next to each other. Theo and Jack are the two across the hall." She moves to the other side of the room and opens a door. "Look. I even have my own bathroom, so I figure Mom can't be too pissed about me sharing the house with guys. It won't be that different from the dorms."

I step outside onto the balcony. "Sure, it won't. I wouldn't go with that rationale, but I doubt your mom will have a big problem with it. Let her know how close I am and that I'll keep an eye on you." Even those words burn like a bitter pill as I say them, because I'm promising her mom I'll protect her, when in reality, I want to corrupt her.

"I don't need a babysitter, Cooper." She joins me outside and leans against the wrought-iron railing behind her, and I have to fight the urge to drag her closer to me.

"I know that, Carys. Trust me." Babysitters don't have these kinds of thoughts about their stepsisters.

Stepsister. Maybe if I keep reminding myself of that little fact, it'll make this easier.

"And you're leaving." Disappointment lingers in her tone. Can she possibly be feeling the same way I am?

Instead of dragging her to me, I move in front of her and run my hands up the warm skin of her arms, needing to touch her.

"I am, but not yet, and Trick and Linc are just a few houses down once I'm gone. If you need anything, call them."

Her eyes close, and her chest rises on a deep inhale. "When are you leaving?"

"Two weeks." I slide her hair away from her face and

wrap my hand possessively around the back of her neck. My thumb rests at the pulse point on her throat. Her heart is racing in sync with mine.

And I don't know that I've ever wanted any woman more than I do now.

It's wrong in so many ways, yet something about it feels completely right.

Like it's the most important thing I'll ever do.

All my goals over the past five years have been structured to get me here. The Navy. The SEALs. Being a part of DEVGRU and being a Tier 1 operator is what I've got my sights on. This sniper training is my next step.

And I feel like I'm being torn in two right now. I need to be here. Need the time to figure out what this is—this current stretching between us. The attraction, which I've so easily pushed down for more years than I'm willing to admit, has exploded into so much more, and I'm not sure how it happened or why. But there's no denying it's there. And judging by how Carys's pulse is pounding out of control, she feels it too.

Her hands dance over my shoulders before they skate down my arms, and my instincts are telling me she's right here with me.

"Carys . . . where are you?" Emerson's voice drifts through the open doors onto the balcony, and Carys pushes me away abruptly.

"We're out here, Em." She stumbles around me on unsure footing but slips away when I reach out to steady her. She goes back into the bedroom, leaving me to watch her go.

What the fuck am I thinking?

Maybe the timing for this training couldn't be better.

Maybe time away is the best thing I could get now, to clear my head and figure out what the hell I'm doing.

Carys pops her head back outside, smiling nervously. "Hey, we're going to lunch. Wanna come?"

"Sorry. I've got to get back. We're training soon." That's a lie. We've got this week and the next off before the team starts training again. But she doesn't need to know that. I need space before I do something I can't take back. "I'll call you later. Make sure you lock that door behind me." Without thinking about it, I kiss the top of her head and walk away, but not before I catch the look of disappointment on her face.

This is not how today was supposed to go.

CARYS

"Thanks, Mom. I appreciate it." I'm snuggled in my favorite chair, with my laptop resting on my lap, and my mom's beautiful face smiling at me through the screen. She and I both have chestnut-brown hair with natural red highlights. My brother, Aiden, however, is a full-blown ginger.

I waited to FaceTime with her tonight until after Emerson left to spend another night at Linc's house. In the five nights since the party last weekend, she's slept here precisely one time. Sunday. It's crazy to see her like this. When she's actually here, she's talking about him. I'm not sure if she's in love, lust, or completely infatuated.

And since I didn't want any distractions during this video call, it was easier to wait for her to leave before calling. I wasn't expecting my mother to accept this new living arrangement as easily as she has. She and Aiden like to treat me like the baby of the family. Which I guess I am. Or at least I was until Callen was born. She says Aiden and I will always be her babies, but I think that myth was debunked when my brother walked in on her and Coach naked in the kitchen. Poor guy. We'll never let him live that down.

But I also think my time away this year helped her see that I'm not a child anymore.

At least I hope so.

"Oh, honey. You're a smart woman with a good head on your shoulders. Did you really think I'd have a problem with you moving in with Emerson's brother? I trust you. And I miss you so much. Just a few more weeks until I get to see you again." The smile on her face puts my nerves at ease.

My stepfather, Coach, sits down next to my mother at their kitchen table with a wide smile on his face and his black Philadelphia Kings polo shirt on, like a uniform he always wears.

"Hey, kiddo. How are you doing?" Coach is a good-looking older man with dark hair and darker blue eyes. He could easily be confused for someone half his age if not for some salt-and-pepper tendrils starting to show around his temples. My oldest stepbrother, Declan, looks like him. Cooper takes after their mother with his blond hair and baby blues I get lost in at night when I close my eyes.

"I'm good, Coach. Finals are done. I've got a week off before summer classes start." Coach slid easily into the position of stepfather and has been more of a dad to me in the few short years since he and my mom moved in together than I've ever had. My bio-dad left when I was a baby. I barely remember him. But Coach has never awkwardly tried to fill that void. Instead, he's treated me exactly the same as his own daughter, and it happened naturally.

He's a good man. Not my father but someone I love like one.

How disappointed would he be in me if he knew all the naughty things I'd like to do with his son? Things I know will take our family dynamic and spin it like an F5 tornado. What the hell does that say about me?

"So you're moving in with boys?" He makes it sound like we're ten years old, but a smile tugs at my lips anyway.

"Yeah, Coach. Emerson and I are moving in with her brother and his friend, Theo. They're the guys from the band I've been singing with. I've told you about them." I adjust my MacBook on my lap, then add, "They're good guys. I think you'd like them."

"Uh-huh." He looks at me with less-than-convinced eyes. "Just remember that no man will ever be good enough for you, kiddo. And keep your bedroom door locked." He pauses for a moment, then adds, "And maybe a baseball bat under your bed."

Mom smacks his arm. "Leave her alone, Joe."

He drags Mom over onto his lap, and I look away before they start kissing. Wanting her to be happy and having to witness them kissing are two completely separate things, and we've all seen enough of their PDA to last ten lifetimes. "Okay, you two. I'll talk to you later. Love you."

"Love you too, honey."

I close my laptop and sigh. Okay, that was way less painful than I thought it would be.

It's time to start packing up my things.

I've spent the last nine months of my life here. It hasn't always been easy being three thousand miles away from everyone and everything I know and love, but it was the right move.

I think I'm going to look back on this as the year I figured out who I wanted to be and what I wanted to do. Here's hoping it doesn't take me another year to figure out my next steps.

A few hours later, my phone rings with an incoming text from Emerson.

Em: Linc said the team would help us move tomorrow.
Carys: The team? Like the whole team?
Em: Umm . . . yeah. I guess.
Carys: We don't have that much stuff. I'm almost done packing. All I've got are two suitcases, three plastic totes, and my clothes I was planning to leave on the hangers.
Em: CC, when a man offers to lift heavy things, you let him lift the heavy things and then watch those sexy muscles work. I'll be home in the afternoon, and they'll be with me.
Carys: And when do you plan on packing?
Em: Have I told you how much I love you yet?
Carys: YOU OWE ME.
Em: I've got scoop.
Carys: What kind of scoop?
Em: Coop scoop. He asked about you and Theo. He wanted to know if you two dated.
Carys: And what did you tell him?
Em: That you guys had hooked up.
Carys: You're evil. Why would you do that?
Em: To see if he'd get jealous.
Carys: And . . . did he?
Em: Oh yeah. Not a happy camper. Not even after I told him it was last year, and now you guys are just friends. No way that boy isn't interested in you, CC.
Carys: Fine. I'll pack your stupid stuff.

I look at the time on my phone and contemplate calling my best friend, Daphne. But it's nearly midnight in Kroydon Hills, and she's not the nicest person when she's woken up. Damn it.

He seemed jealous. What am I supposed to do with that? Is he interested? I mean . . . I was already starting to think he might be. A hope I've been scared to have takes hold in me. It may only be a small thing now, but everything has to start somewhere.

How do you know when to take the leap?

How do you know if it's worth the risk?

COOPER

Carys's dorm didn't seem as small the other night, when it was just the two of us in here, as it does now with Axe, Linc, Trick, and me all inside the door, waiting for instructions. The girls don't seem to have that much to move.

Emerson circles her arms around Linc's neck and whispers something in his ear before he smacks her ass and grabs three suitcases. "Come on, guys, let's get this done and get out of here."

"Oh yeah, Linc. What do you get when you get this done? Ya gonna share with the team?" Axe grabs a couple of bags and follows behind Linc.

"Fuck off, Axe." Linc's definitely not sharing this time. Pretty sure they've shared a few times before, but he's possessive as hell around Emerson already. She means something to him. Something big . . . important. And Linc isn't the kind of guy who gets attached. He's had a shit life, and I count myself lucky to have him as one of my friends.

The door shuts behind them, and Emerson tosses two plastic totes at Trick. "We really appreciate your help, guys." She adds one more on top of the pile, effectively covering his eyes, and opens the door for him. "Follow my voice to the elevator."

Carys is bent over in the closet, wearing gray cotton booty shorts, the curve of her ass peeking out, and a black Kings T-shirt with *Sinclair* written across the back and

Declan's number displayed under it. The fucked-up caveman in me doesn't like my brother's number on her back, even if my name is above it. But the logical side of my brain knows this is my stepsister. Declan's stepsister. And it shouldn't matter that she's wearing that shirt.

Fucking logic's got nothing on how I feel since she invaded my every waking thought and half my damn dreams a week ago. If her brother knew the thoughts I'm having right now . . . Well, he'd kill me, and rightfully so.

Fuck. It's like my damn heart is going to war with my brain.

And when did my heart get involved?

I clear my throat, and thankfully, she stands up. "What do you need me to carry?"

Carys points toward the box on her desk. "That's my sewing machine. Could you please be extra careful with it?"

"Sure."

She smiles at me. "Thanks for your help, Coop."

And *damn*, that smile gets me every time. I run my hand over the back of her head and under her hair before squeezing the back of her neck. "Whatever you need." Three simple words that I mean from the depths of my soul. I'm not sure when my feelings changed, when they went from awareness to attraction that's now turned into pure need. But they have.

Something about this innocent exchange just did me in. I wrap my hand around the back of her neck and run my thumb over her fluttering pulse. Carys releases the prettiest sigh just before the door slams open, and I drop my hand back down to my side like I need to sever a connection before I get shocked.

Carys's emerald-green eyes are wide and locked on me.

Questions linger behind them.

Yeah, baby. I've got them too.

But instead of answering any of them now, I pick up the box with her sewing machine in it and carry it down to my Jeep.

It doesn't take long to get the girls' things moved over to the new house and for Carys and Emerson to direct us where their boxes need to go. Once everything is in and situated, Emerson grabs her keys. "Okay, CC and I are going to Target to get some new sheets and necessities. Buuuuut . . ." she drags the word out. "We'd love you guys to come back tonight for a thank-you dinner."

Linc throws his arm around her waist. "You cook too?"

"Ha. That would be a big no." Carys snorts and cracks up with laughter.

Seeing her so at ease in her own skin makes me smile.

Emerson sticks her tongue out toward Carys. "Nope. Not a cook, but . . . I order a really mean takeout. The booze is on you guys, if you want it though." When Axe opens his mouth to speak, she silences him by pointing at herself. "Twenty," then points at Carys, "And nineteen for a few more days."

Shit. I forgot her birthday is coming up.

"You want pizza or sushi?" No sooner do the words leave Emerson's mouth than all of us answer.

"Pizza."

When the guys and I walk back into our house, Trick whistles for Wanda and takes her outside, Linc grabs beers from the fridge and tosses them to Axe and me, and I turn to Axe. "You do know you don't live here, right?"

He flicks his bottle cap across the room and into the sink. "Course I do. But Trick pays someone to grocery shop and clean the damn house. If I go to my place, I have to do it myself." He sits down on the sofa and grabs the Xbox remote. Axel hates being alone. We all know it, but he'll never admit it.

"Gonna tell us what we interrupted earlier, Coop?" Linc moves around the living room, grabs one of the other gaming remotes, and drops down onto the recliner.

I fight the urge to tell him to fuck off, to give me time to figure shit out before it becomes the next thing the team focuses on for entertainment. I never cared before. But Carys is different. Everything about her—about this—is more. And it's not up for discussion because I'm not sure I'd be able to control myself if one of them said the wrong fucking thing.

Axe stops mid-sip of his beer and stares. "What'd I miss?"

Linc cues up the game. "You were hitting on the hot blonde across the hall when Trick and I walked in on what looked like . . . I don't know . . . a moment, I guess, between Coop and Carys."

"What the fuck ever, man. A moment? Seriously? Do you need a tampon and some chocolate to go with the vagina you've magically grown?" Axe is a fucker, but he's a funny fucker . . . until he turns his sharp eyes on *me*. "And what the fuck is up with you and Miss Goody Two-shoes? Cause you seem interested in a chick you introduced as your sister, man."

"She's my stepsister. And our parents didn't get married

until I had already moved out here. So it's not like that." I'm not sure if I'm trying to convince him or me.

Axel kicks his feet up on the coffee table, totally relaxed. "Still your stepsister, however you slice it, Sinclair. I'm thinking that's a whole level of complicated you may not want to deal with."

I wouldn't want to deal with it if things were different.

But they're not.

She's not.

And I'm pretty sure this thing between us could be worth it.

Worth the risks. Worth the headache. Worth everything.

"Coop . . . ?" When I don't answer, Linc laughs . . . hard. "Oh shit. I want to see Murphy's face when you tell him you've got the hots for his little sister. Fuck me, that's gonna be funny."

"How about you let Carys and me talk like adults before all you assholes laugh at the fallout?" I leave the two of them to play their video game and go into my room, frustration bubbling to the surface. I love my teammates like my own brothers. But we just lived on top of each other for six fucking months, and right now, I could use a little space to breathe.

Maybe it's guilt that makes me send a text to the group chat I have with the guys back home.

They're living the life I could have had.

The life I would have had if I'd have chosen differently.

But that was never the life I wanted.

Coop: Yo Bash. Did you graduate yet?
Bash: It's official next week. But Coach already has me working out with the Kings.
Declan: Unofficially. Just wait until preseason starts. You

still won't know what hit ya, but you'll be glad you got those extra workouts in.

Bash: Relax, Dec. I wasn't complaining. Besides, Lenny's been rubbing my sore muscles every night.

Declan: Belle used to rub my muscles.

Bash: What happened?

Declan: My sweet wife gave birth to a terrorist. He refuses to sleep, and he never gets off her damn boobs. I love him. He's perfect and amazing. But I want my wife back.

Murphy: Stop knocking her up then.

Brady: Yeah. There's these things called condoms. Want me to get you some?

Declan: Fuck you all.

Bash: At least you can't get us pregnant.

Murphy: Hey Coop—have you seen my sister? How's she doing?

Coop: Carys is good. She just moved into a house with her roommate. How are the girls?

Murphy: Sabrina leaves for Georgetown in two months. She's excited.

Brady: Nattie just put the book she wrote up for preorder. She's already halfway through the next one.

Bash: She let the girls read it, and it got Lenny all kinds of hot and bothered. I'll have to thank her for that.

Murphy: Yup. Sabrina too. Wonder where she got the inspiration for that?

Coop: Fuck off, Murph.

He knows I hate when he talks about my twin sister and Brady fucking around.

Wonder how much he'd hate to know what I was thinking about lately?

Brady: We may have tried a scene or two. Nat wanted to make sure she described them right. LOL
Declan: Dude. That's my little sister. I don't need to know that.
Brady: Coop, man. You coming home for beach birthdays this summer?
Coop: I'm gonna try, but I'll be in training. I don't know if I can fly out for the weekend yet.
Declan: Try harder man. We miss you.

After a few minutes, Brady sends me a separate text, just between the two of us.

Brady: Hey, man. Can you talk?
Coop: Yeah

My phone rings with an incoming FaceTime from Brady.

"Hey, man." Damn, I miss these assholes.

"Yo, Coop. Dude, you need to shave. Wait . . . or are you growing that just to look older?" Brady laughs and shuts the door behind him before sitting down on his bed. "Listen, I've only got a few minutes, and Nattie's downstairs. But if there's any way you can get to the beach for Fourth of July, you've got to do it." Brady's voice sounds almost hesitant, like he's nervous.

"I won't know until I'm at the training, but I'll try. What's going on?" It's not like Brady to beat around the damn bush like this, and my curiosity is piqued.

He opens the drawer of his nightstand and removes a blue box.

Holy shit.

He cracks the box open and holds it in front of the screen. "I'm going to ask her to marry me, and I know it would mean so much to her if you were there, man. To both of us. I understand if you can't make it. But try, if you can. Okay?"

"Damn." I'm actually a little choked up. This guy, who's been like a brother to me, is going to marry my sister. "You remember what I said when you told me you wanted to date her?"

"Yeah. You told me not to hurt her." Brady closes the box and shoves it into the back of his drawer.

"I also told you, you were a good guy. You're a good man, Brady. Take care of my sister."

"Always, man. I'll never be good enough. But no one will ever love her more." He swallows. "Wow. I feel like I just asked your dad for permission."

"What did he say when you did?" I can't imagine Dad not being happy for Nat. Brady's loved her for years.

"I wanted to tell you before I asked him. But if you ever tell him that, I'll fucking kill you."

Yeah. He could try.

"I won't say a word." Nattie's voice calls out for Brady in the background.

"Gotta go, Coop."

"Yeah. See ya, man."

We end the call, and I stare at my phone.

My sister's getting married. What's that going to be like?

I lie back on my bed and close my eyes.

Soon, images of Carys invade my mind. Her at the end of an aisle, looking at me with glittering green eyes. Her pregnant, then holding our baby . . . Holy shit. Our baby.

I'm not sure how I didn't realize it before.

Why I didn't see it?

This woman is my endgame.

And fuck anyone else who tries to tell me I'm wrong.

CARYS

Anyone who says they can't find what they want in Target is blind or lying. Emerson and I managed to fill two entire carts, and we probably could have kept going if we had a little more time and room in the car to get it all home. Unfortunately, it's basically where your sense of time and your original to-do list go to die.

I'm not even sure how many hours later it is before we get home. Our blankets and sheets have been washed and should be done drying soon. I set my bathroom up first because I was in desperate need of a shower. If the guys weren't coming back for dinner, I'd have taken a long bath in the claw-foot tub calling my name, but I'd have never been dressed in time for dinner if I'd given in. I've missed soaking in a bath since I moved to San Diego. Obviously, that's not something I got to enjoy while I was living in the dorms. But here, my bedroom has its own en suite bathroom with a black-and-white subway-tiled standing shower and a white clawfoot tub.

Knowing that and with that tub in mind, I went a little goofy at Target, and I now have three oversized apothecary jars filled with bath salts, bath bombs, and bubble bath sitting pretty on the counter next to my favorite island mango candle.

All I need is a book, and it's my own version of self-care.

I can't wait to soak in that tub for hours, lost in a book.

But tonight isn't going to be that night.

Instead, I showered quickly and ran a towel and a wide-tooth comb through my hair, then stared at my lingerie drawer. A sense of pride washes over me as I look at the beautiful pieces Chloe and I've created. After a minute, I decide on a tiny, silk black-and-white thong and a white silk push-up bra with contrasting black lace cupping the top of my breasts. No one will see my lingerie, but having them on is like wearing a shield. I feel stronger and more confident knowing they're there.

As I turn and look at myself in the full-length mirror, I can't help but wonder what Cooper would think if he saw me in this. I shake off the goosebumps that break out across my skin at that thought and throw on a pair of hip-hugging black leggings and a cropped, ribbed, charcoal-gray tank. It's casual but cute, and after a night spent packing up my room and very little sleep, it's as good as it's going to get. A swipe of mascara and some Chap Stick, and I'm good to go, just in time to hear the doorbell ring.

"CC, can you get the door?" Emerson hollers from her room. "I'm naked, and I think it's the pizza."

What would she have done if it wasn't the pizza guy at the door? Answered it naked? If she knew it was Linc, she absolutely would have. Without question.

Em has no shame.

She's one of the most confident women I know.

I'm trying to be more like her.

However, Linc won't be alone tonight. And whoa momma—does the idea of Cooper Sinclair seeing my roommate naked make my stomach churn.

I skip down the steps and hurry to the front of the house, but when I peek through the peephole of the arched wooden door, it looks like I already missed the pizza man. I open the door and step to the side.

"Hey, guys."

Cooper stands on the other side of the door in a plain gray tee with NAVY written across the front in black font. His black Philly Kings ball cap sits backwards on his head as he steps through and offers a wide smile.

"Pizza guy showed up at the same time we did." He lifts the boxes a little higher with a shrug, then looks back at the guys while they share a secretive laugh. "I think we might have scared him." He drops a quick kiss on the top of my head as he passes by with four pizza boxes in his hands, headed toward the kitchen.

In the span of six days, we've become people who touch . . . who linger.

And I'm all for it. But I'm also a woman who knows how she feels and has felt this way for years.

The question is, do I try to talk to him about it before he leaves for his training?

My gut says yes, a resounding yes. But I'm not sure my nerves will allow it.

Linc follows Coop in, holding two takeout bags and leading the way for Axel and Trick, who both carry beer.

"Thanks, guys." I shut the door and lock it before joining them in the kitchen.

Cooper's eyes warm my skin as they linger on the bare stretch of my stomach exposed between my leggings and my tank.

I fight the urge to cover up and hope I'm not turning ten shades of red. Damn fair skin. Every time I get the least bit embarrassed or excited, not to mention drunk, I turn into the living embodiment of a tomato.

Hoping no one will notice my reaction, I busy myself finding the paper plates and napkins we bought earlier. When I open one of the upper cabinets, the plates sit on the top shelf. Emerson has no concept of what short people can and can't reach. But before I can stretch up on the tips of my toes to grab them, Coop moves behind me, crowding me but not touching me. Close enough that his warmth engulfs me when he grabs the plates above my head with ease.

His lips brush over the skin of my ear, and a shiver rips down my spine when he whispers, "I should buy you a step-stool as a housewarming present."

I spin slowly around, and he takes a small step back without looking away. "Maybe I like having you around."

His face changes from goofing around to more guarded. But there's something there. "I won't always be able to be here, Carys. Not with my job."

"I know what your job is, and I know what it means to you." If he's trying to warn me, it's not working.

With an almost imperceptible tip of his chin, his face relaxes, and a small smile slips into place before Axel calls his name. Then, with lightning-quick speed, Cooper's hand grips my hip and moves me an inch away from him before he catches the beer tossed his way.

"Dude, Axe." Coop chuckles. "How the hell can you have such great aim with a gun and such bad aim with a beer?"

"Fuck off, Sinclair. Let's see if you can touch my numbers when you get back from sniper training. Then we'll talk." Axel grabs two slices of pizza, adds some onion rings to his plate, then takes his beer and follows Linc and Emerson through the door to the back deck.

I reach out and fist Cooper's t-shirt while my heart lodges in my throat. "You're going to sniper training?"

"I'm just gonna . . ." Trick motions toward the door the others just walked through. "I'm gonna . . . Yeah." He looks from me to Coop. "Good luck, man." And he's gone with the rest of them.

"Doesn't that make you a target?" I've read everything I could about SEALs since Cooper went to boot camp with the intention of making the teams, and I know what this means.

He puts his beer down, then wraps his hands around my waist and lifts me easily to sit on the counter, and before I even realize what he's doing, he's positioned himself between my legs. In any other circumstance, I'd be all for this, but not when I can't stop picturing him hurt or worse.

"Coop—" I try to force my voice to sound calm but fail miserably before he cuts me off.

"Nope. My turn." Cooper rests his hands on either side of my thighs, crowding me again. "I need you to listen to me, Carys. I need you to really hear me. Okay?"

With shaking hands, I reach up and remove his cap.

Needing to touch him.

Unable to deny the connection there.

"Yes, I'm going to sniper training. You can never have too much training. Can never be too skilled. I have the best training the United States government has to offer, Carys." His voice is firm and leaves very little room for question.

He stands between my dangling legs. His strong, callused hands rest on top of my thighs. This is the closest we've been since the night of our parents' wedding, and I love it and hate it all at once.

"Every time we go down range, there's a risk. But my team is the best of the best, and we're gonna do everything to make sure we all get home safe."

Emotion clogs my throat at the mention that it won't always be safe, and I have to swallow the threatening tears.

"Promise?"

He tucks a lock of my hair behind my ear and holds the back of my neck in a possessive grip like earlier. A move that is so perfectly Cooper, and God, do I want him to be possessive of me.

"Yeah, baby. I promise."

If he didn't already own my heart, this moment right here would be the moment that sealed it. But just when my heart soars, thinking he might kiss me, the back door opens, and Axel walks in, abruptly ending whatever could have been in this moment.

"Come on, future baby momma. Pizza's getting cold, and your girl sent me in here to get the two of you." Axel grabs the pizza boxes with a shit-eating grin on his face as he winks. "Now hurry it the hell up."

Coop offers me his hand as I hop off the counter, his eyes still holding me captive. "We're not done yet, Carys."

"We haven't even started yet, Coop."

But I think we're finally about to.

COOPER

I thought Carys and I would have a chance to finish our conversation before the night was over. But I should have known better. Axel dominated her attention for the next few hours. And while at first it pissed me off, I started paying closer attention to her reactions to him. Once I realized she was tolerating him the way she does her brother, it was easy enough to laugh along and let go of my jealousy.

Even if I'm gonna put an end to that shit real soon.

Every time Axe called her "future baby momma," I wanted to kill him.

Never felt that way over any girl before.

But Carys isn't just any girl. She's mine. Soft and strong, with a heart bigger than anyone I've ever known. And if I really want to give this a shot . . . If I'm right and she feels the same way, this won't be like any other relationship has ever been. It can't be.

Carys Murphy isn't a girl you hook up with—she's the girl you spend your life with.

She's been yawning for the past hour, trying to hide her exhaustion. So, when Linc and Emerson head upstairs to Em's room, the guys and I call it a night. But as the others walk away, I stop and look at the woman curled up in the corner of the couch.

"Hey." Taking her hands, I pull her to her feet. "Go to

bed. Don't make me worry that you're falling asleep out here, okay?"

She covers another yawn, then leans her forehead against my chest. Her hair falls forward, covering her face, and the sweet fruity scent of her grapefruit shampoo catches in the wind for a moment. But it's long enough for me to realize I want more.

I need to know if her skin tastes sweet too.

"What are you doing tomorrow night?" I ask.

"What?" She pulls back, and sleepy, soft green eyes blink up at me through long dark lashes. "I'm singing at the Rathskeller tomorrow with the band."

That could work. "What time do you guys go on?"

"Eight o'clock. Why? Are you and the guys gonna come?" She yawns again, and I turn her toward the back door, a plan forming in my head.

"Go to bed, Carys. Lock the door behind you."

Her head swings around, and those green eyes sparkle under the moonlight. I swear I can tell exactly what this woman is thinking from her eyes. They show everything. "You're awfully bossy, Cooper Sinclair. How did I not know that?" She might be giving me hell, but she's enjoying it, so I don't care.

"Lock the damn door, Carys." I shove my hands into my pockets to keep from reaching out to her. I need to stay exactly where I am, because if I move now, I'll be crossing a line I want her wide awake for. And I need to see if we're both on the same page before that happens.

"Fine," she huffs. "Bossy and moody. Night, Coop."

"Goodnight." I stand with both feet firmly planted until she's closed and locked the sliding glass door behind her. She doesn't look back as she moves up the stairs. And I wait until she's completely out of sight before I leave.

When I walk in the front door of my house, Trick's in

the kitchen filling Wanda's water bowl with Axel nowhere in sight. "Axe already gone?"

"Yeah. He went home. Sometimes I think Wanda's better trained than he is." He puts the bowl down in front of the dog and scratches behind her ears. "Isn't that right, girl?"

Wanda cocks her head, and I swear, one of these days, that dog is gonna answer him. I shake my head at that thought. "Okay well, I'm going to bed."

"Hey, man. Wait. Axe asked me to pass along a message." He straightens and leans against the wall behind him. If he's waiting for me to squirm, he'll be waiting a long damn time. "He said to make your move or lose your chance. Think he was talking about Carys." Trick smiles a crooked fucking smile, and I have to remind myself not to punch the messenger.

Fucking Axel thinks he's got a chance with my girl.

Not happening.

I might have needed to work through a few things before I figured my shit out, but I'll fucking kill him before I let him near her. And when I empty my pockets on my nightstand and see my phone lit up with a text, something in me settles.

Carys: Text me when you get home, bossy.
Coop: Now who's worrying about who?
Carys: I've worried about you since you joined the Navy, Coop.
Coop: Don't worry. I've got this. I'll always come back.
Carys: Who are you coming back to?
Coop: You going to be waiting for me?
Carys: Maybe.
Coop: I'll see you tomorrow night, Carys. Sweet dreams.
Carys: Good night, Cooper.

The Rathskeller is packed when I walk through the door Friday night, but it's easy to find the guys at the bar. Even Rook is here tonight. And he's not big on . . . well, he's not big on people in general. When I join Rook, Axel, Trick, and Linc, Axe eyes me like a bug he'd like to squash.

"No flowers for our girl?"

"She's not your girl." I slide in next to him and flag Brenda down for a beer. "And it's not a dance recital. You don't bring flowers."

"What the hell do you know about dance recitals, Sinclair?" Rook eyes me skeptically.

"More than you. My twin has been dancing since she could walk. And my sister-in-law owns a ballet studio. I know more than any man should ever have to about dance recitals. Just trust me."

Rook shivers. "Yeah . . . not something I had to worry about growing up." He's one of six brothers who, according to him, have been trained to be military men since they were little. Guess dance wasn't exactly part of his life.

Emerson struts toward us, her eyes locked on Linc, and you'd think, based on how she practically runs to him, it had been more than a few hours since they were together. But before I have time to give that too much thought, the band takes the stage, and I zero in on their lead singer.

She looks . . . holy shit. I have no words.

Carys is wearing another miniskirt, like last week, but that's where the similarities end. Instead of leather, today's skirt is denim. She switched last week's knee-high boots out for a pair of pink Doc Martens, and stretching tight across her chest is a cropped, pink Philadelphia King's t-shirt with a sparkly gold logo in the middle. Her shiny hair hangs in curls down around her shoulders, and it shimmers under the lights as she takes the front of the stage.

The guy she doesn't live with starts off with a familiar guitar solo, and Carys sways back and forth to the music before she takes the mic in her hands and opens her mouth. The first few words of "Sweet Child O' Mine" float throughout the bar, and the crowd goes wild just before Jack and Theo join in. A roar flows through the crowd, and her responding smile warms somewhere deep in my soul.

She dances around the stage as she sings, moving from each guitarist to the drummer and back. Then, she's holding the microphone out to the crowd for them to sing along with the chorus. "She's fantastic," I say to no one and everyone, completely in awe.

"So, you manning up and taking baby momma home with you, or am I?" I know Axel's kidding, but I throw my elbow back into his gut anyway and enjoy when he doubles over, coughing.

"Ooh. Guess it ain't you, Axe," Trick laughs.

"Lay off the baby momma shit, and I'll let you walk out of here tonight. Call her that again, and we're gonna have a problem, brother." I cut my eyes to him, and the fucker's eyes are watering as he decides which he wants to do more —breathe or laugh.

Once he catches his breath, he stands tall and looks around at the guys. "Pay up, assholes. I was right. It took a week." He opens his palm and shoves it in the guys' grumbling faces as each one pulls a twenty out and slaps it down. "Told ya."

"What the hell are you talking about?" Emerson asks as Linc moves her from his lap to grab his wallet from his back pocket.

Axel drops the money down on the bar and wiggles his eyebrows at Brenda. "Brenda . . . love of my life. Drinks are on me for the team tonight." He stretches over the bar like he's going to kiss her until she smacks him with her towel.

"Drinks are on Axel, boys. What are ya having?" She lines up a row of shot glasses, knowing us all too well.

"Well, since you asshats are betting on me, I think this calls for some Don Julio."

Once the tequila is poured, we raise our glasses.

"To claiming the girl," Rook offers. "It's about mother-fucking time."

"To claiming the girl," the guys repeat.

"Woo! I'll drink to that." Emerson throws her shot back, then grimaces from the burn before her eyes grow wide as they catch on something across the bar. "Oh my God. Dad?" She jerks away from Linc and runs over to Stone Madden and his entourage, who just walked through the doors of the Rat. He's wearing a hat pulled low over his eyes. Guess it's his attempt to go unnoticed. Shame it's not working. Everyone in the back half of the bar noticed him as soon as he walked through the door.

Rook stands from his stool and stares hard at Linc. "Her dad is Stone Madden? What part of low profile do you not understand?"

Linc watches his girl. "Relax, man. My profile *is* low. Em isn't the famous one." His argument doesn't satisfy Rook, but the team's number two doesn't push it for now because Emerson walks over with her dad, followed by the lead singer of Black Stone, Eddie Black.

Ho-ly. Shit. They're rock royalty.

Stone's girl from the other day is attached to his arm, and Emerson has hers linked through Eddie's as she makes the introductions.

But before she can finish, Eddie whistles. "Wow, look at Jacky boy up there. He remind you of us at that age,

Stone?" Eddie crosses his arms over his chest and watches the stage with an eagle eye. "Who's the singer?"

"That's my roommate, Carys. Jack's trying to convince her to join the band." Emerson beams with pride for Carys. "And he hates when you call him Jacky."

Her dad orders a round of beers and hands one to her, not caring that she's not twenty-one. "What do you mean trying to convince? She's a fucking natural up there. Great voice. Great look."

"Great legs too," Eddie laughs, and rock royalty or not, I want to punch him in his pretty-boy face.

"She sings for fun. She doesn't want to be in a band. Carys is helping the guys out while they try to replace the last guy." Emerson runs her fingers over the lacey black shirt she's wearing. "She wants to design clothing. She made me this last weekend."

Stone's girlfriend rubs the ribbons between her fingers. "She made this?" She looks questioningly at Emerson. "This is fantastic. Where does she sell her designs?"

Before Emerson can answer, Eddie does. "Fuck designs. That girl was born to be a star. You can't teach what she's got."

Emerson pats his chest condescendingly. "I'm telling you, this isn't what she wants. She's just filling in."

"We'll see about that." He stares at Carys like he's judging one of those contests on TV and he's got her golden ticket in his pocket.

I want to tell this guy to back off, but I'm not going to be the guy who causes a scene while Carys is on stage. Instead, I remove myself from the crowd and move down the bar to stand next to Rook.

"Ignore him, Sinclair. Dude's an overprivileged asshole. Trust me, I know the type."

"Yeah . . ."

We're quiet for a minute while we watch the band.

Carys transitions to a P!NK song. Her voice builds, and she closes her eyes as she reaches for the high notes, sending goosebumps over my skin.

"That's my baby momma," I hear yelled into the crowd, and if it weren't for the smile gracing her beautiful face when she hears it, swear to God, I'd fucking kill Axe.

CARYS

WHEN SIX DAY WAR PRACTICED THIS MORNING, WE DECIDED to have a little fun with tonight's closing song. Jack and I finish the set with a cover of "Cheap Thrills." And as I raise my hands over my head and bounce along with the chorus, my smile grows bigger than I ever thought it would. If last week was a rush, our performance tonight has been a high, higher than any I've ever had singing for a crowd.

When we leave the stage and step into the back hallway, my sweaty hair is sticking to my even sweatier face, but I feel freaking fantastic.

"Guys . . . Wow! I can see how you can get addicted to that high."

Jack hauls me in for a quick hug. "Told you so. Give me a few weeks, and you're never gonna give us up." If I'm not careful, I could totally see him being right, and I really don't want to fall into that trap. "We're like an STD you can't get rid of, CC."

"Ew, gross." I shove him away. "Not winning yourself any points there, Madden."

"Dude." Theo twirls his drumstick between his fingers like they're an extension of his body. "Your dad brought Eddie Black with him tonight. Did you know he was doing that?" Anxious energy is rolling off him in waves.

"Seriously, I didn't even know Dad was coming." He grabs his bass from Lucas. "I would have told you if I did."

Lucas scoffs, holding tight to his guitar case. "I'm glad I

didn't know. I had a hard time controlling my nerves once I saw them."

"Don't look at their faces." All three guys stop what they're doing and stare at me.

"What?" Lucas is a newbie like me. But I know he's hoping this leads to a permanent place in the band.

"Don't make eye contact. Instead, look right above everyone's heads. That way, they all think you're looking at them, but you're not. It helps control the nerves. Trust me. I might be new to the whole band thing, but I've been on stage my whole life. That's my trick. Avoid eye contact."

"Well, damn." Theo stands there, staring until Jack kicks his foot. "You've basically played a stadium."

I can't hold in my laugh. "I wouldn't go trying to score us a spot at Wembley just yet."

We get our gear packed up as quickly as possible so Jack can say *hi* to his dad, and Theo and Lucas can schmooze the rockstars before they leave. I'm not sure what it says about me that the only person I want to see tonight has absolutely nothing to do with rockstars.

Another reminder that the rockstar life really isn't for me.

Once we push through the crowd dancing to the music the DJ spins, I see our group taking up the entire back corner of the bar. Well . . . I notice the whole group, but I only see Cooper. Everyone around him is talking, laughing, and drinking. But not Cooper. He's staring at me with a look in those baby-blue eyes I desperately want to believe is need because want and desire don't even exist in the same stratosphere as the need I have for him.

Need is so much more.

But before I can make my beeline for Coop, Jack grabs my arm and tugs me behind him to talk to his dad and Eddie Black.

They talk about the band.

About the sound.

The need for original music.

Jack tells him about the songs I've helped him and Theo write this year. We only perform a few in each set because the bar crowd wants the covers. It's a smart move on the guys' part. Give the crowd what they want, but add a little of your own music each week, so they start wanting more of that too.

Stone and Eddie try to convince me that I'd be crazy to pass up the opportunities I'll get as part of Six Day War. They talk about labels and touring.

And the entire time, I feel Cooper's eyes on me.

Two bottles of water later, I excuse myself to use the ladies' room . . . And to give myself a break from this full-court press from the band and Stone and Eddie to get me to change my mind about sticking with them. They don't seem to be listening to me at all, which is pissing me off. And I really do have to pee. So, it's not a complete duck-and-run plan.

The bar is more packed now than it was during our set, and I push my way through the crowded dance floor full of writhing bodies and drunk coeds. The bathroom is tucked away in the back hall, near the stage. And thank goodness, it's empty because at this point tonight, I'm in no mood to wait in a line of people just to pee.

Once I've washed my hands and run a damp cloth over my face, I flip my head over and run my fingers through my hair to try to fluff it up a little. My thin hair has very little body to it on a good day, and a good day died under the heat of the lights earlier. I tug my skirt down just an inch on my hips and adjust my bra, so what little boobs I have sit a bit higher because it can't hurt. And screw anyone who says they're not at least a tiny bit vain. Because

I like to think I'm low-maintenance, but I still want to look my best.

When I open the door and step out into the hall, I manage to crash face-first into a wall.

Well, not so much a wall as someone's chest.

A large someone.

Oh shit.

A man I don't know grabs both my shoulders and crowds me against the wall.

I look around, but there's no one else in the hallway. And the music is so loud, I don't think anyone will even hear me if I scream.

"Has anyone ever told you, you have the voice of an angel?"

COOPER

TRICK AND ROOK ARE ARGUING OVER SOMETHING. I SHOULD be paying attention to what, but I'm not. Carys went to the bathroom almost ten minutes ago, and I haven't seen her since. I watched her push her way through the crowd, but once she was on the other side of the dance floor, I lost her as she turned down the hall, and something about it isn't sitting well with me.

"Right, Coop?" Trick asks.

I have no clue what the hell he said before that and nod my head as I push off the bar and follow the path Carys took a few minutes ago. But with every step, warning bells start to go off in my mind, and I pick up my speed.

Then I turn down the hallway.

Carys is pinned against the wall by a large man.

He's five foot ten, two hundred and fifty pounds.

He looks sloppy drunk.

Physically, he's no threat.

I can easily take him, but I can't be sure he doesn't have a weapon.

His face is too close to hers.

His body is invading her space.

Her delicate palms are flat against his chest, and her eyes are wide with fear while his fingers run through her hair.

I step between them before either one realizes what's happening.

With a hand to his chest, I shove him back, and he crashes to the floor.

When she tries to step around me to see what's happening, I reach back to stop her. Squeezing her hip, I wait to see how this dude reacts and if he's going to reach for a weapon.

His eyes are less than focused one minute, then full of fear the next. "What did you do that for?" He sounds like a big kid. "That hurt."

"Coop." Carys tugs at my shirt. "I don't think he was trying to hurt me."

The guy runs a hand over the back of his head. "I just wanted to tell her she sounds pretty when she sings."

Carys laces her fingers through mine and carefully moves around me. "Thank you."

"Hey." I'm not as forgiving as she is. "Don't ever put your hands on a woman."

He gets to his feet and backs away from us. "I'm sorry."

We watch as he stumbles down the hall. Once he's out of sight, she leans back against me, letting me take her weight.

I scoop her into my arms before she falls. "Is there a back door here?"

"I can walk, Cooper." Her clammy skin and shaking body tell me otherwise before she points me toward the end of the hall.

We round a corner to an old metal door that dumps us in the back parking lot not far from my Jeep. I carry Carys to it and open the back gate, then set her down on it. Gently, I run my hands over her arms and down her sides, checking for injuries. The air outside sits heavy against our skin as a storm gathers in the distance.

"Are you hurt, baby? Did he hurt you?"

"No. He didn't hurt me." She crinkles her nose, causing

the light dusting of freckles on it to bunch up. "I'm okay. He just scared me. I don't think he realized what he was doing. He seemed like he just wanted to talk but had no clue that he was scaring me. Maybe he drank too much. Maybe he's socially awkward. I don't know. But I don't think he was trying to attack me."

"Baby." I run my hands over her head and ghost my fingers across her face, needing to know for myself that she's really okay. "Do not ever make an excuse for a man who doesn't know to keep his fucking hands to himself. That is never okay." I hold her possessively in my arms and breathe her in as I try to get myself under control.

Thunder crashes in the distance as if it's channeling the rage that courses through my body. It's a living, breathing thing, threatening to explode if I don't lock it down. "If something happened to you . . ." I leave the rest of the sentence unsaid, unwilling to think about the what-ifs. Instead, I focus on this woman. This moment.

Carys wraps her arms around my waist and runs her palms soothingly up my back, even though I'm supposed to be taking care of *her*.

"Cooper . . ." Her breath warms my cheek.

I pull back and cup her face in my hands. Her eyes shine with unshed tears that I wish I could take away for her. Make it so she never knows fear. My thumb traces the curves of her face.

She closes her eyes, and those long lashes kiss her perfect skin as she slowly drags her teeth over her trembling lower lip and leans into my hand. Then on a whisper, her eyes open and she asks, "Do you want to kiss me, Cooper?"

"More than my next fucking breath, Carys." I'm not sure I've ever wanted anything more. I fight the urge to crush my mouth to hers.

To take what I need.

What we both desperately want.

What I've wanted for fucking years.

Instead, I lean down slowly and brush my mouth over hers, groaning when her sweet taste explodes on my lips.

Carys moans, and electricity sparks between us. My cock twitches behind the zipper of my jeans before I slide one hand to the back of her head and gently tug her hair, then tilt her head as I deepen the kiss. My other hand grips her waist, dragging her closer.

Needing more.

Wanting everything.

Trailing my mouth along her jaw, I lick the salty sweat from her skin while she claws at my chest, trying to get closer.

The sexy sigh she breathes out when her hands slide up under my shirt and rest on my bare pecs is intoxicating. And my dick grows hard as steel, wanting in on the action.

As if sensing what I need, she wraps her legs around my waist and her arms around my back. She rubs her chest against mine with a moan at the delicious sensations of her soft curves fitting perfectly against the hard planes of my body. Our tongues dance a slow dance. Learning. Exploring. Setting every fucking nerve ending ablaze, like a live wire skipping across a street, ready to set fire to whatever it touches.

Her nails dance across my waist and tug at my belt as I run my tongue down her neck, stopping to trace lazy circles over her racing pulse.

Carys clings to me, grinding against me.

The heat of her pussy tempts me to take this further than we should.

Not yet.

Not here.

Not like this.

She deserves more. Better.

She deserves flowers and dinner. Promises.

She doesn't deserve the back of a Jeep.

"Carys . . ." Unfocused eyes stare back at me, scorching my soul. "I—"

My phone rings in my pocket, and it's not just any ringtone.

Fuck.

I pull back and rest my head on top of hers as she groans. "Ignore it, Coop. Please tell me you're going to ignore it."

"I wish I could." I yank my phone from my jeans and look at the screen. "It's Command. We've got to go in."

"Now?" Her hands fist my shirt. "Like . . . you need to go *in*, in? Like you're getting sent somewhere now?" Her words are fast. Clipped . . . and scared.

I expected frustration, but what I see instead is fear, and I never want to be the reason this woman is afraid. "Yeah, baby. I've got to go in. We all do. It's part of the job. Can I drive you home first?"

She kisses me again nervously and runs her hands over my face. "Will you let me know before you leave?"

"Yeah. I'll let you know as soon as I can." Her eyes well up with tears. "Please don't cry."

Carys sniffs as she forces her tears back and sets her shoulders tight. "Thanks for saving me tonight, Coop."

I kiss the freckles on the bridge of her nose, then haul her against my chest.

A week ago, I'd have been thrilled to get spun up again already.

Funny how quickly your perspective can change.

An hour and a half later, we've been briefed on a mission gone wrong.

Alpha Team—a unit out of Virginia Beach—has been in the Sudan on a mission, but their cover was blown by a former British special agent.

Charlie Team is being sent in to pick up where Alpha Team left off.

Once Command gives the orders and clears out of the room, Ford stands there, arms folded over his chest, staring at me. "Sinclair. You're supposed to be on a plane for sniper school in two weeks. If you miss the start, you can't just drop in when you get back. We understand if you want to skip this one, so you don't risk fucking that up."

I close my laptop in front of me and stand up with it in hand. "Not a chance, Master Chief. I'm not letting you guys have all the fun without me. Axe would never let me live it down."

"Damn straight," Axe adds with a fist bump.

"OK. It's settled then, boys. Our flight leaves at zero-five-hundred. Get your shit in order." Ford gives us our marching orders, and we all exit the war room, then grab our phones that have to be left outside the door.

I turn it on and quickly look at the screen. There's one message from Carys.

Carys: Please be safe.

I have a choice to make.

Coop: You still awake?
Carys: Yes.

Coop: Can I stop by?

Carys: I'm already waiting.

The need to see her before I leave is so strong that it's the only thing I think about as I drive to her house and park my car on the street directly behind Linc's. I figured this was where he was going too, but we didn't stop to talk on our way out. This is the first time either one of us has had someone to say goodbye to before a mission.

Before I make it to the front door, it opens, and all I see is Carys. Standing in an oversized Kroydon Hills Prep football t-shirt that hangs off one bare shoulder. Her legs are bare, and her hair hangs damp around her shoulders. As soon as I'm close enough, she throws her arms around my shoulders, and I lift her off her feet, walking inside.

She slides her legs around my waist. "How long before you leave?" She holds my cheeks in her hands as a tear tracks down her face, wrecking me.

"I have to be back on base by five a.m., but I've got to stop at my house before I go. So maybe five hours."

Her thumb runs along my jaw. "Come to bed with me, Coop. You need to sleep."

I grab the back of her head and press a kiss to her forehead, then lock the door behind me.

Is it possible to be in love with a woman you've only kissed once?

CARYS

Cooper carries me up the stairs to my bedroom and, with more gentleness than he looks capable of, places me down on the bed. I reach over and grab my phone from the nightstand and turn on my new nighttime playlist.

He reaches behind his neck and drags his t-shirt over his head, and I momentarily stop thinking altogether and stare. His body is a work of art, cut like a marble statue, and my heart speeds up at the sight. He kicks off his sneakers and steps toward my open balcony doors.

"You sleep with these open?"

I tuck my knees up inside my shirt, resting my arms around them, and then tilt my head, fascinated by the movement of the muscles in his back. "Not usually. But Linc and Em aren't exactly quiet." I shrug. "The music helps, but the sound of the ocean works even better."

When he turns and unbuttons the top button of his jeans, my brain explodes.

"Do you care if I take my jeans off?" He says it so casually that I have to bite down hard on my bottom lip to keep in the hysterical laughter threatening to bubble up and burst free.

"If you're trying to seduce me, Cooper, you're doing a freaking phenomenal job."

His eyes go dark with lust, and a swarm of butterflies suddenly take flight in my stomach. "If I was trying to seduce you, Carys, you wouldn't be talking right now." He shucks his jeans and sits down on the bed with his back against the headboard before reaching for me. The chunky black watch he wears is a stark contrast to his tanned skin and looks sexy as hell on his wrist. I don't think I've seen him without it since the first time I saw him at the bar.

I lean over the nightstand and switch off the light, bathing us in darkness. There isn't even moonlight filtering in through the storm clouds gathering over the ocean. And as Coop holds me in his arms, a loud boom in the distance is followed by a bright bolt of lightning over the churning waves. The first fat drops of rain start to fall, playing a staccato beat against the wrought-iron railing of the balcony.

I tentatively trace my fingers over his chest, trying to shake my wracked nerves. The cocooning darkness of the night emboldens me.

"Do you ever get scared?" I whisper, wanting to know but terrified of his answer.

"Yeah," he answers just as quietly. "Fear is healthy. It reminds you you're alive." He absently plays with my hair, running his hand through the length of it, then twirling a lock around his finger before tucking it behind my ear. "But then the adrenaline kicks in, and your body does what it's trained to do. It's when the adrenaline rush is over that your mind starts to wander. Starts to remember . . ."

His body is warm and relaxed, and I'm finding it hard to believe he's here, next to me right now, but who knows where he'll be tomorrow.

"Coop . . . what changed?" I can't believe I'm asking, but I need to know. "Why now? What made you look at me now?" My words stay soft. Unsure.

Cooper presses his lips to the top of my head before answering, and I inhale his clean scent, memorizing it, so I can still smell it once he's gone. "Do you really think I only just saw you, Carys?"

I tilt my head back and run my hand up his neck to the back of his head. If I ever want this to be more, I have to be honest. "I guess I do. This last week has been different. You've been different."

With an almost imperceptible shake of his head, he agrees with me. "I guess I have, but so have you. When I met you, you were a freshman in high school. Your brother was my best friend, and I was about to turn eighteen. There was no way anything could have happened then, but I promise you, I saw you. I always saw you." Coop crosses his legs at his ankles and gets comfortable.

"I saw how you would beam up at Murphy any time you two were in the same room. I paid attention to the way you'd talk about being a Broadway star one day and saw every single show you performed on Kroydon Prep's stage once I moved to town. My favorite was *Rent*. You killed it, but I didn't like when you had to die for a minute at the end."

A cool breeze blows in through the doors, and goose-bumps scatter over my bare skin.

Not as much a reaction to the cold as the realization that this man has always seen me.

"I watched you get quiet when there were too many people around. The way you prefer to be surrounded by people you know, people you feel safe with. I know the freckles across your nose and cheeks get darker in the summer and you hate the ocean at night. I've been watching you for a long time, baby. But our family situation is complicated. I haven't figured out how we're going to deal with all that yet. But seeing you last week . . . away from everyone else." He trails the tips of his fingers along my throat, and I shiver as the heat building between us comes close to incinerating us both.

"You're not that kid anymore, Carys. Neither of us is."

I lay my face against his shoulder and hide my eyes. "I saw you too, you know?"

Laughter rumbles up his exquisite chest. "Yeah. You weren't as good at hiding it as I was."

"You asshole," I laugh and try to yank away from him, but he tugs me back.

"Hey, now. Don't be like that. I liked the way you looked at me."

We lie in the quiet of the room, listening to the storm outside play its own tune as sleep slowly tugs at the two of us.

"Sing me something, Carys," he whispers as the weather rages on.

Without overthinking it, I sing the old Lifehouse song we danced to years ago while I run my fingers over his chest. And by the time I sing the last words of the song, his breathing has evened out, and his strong, hard body has relaxed around me.

Everything but the grip he has on me.

That's tighter now than it's ever been.

On my body and on my heart.

When an alarm rings softly from Cooper's phone hours later, I brace myself. He's leaving, and I don't know where he's going or when he's coming back. I don't know how to do this, but I'm about to learn.

Baptism by fire and all that good stuff.

His blue eyes crack open and meet mine. "I'm sorry."

His voice is rough with sleep, and I want nothing more than for the two of us to lie back down and block out the rest of the world while we hide under the covers. But that can't happen. "I didn't mean to wake you." He sinks back down into the mattress as if reading my mind, then pulls me closer.

I burrow deeper, needing to be as close to him as possible. "Don't worry about it. I've been awake."

Cooper's hand slips under my nightshirt, skims over my lacy cheeky panties, and stops on my rib cage. He doesn't move it any higher. Doesn't so much as hint that he wants what I'm dying for. "Were you watching me sleep, beautiful? Sounds kinda creepy."

"We've already established that we both like watching, Cooper Sinclair. Don't tell me the big bad SEAL gets creeped out by little old me."

"There are so many things I want to watch you do, baby." He has a devious glint in his eyes as he lowers his mouth down to mine and slides his tongue along the seam of my lips, silently begging for entrance that I'd never refuse. Then he rolls me under him.

Nothing has ever felt as good as Cooper's weight on my body.

His chest against mine.

The strength of his arms wrapped around me.

And when the sleep timer on his phone chimes again, reminding him it's time to go, I want to cry that this moment is over too soon. Cooper rolls over and silences the alarm on the nightstand. "I'm sorry, Carys. As much as I wish I didn't have to leave, the Navy doesn't accept excuses."

I skim the tip of my pointer finger over the lines of his muscled chest and down to his abs, stopping at the edge of his boxer shorts. "Promise you're coming back?"

"Nothing in this world would stop me from coming back to you. Not now that I have you." A predatory smile stretches across his face before he kisses me again.

Excitement and fear go to war with each other deep in my stomach. "I've wanted you for years. I've waited for you, Cooper Sinclair. Don't you dare break that promise."

"When I get back, we'll figure everything out. I promise." His eyes dance between mine. "Okay?"

"Yeah." I refuse to let him see me cry. If I want this—want him—I'm going to have to get used to Cooper leaving. Even if I hate it with every fiber of my being. I know what he does for a living. What he's always wanted to do. And I think I have a pretty good idea how much he loves it. So, instead of being weak and needy, I stand from the bed and hand him his shirt.

Once he's dressed, he closes my balcony doors. "Don't sleep with them open while I'm gone, okay?" He grips the back of my neck and draws me to him.

I reach up on the tips of my toes and press my lips against his. Sealing our promise. Soaking him in.

He kisses me reverently before he lets me go. "See ya soon, mini-Murphy."

"Oh my God," I laugh. "I haven't heard that in years."

Coop's smile stretches. "I got you to laugh."

"You did." I touch my lips with my fingertips. "Be safe, Coop."

He nods once, then walks through my bedroom door, closing it behind him.

He didn't say goodbye.

We didn't say goodbye.

Maybe that's better.

I drop down onto my bed, and the first tear falls. Once the gates open, there's no stopping the waterworks. After a few minutes, my bedroom door cracks open, and Emerson climbs into bed with me. Matching tear-tracks run down her cheeks.

"They're going to be fine. Right?" Her last word gets caught on a sob.

"They're going to be fine." I'm not sure if I'm trying to convince us or willing it to be true.

But I refuse to accept that the universe would finally bring us together, only to take him from me now.

CARYS

A week later, I'm tucked into the corner of the sage-green sofa with a cup of hot tea and my sketch pad when Jack comes upstairs from the basement studio. He holds his Gibson acoustic in one hand and a well-worn notebook in the other. There's a chewed-up pencil stuck behind his ear, and judging by his bloodshot eyes, I'm pretty sure he hasn't slept yet. I'm learning that's not uncommon for Jack. According to him, his creative juices flow best at night.

Which is the complete and total opposite of me.

It's been easy to throw myself into work, but instead of staying up all night, I've spent the past week waking up at the crack of dawn to work on new lingerie ideas. It's an easy way to block out the fear I've felt every day Cooper's been gone.

Jack and Theo moved in a few hours after Cooper and Linc left last Saturday. They had way more stuff to move than Em and me. They also had half their fraternity here, helping them throughout the day and late into the night.

Emerson and I didn't bother joining them. Neither of us was going to be good company that day. But this is their home too, so we weren't going to ask them to have everyone leave either. Instead, we Grubhubbed ice-cream supplies from the local market and binge watched *The Witcher* while we ate our feelings.

I let myself have that one day to wallow, then woke up

Sunday, laced up my running sneakers, and went for a three-mile jog on the beach before anyone else had even gotten out of bed. Running in the sand sucks, but the sound of the waves lapping at the shore makes up for the extra burn in my thighs.

An entire week has come and gone since then, and still no word from Cooper.

No call.

No email.

No text.

And yup, I've become *that* girl. The one who checks her phone obsessively to make sure it's charged and that I haven't missed anything. I'm getting on my own nerves. So, when Jack sits down next to me and places his black-spiral notebook in my lap, I put my sketch pad down and read over the words on the page.

The song is new.

His handwriting is about as legible as my two-year-old brother's.

Yet somehow, I manage to decipher it.

It's good. *Really* good.

"Can you sing the chorus for me? I need to work out the chords here." He points to the page with the chewed pencil, and I read it over and wait for him to count us off.

Jack still hasn't given up on me sticking with Six Day War, but he has put some feelers out at school. In the meantime, we keep practicing, and I'm still helping them with their original music. I keep telling Jack he's got a month before I go back to Kroydon Hills for July, but he doesn't seem to be in any rush.

When we repeat the chorus, he adds in a line of harmony and taps his palm in time against the Gibson. Theo joins us from the kitchen and uses his hands against the coffee table as a makeshift drum kit while we work out the song. By the time we've finished, Emerson has joined us and is sitting on the edge of the couch with her phone in front of her face, recording us. No doubt, uploading it to the band's socials. She swears she's on my side and fully supports my not wanting to sing lead with the band permanently, but you'd never know that based on the pics she's shared this week.

One of the videos of us singing at the Rat last Friday went viral already.

It's not really helping to convince Jack that I'm not the singer he's looking for.

Jack grabs the book from my hands, jots a note down on the page, then closes it. "You think we can have this ready for the Rat this week?"

I sip my tea with honey and lemon, a trick a voice teacher taught me years ago. "Works for me."

"Yeah," Theo agrees. "Me too."

My phone rings, and Em and I both scramble to see the screen. Chloe's name flashes across it, and we each let out a quick breath. Neither one of us is good at waiting.

"Hey, Chloe." I head out to the backyard. "What's up?"

"Good morning, Care-Bear. Why do you sound miserable?" Chloe has never been someone who sugarcoats things. She lacks a filter and is the ultimate *take me as I am* girl.

She's a year older than me, but I kinda want to be her when I grow up.

"Sorry. Didn't sleep great last night. How are you?" I haven't said anything to her about Cooper yet.

Not yet. I don't know how any of them will take it, and I'm not willing to deal with that complication yet. We need time to figure out what we're doing before being put under a microscope for the entire family to study and feel like they have a say in. And everyone will have an opinion.

Especially my brother. Aiden is going to throw a fit to rival Callen's biggest tantrum.

Ironic since I'm the one he likes to treat like a child.

We're so screwed.

This sounds good in theory, but it means we're keeping something from the people we love. We need more time in the same damn place before we can tackle that shit.

Even though she's not technically family, Chloe's brother, Brady, and my stepsister, Nattie, have been together for years. Kroydon Hill's *It* couple. Making Chloe extended family, whether she wants to be or not. The difference between Chloe and me is that she's always been accepted as part of our brothers' group of friends.

She's one of them, but I've always been treated like a little sister.

Someone to protect, instead of an equal.

"Did you finish up those French-lace sets last week? Because I think I found a buyer who wants them in her boutique in the city. I want to show her a sample before we discuss cost." Of the two of us, Chloe is the sales brain behind our brand, Le Désir. She's handled most of the business aspects and let me run wild with the designs. Yes, we're each doing both, but it's been surprising how we've fallen into these roles with ease.

"Yes, ma'am. I'll have them overnighted to you later today. You still playing with bathing suits?" I walk through the back gate and sit down in the cool sand, digging my toes in. It's still early here, and the sun hasn't had time to warm it yet.

"Yeah. I've gotten a few done. I sent you the designs Friday, remember?"

Shit. She did, and I never responded.

"I'm sorry. Summer classes already started, and I got caught up trying to get all my reading in. Seriously, Chloe, I hate school. I wish I could just take the design classes and ignore the rest."

"I know, Carys, but you're only a year in. Suck it up, buttercup. You've still got three to go." Paper rustles on her end of the line, followed by a loud thud. "Shit. Sorry. Damn phone. Listen, overnight those sets. Then look over the swimwear. Tell me which you want me to make you for vacation, kay? See you in three weeks, right?"

"Yup. See you soon." I end the call and sit there for a moment, contemplating my next moves.

Jack and Theo want me to agree to join the band, so they can stop searching for a replacement and start building on the momentum we've got going.

Chloe thinks I've got to finish school because she knows my mom.

My mother may have been strangely chill about me moving in with guys, but if I tell her I'm dropping out of college after only one year, I have a sneaking suspicion she'd go ballistic.

I've got to figure out what I want.

When I ask myself what I want to do, the answer is always the same. I want to design lingerie. Maybe bathing suits too, with the occasional dress thrown in for special events.

But what about school?

It's easy to say you don't want to finish out your degree, but do I mean it?

I think I might. But I'm not ready to make that call yet.

To deal with the consequences of making that call.

Guess that makes me a *coward*.

I like what being in California has given me.

A chance to figure out the person I want to be, far away

from home and the expectations surrounding me there. I've loved my design classes. But I've hated everything else related to school. However, that said, I don't know if I can give up yet.

No promises that I'll finish my degree. But I'll give it a little more time before I make that decision. I've got a summer full of classes so I can at least cut back on how many years I'll need to be in school. Of course, that means this summer is going to blow.

After a few more minutes of my mini pity party, I stand and wipe off the sand off my butt, then turn toward the house. But instead of moving, I stop and stare. Cooper is standing in the sand a few feet in front of me, outside of our back gate. He's dressed in his pale tactical camo pants, and a long-sleeved matching tan and camo polo shirt. Black aviators hang down from the v of his shirt, and my breath catches in my lungs at the sight of him.

He crosses the sand in two strides.

He looks like a man who just found his salvation, and my knees threaten to buckle from the emotion in his eyes. "Hey." Cooper cups my face in his hands, and I melt at the warmth.

"Oh my God, Cooper. You're back." I grab hold of his wrists, then trace my finger under his eye. "What happened?" He's got a butterfly stitch beneath his eye and a slight bruise on his cheek.

"Nothing. I'm fine. I just needed to see you." He holds me gently against his chest, keeping me there like I'm the most precious thing in the world. "You okay? How's everything been?"

I squeeze him tighter, needing to assure myself he's here. He's real. This isn't a dream. "I'm better now that you're back. I know you're trained for this, but not knowing what was happening or where you were was so much harder than I was prepared for."

"We didn't exactly have time to talk about any of that, did we?" He takes a step back and holds his hand in mine as we walk back to my house. "I really wish we'd have more time today."

"What?" I ask, confused.

He holds the gate open for me, then sits down on an Adirondack chair and tugs me down onto his lap.

Strain is evident in the lines of his face.

"What aren't you telling me?"

"Listen, Carys. I don't have a ton of time. We only landed a few hours ago, and as soon as we all finished our reports, I came here to see you. I have to be on a plane today that's leaving at fifteen-hundred for that training I told you about, and I still need to go home and pack."

My heart drops, and a sense of déjà vu takes hold. "You're leaving again? You just got back."

"I have to. I knew this could happen when I agreed to join this last op. Ford offered to let me skip out, but I could never do that to the team. I had to go."

"How long will you be gone?" This is it. This is what being with Cooper Sinclair is going to be like.

He wraps his hands around me, snaking them under my thin red tank, and rubs calming circles over the small of my back with his callused thumb. "Six weeks. Maybe seven. I'm not sure."

I lay my head on his shoulder, trying to hide the way his words crush my heart. "Okay."

"I'm sorry."

"We'll figure it out." I squeeze him tighter and repeat the words again, not sure if I'm trying to convince him or myself.

Coop: Hey baby. How was your first day of summer class?
Carys: Long. Remind me when I'm ever going to use astronomy in the real world.
Coop: You're taking astronomy?
Carys: I needed a four-credit lab science. It sounded easier than biology. How's training going?
Coop: I made my ghillie suit today.
Carys: Your what?
Coop: It's a suit that's supposed to camouflage you.
Carys: Now we're both officially designers. LOL

The dots on the message start and stop a few times before he finally answers.

Coop: I've got to go, Carys. I'll call when I can.

Carys: Seriously! When am I ever going to use calculus in my everyday life? Have I mentioned that I hate school?
Coop: I'm using it every day right now.
Carys: For what?
Coop: You really don't want me to answer that. Tell me something good.
Carys: The video Emerson posted of us performing last weekend went viral. That's the third one.
Coop: You thinking about staying with them?
Carys: Nope. But I was wearing one of my own designs this time, and that got Chloe and me a ton of attention. It's

got me thinking about taking time off from school, even more so now than I was before.

Coop: Want to talk about it? What are the pros and cons?

Carys: Pro – I can concentrate full time on Le Désir. Designing makes me happy. The entire process from the original concept all the way through to the sale of the new design to a boutique. I love it.

Coop: What's the con?

Carys: Mom's going to have a cow if I drop out.

Coop: Talk to your mom, baby. She might surprise you.

Carys: When did you turn into the person I want to talk with about everything?

Coop: About the same time we both got our heads out of our asses.

Carys: I miss you.

Coop: Miss you too.

Coop: I hit a target today from a thousand meters. Undetected.

Carys: That's incredible. What does that mean?

Coop: It puts me one step closer to my ultimate goal.

Carys: And that would be?

Coop: I want to be a Tier 1 operator. I want to be the best of the best.

Carys: Does a higher tier equal more danger?

Coop: Not necessarily. It's why we always train. To be ready for anything.

Carys: Please be safe.

Coop: Always.

Carys: I got a B in Calc. Feels like an A. LOL. So freaking excited to be done with math.

I wait for Coop's response, but it doesn't come.
Even hours later, there's no answer.

Carys: Miss you.

I try not to let his silence bother me. Logically, I know he's busy, and there'll be times he can't answer me, but the girl who's loved him from afar for years, without any inkling of him returning my feelings, still worries that he doesn't feel the same.

The ringing of my phone cuts off the music playing in my AirPods Saturday morning while I work on a five-mile run. I pull it out of the pocket of my leggings and stop running. My heart does a little dance when I see it's an incoming FaceTime from Cooper. "Hey, handsome."

"You okay, Carys? You're all red." He scratches the scruff that's getting out of control on his face.

"Just running." I take a deep breath. "It's hotter outside than I thought, and I'm finishing up five miles. Is everything okay? You went radio silent there for a few days."

He winces. "Sorry, baby. We've been in the field."

I try to slow my racing heart. "Don't apologize, Coop. I get it. What were you guys doing?" The look on his face tells me right away that he can't talk about it. "Don't worry about it."

"You're heading back to Kroydon Hills soon, right?"

"Yeah. I can't wait to see everyone. Do you think you're going to make it?" I practically hold my breath, waiting for his answer, desperate to see him again.

"I think so." A siren sounds in the background, and Cooper's shoulders sag. "I've got to go. Talk soon."

"Be safe, Cooper."

The call ends, and I say a silent prayer.

CARYS

I never knew what a bitch time could be. That it could fly by and yet drag on simultaneously. I ended up adding a design class to my summer schedule, upping my class total to three for the month of June. It's better to get them out of the way now while I don't have anything else going on.

San Diego University of the Arts offers two summer sessions, and the first ended yesterday. Just in time for me to pack my bags for home. The July session starts on Monday, and I've enrolled in two more classes for it, but I'm taking them both virtually.

Between the classes I took over winter break last year, the ones from this summer, and the ones I hope to take next winter, I should be able to knock out an entire year of school and graduate in three instead of four.

Anything to get this over faster.

I shut my suitcase and push down with all my strength so I can actually get the zipper to close around the case overstuffed with clothes. Then I grab my carry-on and purse and check my text messages.

Mom: Can't wait to see you. Have a safe flight. Your brother is meeting you at the airport.
Aiden: That should read, your favorite brother.
Declan: Make sure you go to the right gate this time.
Aiden: That was a onetime thing.

Carys: It's the same gate as last time.
Aiden: See? I can't mess it up.
Nattie: I have faith you can and will, Murph.
Aiden: That hurts, Nat.
Carys: You'll survive, big brother. See you soon, guys.

I tug my suitcase from the bed, letting it hit the floor with a loud thump. A second later, Theo pops his head through my open door.

"Hey, let me grab that." He picks up my suitcase and carry-on, then eyes me skeptically. "Geez, CC. Did you leave any clothes in your closet?"

Emerson and Jack left a few days ago to spend a few weeks in France with their mom, leaving Theo and me alone in the house. I wasn't sure if Em was going to go or not. She really didn't want to leave Linc, but her mom guilted her into it. She's good at that, according to Jack. But now, as Theo carries my stuff to the front door for me, I feel bad about leaving him here alone. He's stopped acting like a horny jackass and turned into a good friend. I asked him once if he wanted to come home with me, but he wasn't interested. "What are you going to do with the house to yourself this month?"

"Probably pick up a few extra shifts. Maybe try to get a few songs written." He puts the bags down by the front door and squeezes me in a bear hug. "Have fun, CC."

"Thanks. You too." My phone vibrates with an incoming text, letting me know my ride is here. "See ya in a month."

The flight from San Diego to Philly International is supposed to take a little over five hours. But that doesn't include the extra hour we spent taxiing on the runway before takeoff, for some unexplained reason. By the time we're finally allowed off the plane in Philly, I smell like stale air, am exhausted, and my stomach is growling.

Never a good combination.

Hangry is a real thing.

And it's not pretty.

I texted Aiden to let him know I've landed and should be out soon, and I half expected him to not be here for me when I finally step foot outside the airport exit. But there he is on the other side of the sliding doors, parked in the pick-up zone, leaning against his black Cadillac Escalade, holding my equivalent to a bouquet of roses . . . a paper takeout bag from Tony Luke's.

It's been about six months since I've been home, and I guess I missed him more than I knew because without thinking it through, I drop my bags and throw my arms around all six feet plus of my giant ginger of a brother and squeeze.

"Missed you too, Care Bear." One big arm squeezes me to him, while the other—holding the heavenly goodness that only a roast pork and broccoli rabe sandwich smothered in provolone cheese can contain—hangs down by my side. "Come on, kid. Time to go home."

He opens the passenger door for me and places the Tony Luke's bag on my lap once I'm seated, then throws my suitcase in the back and joins me in the front seat. I might have left California at eleven this morning, but between the three-hour time difference and the long flight, the sun has already started to slip behind the horizon as he drives through the streets of Philadelphia on his way to

Kroydon Hills, yammering on about everything and anything.

Football, Sabrina, her big move to Georgetown . . . and the football draft next year. My big brother is a big goofball who hates silence. Whoever said girls talk too much never met Aiden Murphy. I try to concentrate on everything he's saying, truly, I do, but as the busy city streets transition to the slower pace of our lazy hometown, nostalgia takes over, and I realize how much I miss this place.

"Are you listening to me at all, Carys?"

"Umm . . ." I stall, grasping for a nugget of what he just said. "Of course, I am. But there's not much you can do about the Secret Service, Aiden. You're engaged to the daughter of the president. It's all part of the package. And she's moving to Georgetown at the end of the summer, so stop complaining that they're annoying you. Soon enough, she's going to be three hours away. And you'll be wishing she wasn't, and you'll miss those agents."

Aiden glances at me quickly before looking back at the road. "I wasn't complaining about Sabrina. Just the suits," he pouts.

"Yeah, well, the suits are there to keep her safe. I'm sure she doesn't love it either, but it's not like you didn't know this was a possibility when you started dating." They've been together for three years, and Sabrina's dad started his campaign for the presidency about six months after they got together.

"Dude, retract the claws, kiddo." Aiden will never see me as something more than the little kid who used to follow him and his friends around.

I lift my hands in the air and wiggle my fingers. "No claws. Just reminding you to be grateful for what you've got."

He turns into Mom's neighborhood. "I don't know if I like you being the wise one. That's my job."

I cover my mouth to hide my chuckle. "Your job was to scare away the monsters when I was little, and you did it well. Maybe now you can just try seeing me as a friend." I watch the emotions flit over his face as my words sink in, but I can't quite make out what he's thinking as he turns into Mom and Coach's driveway.

"You know how Cooper always tortures Brady about dating his sister?" he finally says.

I force my face to stay neutral at the mention of Cooper, hard as it may be. "Yeah . . . what's your point?"

Aiden turns the car off and twists to look at me. "There's something about protecting your sister that's ingrained in us at birth. And it's worse for me because you're my baby sister, not my twin."

"I'm not a baby, Aiden. I'm three years younger than you, and you and Sabrina were already living together by the time you were my age. And I'm not sure how we even started talking about this." I grip the bag of food tightly, ready to make a quick escape, but he stops me with a hand on my arm.

"I know you're not a kid anymore, Carys." He swallows. "Fuck, you've been on your own for a year. I get it. But old habits die hard, and it's weird as hell for me to hear you be the voice of reason." Aiden cringes. "Just promise you'll never talk to me about sex, and I'll promise to try to treat you like an adult instead of a kid. Okay?"

He offers me his hand, and I stare at it like a snake I'm expecting to attack.

Is he for real?

I didn't have to fight for this.

I wasn't even the one to bring it up. He did that all on his own.

Instead of shaking his hands, I lean over the center console and circle my arms around his beefy neck. "I love you, Aiden James."

"Love you too, Carys Catrina."

When I walk into the beautiful brick house, the high-pitched squeal of my little brother matches the cadence of his chubby feet pounding against the hardwood floors. His body takes him faster than he can stop, and he flings himself across the room at me.

"Care Bear, you're home."

I drop my bags and squat down to catch him. "Callen, be careful." I pick him up, and he wraps his arms and legs around me like a koala bear. I press my lips to his floppy black hair that still has that sweet baby smell and inhale deeply. "I missed you so much, Cal."

Mom follows Callen into the room and throws her arms around us both, kissing my cheek. "Oh honey, I've missed you."

"Me too, Mom." There's something about being hugged by your mom . . . it just makes everything better. I close my eyes for a minute and soak her in until Callen starts to wiggle in my arms. I look up and find Coach watching us from across the room with a warm smile. "Hey, Coach."

"Good to have you home, kiddo." He joins our little group hug and tries to tug Callen free. "Come on, Cal. It's time for bed."

Chubby legs hold me tighter as he begs, "No, Daddy. I want Carys to read me a story."

I run my hands over his silky, soft hair. "One story, then bed. Okay, big guy?"

"*Ferdinand,*" he squeals.

"That's my favorite too," Aiden adds. It actually *is* his favorite, always has been.

"Come with us, Murphy." Callen has obviously been spending too much time around the guys, if he's calling Aiden by our last name now, like they do.

Mom's hands sit on her hips as she tries to force a stern face to hide her smile. "Callen Joseph, what have I told you?"

Callen's head whips around to Mom. "Always say please." Then he smiles up at our big brother. "Please, Murphy."

Aiden chuckles, and Mom pinches his ear. "Ow, shit." He tugs Callen away from me and sits him on his hip. "I think Mom means you're not supposed to call me Murphy, little man."

"But Dad calls you Murphy. So do Declan, Nattie, and Cooper." The kid's not wrong.

Mom clears her throat. "Time for bed, sweet boy." She kisses his and Aiden's cheeks, then cups my face. "I'm so glad you're home, Carys."

"Me too, Mom." Me too.

Standing here, surrounded by the people I love, I realize how much I missed this.

Hours later, after Aiden's gone home and Mom and Coach have gone to bed, I pull out my phone and text Cooper.

. . .

Carys: Hey. I'm back in Kroydon Hills. And Callen was already talking about you. I told you they wouldn't forget you.

Cooper: Hey baby. Wanna FT?
Carys: Sure.

We've tried to FaceTime a few times since he's been gone and have been filling in where we can with texts, but I want to see him in person. A minute later, the screen changes to an incoming call. I swipe to answer and am greeted by Cooper's handsome face with damp hair and a towel around his neck. A swarm of butterflies takes flight in my stomach just from looking at him.

"God, it's good to see you, Carys." That seriously sexy tone of his makes me practically purr. "How was your flight?"

I move a pillow behind my back and lean against the white-iron headboard. Relaxed. "The flight was long, but it wasn't bad. Aiden met me with Tony Luke's when I got in the car, so that made it better. Are you still planning on surprising everyone this weekend?"

"So far, so good. I should get there sometime Saturday, but I've got to get back here late Sunday night."

I wish I could reach through the screen and just touch him, to remind myself he's real. "I can't wait to see you," I whisper the words, scared to jinx us.

Nervous something will happen and he won't make it home.

Petrified something will go wrong and someone will find out about us.

But I'm willing to take the risk.

"You sure you don't want to tell everyone about us?" I guess he's worried about the same thing.

We need to figure out what this is before we talk to them.

Cooper doesn't love the idea, but he's agreed to wait for now.

"Yeah, I'm sure. Maybe we'll be able to sneak away." I smile coyly. "Are you going to stay with Mom and Coach?"

"You're gonna get me in so much trouble, Miss Murphy." There's no malice in his words. Just a twinkle in those baby blues, promising all sorts of things we've yet to discuss.

"Only if you're lucky, Coop."

Coop reaches over and turns off the light, leaving him bathed in darkness and the light of his phone. "Sing something for me, Carys."

I do the same thing and turn off my lights, crawling back into bed, then sing my take on one of my favorite songs, "Kiss Me," by Ed Sheeran. I bring it up a few octaves and sing it lighter than the original. Coop closes his eyes, and I wonder if this is love?

The two of us lying here in separate time zones.

Wishing we were together, but making it work however we can.

Will it always be this way?

COOPER

"I'll be there, man. I caught a military flight to a base in Delaware, and now I'm sitting in traffic, trying to get to you guys." I haven't even crossed the damn bridge to get into New Jersey yet, and traffic has been at a standstill for nearly an hour. "Did you really have to propose on a holiday weekend? It's like the shore traffic is on roids, it's so bad. I saw a grandma flip somebody off for trying to get in front of her."

Brady laughs like he thinks I'm kidding, but that little old, blue-haired lady looked pissed. And I'm betting that big old boat of a car she's driving could have done some serious damage to the Prius that was trying to cut into her lane.

"Take your time, Coop. I didn't tell anyone you were coming. They're going to freak when you get here."

A horn honks in front of me as the light turns green, and somebody doesn't move fast enough. "I gotta go, Brady. See you in a few hours." I end the call in time to navigate the bumper-to-bumper cars with a stupid smile on my face. I'm happy for my sister and my best friend.

It's hard to believe it's been five years since they met and everything changed.

Will Murphy be able to be happy for Carys and me the way I am for my sister and Brady?

When I finally drive over the old rickety bridge into the tiny shore town that our family and friends have slowly begun to take over, I roll down the windows on my rental car and breathe in the salt water and marshy bay air. Brady told me once it was his favorite smell in the world because he knew for a few days he could relax. I get that. Training has been intense. It always is. Not anything out of the ordinary, but I hate being away from the team. Even if improving this skill will only help me keep us safer and make the team better.

It takes another thirty minutes to get through the tree-lined streets of the tiny town. Flags hang from each telephone pole, and red-white-and-blue bunting has exploded all over the streets full of tourists eating lunch at outdoor bistros, weaving in and out of small shops, and pulling wagons full of toddlers to the sandy shores. Dad's house is at the other end of the island, where the properties have views of the beach and the bay. Dad, Declan, and Brady's parents own three houses next to each other on the beach, and they take up an entire block of prime real estate, forming some version of a compound.

I park in Dad's driveway and shoulder my duffle bag before letting myself through the back gate. The doors are locked, but the key is still under the mat—where he always keeps it when they're down here—and I let myself in.

Not the safest move, Dad.

Callen's toys are scattered throughout the house, mixed in with a few dolls that belong to one or both of my nieces, judging by the sparkly pink ballet shoes and matching tutus they're wearing. Gracie and Everly are one week younger than Callen. Technically, they're his nieces, but more often than not, his tormentors. A half-eaten birthday cake sits in a pink Sweet Temptations bakery box on the counter, and an English Comp II book is lying open on the island next to it. I know Carys is trying to get through as many of her core classes as she can this summer, but I cringe, looking at it, and know I made the right decision in skipping college.

I walk down the hall to the bedrooms at the back of the first floor and throw my bag into the first empty one I find. There are three bedrooms down here, two more on the flight above this, and the master takes up the entire top floor. I kick off my sneakers, grab my flip-flops out of my bag, and check the other two bedrooms to see if anyone else is staying down here. The first one's empty, but Carys's sweet scent clings to the air in the second. A few bikinis are thrown haphazardly on the bed that she's left unmade, and a suitcase lies open and full of clothes on the floor.

My mind runs a little rampant with everything I want to do to this woman when I see her again.

We've both hated this time apart, but it's forced us to slow down and get to know each other in a deeper way than we did before. It's incredible how quickly she's become the person I want to talk to every day. The one I call the second I can to share the little things and the exciting things with. The way that I'm desperate to see her face at night, and listen to how band practice went, or what she's working on for Le Désir. She's slowly becoming everything to me the way I'm pretty damn sure she was always meant to be.

And it fucking sucks that I have to remind myself—as I walk down the crowded beach to the tents my family has set up a few minutes later—that I can't even reach out to her.

Not here.

Not now.

Not since we agreed this weekend wasn't the right time for that.

I may have agreed with her when she said she wasn't

ready for the family to know, but I fucking hate the idea of hiding how I feel about her. I'm not sure anything in my life has ever felt this important. And it feels wrong to hide it like a dirty secret. But I'm following her lead . . . for now.

Everly is the first one to see me coming. My two-year-old niece makes me feel like a fucking giant when she drops her bucket and giggles with joy, then runs toward me with her blonde curls bouncing around her face. "Uncle Cooper," she squeals.

I move a little faster to scoop her up before she falls flat on her adorable face. Tiny arms circle tight around my neck as she plants a sloppy kiss on my cheek. "What are you doing here, Uncle Coop?"

"I didn't want to miss your birthday, princess." I blow a raspberry on her cheek and squat down for Callen and Gracie to add themselves to the group hug, wishing all three of them happy birthday.

Man, I missed this.

"I didn't know you were coming, son." Dad holds me tight to him for a moment before my stepmom, Katherine, places a kiss on my cheek.

I take a minute to say hi to Murphy, Sabrina, Lenny, and Bash. Then reach for my beautiful sister-in-law, Annabelle, who's holding my two-month-old nephew, Nixon. I've only gotten to see this little guy on the other side of a screen till now.

"He's perfect, Belles."

"It's so good to see you here, Cooper." Annabelle places him gently in my arms, and wide blue eyes stare back at me, studying me like only a baby can, until a familiar voice yells.

"Coop!"

Belle's brother, Tommy, has grown from a shy nine-year-old boy, when I first met him, to a teenager who will undoubtedly be bigger than all of us eventually. He leans his head on my shoulder, a big sign of trust from this awesome kid who doesn't like to be touched.

"I've missed you, Coop."

I wrap my free arm around him. "I've missed you too, buddy." Nixon scrunches up his face and grunts before the stench hits my nose, and I pass him right back to his mother. "That's all you, Belles."

I look over and see Carys standing next to my brother and Belles, watching me. Big brown sunglasses are pushed up into her long dark hair. A black-triangle bikini with bright-pink straps is tied around her neck and at her hips, and an open white button-down shirt covers her sun-kissed skin. She's a sight for sore eyes, and I want to do more than look.

One of the hardest things I've ever done is step forward to hug her without touching her the way I want to.

Without enjoying her the way I need to.

I keep my hands on the outside of her shirt and awkwardly squeeze. "Hey."

She blushes as she bats those long inky lashes up at me. "Hey, Coop."

We're forced to pull apart way too soon, and I scan our group for my sister and Brady. "Where's Nattie?"

Murphy tosses me a football and tips his chin toward the ocean, where Brady and Nattie are kissing at the edge of the water. I might have chosen to go into the Navy, but football will always be my first love. With a Cheshire-cat grin, I throw a perfect spiral through the air, missing Brady's head by inches before I walk down and join them at the water's edge.

"Stop kissing my sister!" I've never actually minded Brady kissing Nattie. I mean, I don't want to see it. But I couldn't have picked a better man for her, even if it's fun to torture them.

Nattie spins around in shock. "Cooper." She runs and collides into me. "What are you doing here? I thought you couldn't come this year."

I hold her close while she cries and tell her what I can, which isn't much. "I got three days' leave. I basically get a few hours today. And most of tomorrow. Then I'm back on a plane. But I didn't want to miss the family weekend."

Brady smacks me on the back. "It's good to see you, man." He hands me the football. "Nice shot, but you missed."

"Got you two to stop kissing, so you get to live." Lucky fucking bastard. No guy will ever love my sister more than him.

I wonder if Murphy will feel the same way.

CARYS

WHY DOES WATCHING A GORGEOUS MAN HOLDING A BABY make my ovaries want to explode?

I'm not talking toddler, although watching Cooper with Callen and the twins is a sight to behold. But watching him fall in love with Nixon affects me in a visceral way I wasn't expecting. That tiny baby tucked against Cooper's muscled chest as we all pack up to go back to our respective houses may be the most insanely hot thing I've ever witnessed.

Coach wants to grill a big family dinner, but that means we'll eat at 5:00 p.m. because these babies haven't napped today, and most of them are already getting cranky as everyone heads back up the beach to start food prep and shower.

We're spread out among three houses. Brady's parents' place is packed, with him, Nattie, and all their friends staying there for the weekend. I'm a little worried Cooper is going to either stay there or with his brother, Declan, after he hands Nixon back to his parents.

But as soon as Coach follows Mom upstairs, carrying a whining Callen, who doesn't want to take a bath, Cooper steps through the kitchen doors, and my breath catches in my throat.

His black Kings ball cap sits backward on his head, tucking his blond curls down. A sleeveless black tee show-cases the defined muscles in his arms, and a pair of red board shorts stretch across strong thighs and tanned skin.

It's a heady combination, and I swear to God, if he doesn't touch me soon, I'm going to combust.

Judging by the predator-like expression on his face as he stalks toward me, he feels the same way.

He doesn't make me wait long.

His strong arms pin me against the cool stainless-steel refrigerator. Cooper's calloused hands slide under my oversized linen shirt and along my heated skin—sparking fire every place he touches—before he lifts me from my feet and wraps my legs around his waist.

"I missed you so fucking much, Carys. I can't wait another minute."

His words are a balm to all the tattered edges of my soul that formed while he's been gone. The doubt that was creeping into my mind, questioning his feelings. The nerves that our family won't accept it. The fear that it's all going to fall apart before it even starts. But none of it matters now that he's here.

My arms twine around his neck, and I tug off his cap, then run my fingers through his soft blond hair as I crash my lips over his. Molding my body to his, I can't tell where I stop and he starts.

"It doesn't make sense," I pant. "But I feel it too, Coop."

He walks us carefully down the dark hall and into the first bedroom, then kicks the door shut behind him and leans me against it. Blue eyes scan every inch of my face, his breath coming rapidly. "You are the most gorgeous woman I've ever seen." His tongue invades my mouth as he cups my breast and my nipple aches at the feel of his thumb brushing over it.

"Cooper . . ." I beg as I grind my pussy down against his hard cock that's pressing against my core. Only his shorts and my tiny bikini separate us, but it's too much.

I want them gone.

"Shh, you've got to be quiet." He bites down on my bottom lip and tugs. "We don't have much time, and I need to make you come for me. At least once." One hand slides from my hip into my bikini bottoms, and then his fingers drag through my sex, sending me spiraling through the stratosphere. "Your pussy is soaked, baby. Is this for me?" he groans. His words are so quiet, and fuck, they're sexy.

I nod, his dirty words making my clit throb with need as I bite down painfully on my bottom lip to keep from crying out when he slips one blunt finger inside me. Then another. Stretching me. Filling me. His rough thumb rubs circles around my clit, teasing me, while he holds me like I weigh nothing against the wall.

Every breath we take seems amplified by the threat of being discovered, and I've never needed to come so badly in my life.

Chills of anticipation break out over my skin as his fingers work me into a silent frenzy. "Oh, God," I whisper as his fingers curve to hit a spot deep inside me no man has ever touched.

My core tightens as chills caress my skin.

Cooper licks into my mouth. "Shh, baby. No sound, remember?"

I nod my head and get lost in the heavy-lidded heat of his blue eyes.

"Good girl." He pulls his fingers out, and my eyes fly to his, desperate for this not to end. But he just smirks at me, then traces my lips with his fingers, pushing them onto my tongue. "Suck."

I do as I'm told and suck his fingers clean, showing him what I'm dying to do to his cock. My own tart taste coats my tongue.

Cooper's eyes darken, and he groans as I swirl my tongue around his fingers.

He slowly lowers my feet to the floor, then, holding eye contact, drops to his knees, and throws my leg over his shoulder. He shoves my bikini bottoms to the side, opening me to him. Dark eyes look up at me with a wicked grin, and I know I'd give this man anything he wanted and everything I needed. I open my mouth but quickly bite down on my lip to stop from moaning.

"That's my good girl."

His words fan the flame of my already insane need, and I pant, unable to catch my breath as I watch the sinful sight in front of me.

Cooper drags his flattened tongue through my pussy slowly, lapping at me. Then he growls against me, sending vibrations through my body.

I throw my head back, trying desperately to muffle my cries. I should be mortified at how wet I am, but when his tongue spears inside my pussy, I lose the ability to form a cohesive thought and no longer care.

It's his fault I'm this turned-on.

His fault my body is singing right now.

He sucks my clit as his fingers tease me and bring me to the brink until darkness begins setting in at the corners of my vision. And when I think I can't take it anymore, his teeth finally scrape over my pulsing clit, and I explode on his tongue. My back arches off the door, and my fingers grasp his shoulders for purchase.

Completely lost to the moment.

Soundless.

Breathless.

We're quiet.

Only my panting fills the silence.

Until Coach yells from somewhere down the hall, "Cooper, go next door and tell your sister dinner will be ready soon."

Coop drags his tongue through my drenched sex one more time, absorbing the aftershocks wracking my body, then gently lowers my leg to the floor. He kisses the inside of my thigh and smiles devilishly up at me, before yelling, "Okay, Dad."

Holy shit. Life just got complicated.

Coach has always had a thing about having everyone around a table. He loves family dinners more than anyone I've ever met. And with each new person who joins our extended family—by blood, marriage, or luck—he welcomes them and adds another chair. We're eighteen people deep, seated at the giant table on the back deck overlooking the ocean this evening.

There are more conversations than I can keep track of happening at once, yet my eyes are constantly drawn to the man sitting across from me. My cheeks flame red every time he catches me staring at him, but I don't think anyone else has caught on. Annabelle sits to my right, holding her youngest as she tries to eat, so I take him from her to give her a minute of peace.

Or at least I try. As soon as I settle Nixon in my lap, her twins start fighting over a piece of watermelon that ends up being thrown across the table with a shriek and hits Belle in the face. It's hard to not laugh, but most of us try to at least hide our reactions.

Declan stands, with the ultimate dad glare, and orders the girls to follow him into the house while Belle wipes her face. Then, with a sigh, she turns to me.

"Don't be in a rush for kids, Carys." She peeks over at Nixon, who grips my finger with a contented look on his face while he sucks his bottle down with half-closed eyes. "They're cute but brutal."

I look down at the happy little baby in my arms, then at the unhappy toddlers crying in the house. "I think I'll wait a few years before thinking about kids."

Nixon finishes his bottle, and as I lift him to my shoulder to burp the little bugger, he lets out a noise that doesn't come from his mouth. Gross.

Aiden laughs. "Yeah. First, try finding a guy worthy enough to pass the test with all three of your brothers. I mean, come on," he looks over at Cooper, "one of us is a trained badass, and all of us could bench press anyone you try to bring home."

Almost everyone laughs, but I don't find his stupid comment funny. Instead, I stand. "Belles, I'm going to go change Nix's diaper." I glare at Aiden. "Did I ever ask Sabrina if she was good enough for you?"

When Aiden's mouth drops open, I push harder. "Did I ever give you a hard time about any of the skanky girls you dated before the two of you met?" The table gets quiet, but I don't care. "I'm an adult, big brother. I've successfully managed to live across the country for an entire year without needing you or anyone else to step in and handle my life. You can stop acting like you get a say in who I date or what I do whenever you want now." I run my hand over Nixon's back. "Or don't. That's up to you. But understand you get zero say in who I date and how I live my life. Whether you think you do or not."

I move down to the end of the table and kiss Coach. "Dinner was great, Coach. Thank you." Then I walk into the house, passing Declan, Evie, and Gracie as they come back outside.

I hear Dec ask, "What did I miss?"

"Murphy's an asshole," Nattie answers.

Coach groans, "Language, Nat."

"What's an asshole?" Gracie's little voice asks.

I take Nixon into the spare room to change him before I can catch the answer.

I'm lying on the bed a few minutes later, curled up around Nixon. His dark hair and even darker blue eyes tell the world he's every bit his daddy's son. I'm playing with a soft blue elephant rattle, holding it above him and watching his tiny hands reach for it when there's a knock on the door, and he and I both turn our heads.

"Come in."

Belle floats into the room like the former prima ballerina she is and takes a seat on the bed. "There's my boy." She traces her finger down the bridge of his nose, then looks at me. "You okay, Carys?"

I look back down at Nix, embarrassed at my reaction. "I'm fine. I shouldn't have gotten so mad. But Aiden just knows the exact buttons to push."

"Murphy's always been a loudmouth, but he means well. He's just protective of you."

My heart pangs with guilt over how I snapped *and the secret I'm keeping*, even though I meant every word I said and am doing what I have to do. "I know. At some point, he's going to have to realize I'm not a kid anymore." I tickle the rolls of fat on Nixon's thighs right above his knees until he belly-laughs. "We've got a whole new generation of them."

"We do," Belle agrees. "But you were his little sister first. So give him some grace and try to remember that."

I bring my gaze up to her, then sit up. "I really hate when you make sense sometimes."

"I really hate that I used *Murphy* and *grace* in the same sentence." She leans her head on my shoulder. "But he means well. Don't get me wrong. When the time comes, I absolutely think you should rub whatever man you want in his face. But maybe try not to bite his head off in the meantime."

I pick Nixon up and cuddle him to my chest. "Fine. I'll play nice."

Belle takes the baby from me. "Now go have fun next door, and make sure Nattie doesn't drink too much before the fireworks. She'll never forgive herself if she's drunk when Brady proposes."

I grimace. "Does everyone know he's proposing?"

"Everyone but Nat."

Our family sucks at secrets.

I am so screwed.

COOPER

ONCE DINNER HAS BEEN CLEANED UP, THOSE OF US WITHOUT babies who needed to be put to bed sit around a table on the back porch of Brady and Chloe's parent's house, playing Cards Against Humanity while we wait for the fireworks to start. It's a typical hot and humid Fourth of July—with just enough of a cool breeze floating in off the churning ocean to keep us comfortable and yet warn of an impending storm.

There's a slow pace to the night. A level of relaxation we don't typically see back in California, when you're always a call away from getting spun up. Years of friendship envelop those of us sitting out here. These guys see each other all the time. Hell, until Bash proposed to Lenny last spring and officially moved out, most of them lived together.

It's easy to get lost in the comfort of home.

We've been coming here together for years and would typically all watch the fireworks on the beach, but everyone's been given instructions for tonight. Brady wants us to stay here until the first burst of colors explodes in the sky. Then we can join them.

Of course, my sister has no clue what's happening.

"Come on, guys," Nattie pleads. "You can't be party poopers. The fireworks are starting in a minute. Who wants to go sit on the beach with me?" she pouts.

"Sorry, Nat. I got sunburnt today and don't feel like

getting sandy again." Lenny's sitting on Sebastian's lap, not looking anything like the football heiress she truly is. Content in a way I don't know Carys and I can ever achieve in front of these people.

Sabrina stretches and places her long legs on Murphy's lap, then closes her eyes. "I'm just so comfy, Nat."

"Whatever. You guys all suck." My sister turns to Brady, completely oblivious to his nerves. "You'll come with me. Right, QB?"

"Anywhere, Nattie." He tugs her toward the stairs leading down to the beach and grabs the blanket from the railing.

But Nattie stops and looks my way. "You coming with, Coop?"

"Yeah, that would be a no." I tilt my beer toward them. "Have fun. I get enough sand every day, sis."

She pouts for a minute before turning down the steps.

I watch Brady follow her onto the beach, then let my eyes roam over my friends—each coupled up with their girls, happily engaged—then stop on Carys and Chloe whispering to each other. And while she and I agreed we both wanted to keep this thing between us to ourselves for now, I can't help but be jealous of the way my friends can all enjoy being with their women, while I sit on the opposite end of the table, being careful not to get caught staring at mine.

She's wearing a black strapless top, that's tight and crinkly around her chest and loose down to her hips, with a pair of white shorts. None of her laces or bows tonight. Her normally pale skin is sun-kissed, and her dark hair is down and wavy around her shoulders, blowing in the ocean breeze. Her laughter is intoxicating. I want another taste of her skin so fucking bad.

And she has no idea as she sits there, ignoring me.

I tear my eyes away from her when Chloe jumps up and runs inside to grab her camera. "It's almost time," she cheers.

Bash picks up Lenny's hand and kisses her ring finger. "I swear, I figured Brady and Nat would have been the first of us to get engaged."

"Yeah, man. Me too." Murph stands and tugs Sabrina to her feet, then punches me in the shoulder. "You gonna stop giving him a hard time about kissing your sister now, Coop?"

Yeah.

I might need to lay off on that one, considering all the ways I want to make Murph's sister scream.

Nattie said yes, to absolutely no one's surprise.

She's already announced she wants to get married next summer and asked me if I knew when I'd be deployed. I think she might have even picked a date, but I can't be sure. I've never seen my twin so damn excited, and I'm happy for her. I am. But it seems like the happier Nattie and Brady become, the more Carys avoids me.

I know we're complicated, but I don't back down from a challenge. And I've never been so damn sure about anything as I am about my feelings for Carys Murphy.

As the celebration winds down, I watch her hug Nattie, then turn to leave. So, I kiss my sister and say my good-byes, then quickly catch up with Carys on the beach.

"Hey. You gonna leave without saying goodbye?"

"You should go back, Coop. Go celebrate. I'm going to bed." She walks a few steps ahead of me down the sand without turning around, making it past Declan's house and into Dad's backyard before the first raindrop falls. But even the rain can't hide her tears when she finally looks at me.

I pull her back under the covering of the second-floor balcony, hidden from view and the rain, then cradle her head. "You want to tell me what's wrong?"

"Nothing . . ." She sighs and looks beyond me, instead of *at* me, worrying her bottom lip and holding back a sob. "Everything . . . I don't fucking know, Cooper. Maybe this whole thing is a mistake."

Fuck that.

"Eyes on me, Carys." When her gorgeous green eyes lock on mine, I refuse to let them go. "We are *not* a mistake." She takes a deep breath but doesn't say anything. "Tell me what's going on in that beautiful brain, baby."

Her lower lip trembles. "I don't know how we'll ever work, Coop. My brother is a giant pain in the ass, and we're both lying to ourselves if we think he's not going to cause a problem. We're walking through a mine field of family issues if we do this. And what if it doesn't work out? What are we supposed to do then? What does that look like during holidays? *Hey, can you pass the potatoes and act like you haven't made me come?*"

I can't help the laugh that slips past my lips or the glare it earns me. "I don't know that my dad would appreciate hearing about sex over potatoes." I wrap my arms around her, holding her tightly against my chest. "We might want to save that for dessert. *Hey, can you pass the cake and pretend you haven't licked icing off my body?*"

Carys presses her palms to my chest and shoves me back. "I'm serious, Cooper. Promise me if we do this, we'll keep this thing between us."

"There's no *if* about it. We *are* doing this. And I promised you that." I press my lips to hers and enjoy the shivers that travel down her body. "We're going to take our time figuring this out for us before we worry about them."

She silently nods as a bolt of lightning cracks open the dark night's sky, ushering in a downpour of rain. Carys fists my shirt in her hands, and her body sways closer. "Stay with me tonight?"

Fuck.

I know I'll never be able to deny her anything. I capture her pouty lips with mine for just a second. They're soft and warm and so much like coming home.

We step inside the house and scan the darkness of the first floor, checking for Dad or Katherine, before sneaking down the hall to her bedroom. With the door locked behind me, I stalk toward her until the backs of her knees hit the bed, and she sits.

"Carys . . ." The moonlight filters in through the glass doors of her room, illuminating her creamy skin and leaving me speechless.

She tucks her legs under her on the bed and sits up on her knees, making us the same height. Then she tugs her shirt over her head, leaving her bared to me. Her pink nipples become hardened peaks in the cool air, begging for attention, and I'm awestruck.

She's incredible.

And she's mine.

"I'm yours, Cooper." She runs her hands under my tee and shoves it up my body, then drops it to the floor with hers and pops the button on my shorts. "I've been yours for years." Her nails scrape down inside my boxers before she wraps them around my dick and squeezes, sending chills over my skin before she shimmies out from under my arms and drops to her knees in front of me.

She's tiny, barely coming up to my waist. But when she

looks up at me through those dark fucking lashes, I can't think.

I gather the length of her hair in my hand and wrap it around my fist with slow deliberation as she drags her tongue from the base of my cock all the way up to the tip, my blood thickening as my spine pulls tight. "The question is, are you mine?"

The question drags a visceral reaction from me. "You're fucking right, I'm yours. Now show me." I tug her hair with my fist, and Carys swallows me down her throat, sending an electric bolt of pleasure up my body from the base of my spine.

Her head bobs, and her eyes water as she works her way down my cock.

And fuck me, she's such a pretty sight, but this is not how I'm coming tonight.

I tug her head back by her hair until she looks up at me, then lift her and drop her on the bed.

"Did I do something wrong?" Confusion tugs at her, and I press my lips to hers.

Licking my way into her mouth, then down her neck, I worship her perfect nipples and grab her knees. "No, baby. But the first time I come with you, I need to be inside you." I spread her legs, settling in and then lick her cunt through the lace of her thong.

Her tart taste coats my tongue as she squirms beneath me.

"Coop . . ." she whines.

"I need to make sure you're ready for me, baby. I don't want to hurt you."

Her breath comes in quick, short, silent beats.

Shoving the delicate lace aside, I drag my finger along her drenched sex, then push inside her as she moans quietly. When I curl my finger, just like she needs, and suck her pretty little swollen clit into my mouth, I growl against her pussy, and she locks her legs against my head and comes, writhing on the bed.

A silent scream falling from her lips.

So fucking perfect.

"Shit, baby. I've got to get a condom from my room." I lean forward, placing my hands on either side of Carys's head.

Cradling me between her legs, she tightens her hold to keep me close.

As if there were anywhere else on the planet I'd rather be.

"I'm on the pill, and I'm clean. I haven't been with anyone in a long time, Cooper." The softness in her voice begs me to take what she's offering. The gift she's willing to give.

I gently run my thumb over her cheek. "I'm clean too. We get tested for work. I've never been with anyone without a condom. Are you sure, baby?"

Carys shimmies her panties down her legs, then envelops me back between them. "I need you, Cooper. Just you. Nothing between us." She presses her tits to my chest, clawing at my back, trying to get closer. Her tongue skates over my ear as she whispers, "Don't be gentle."

CARYS

A CRACK OF LIGHTNING ILLUMINATES THE ROOM AS COOPER drags the thick head of his cock through my sex, coating himself in my wetness. Sliding up and down, teasing me until I grasp the sheets in both hands, ready to scream. But as I open my mouth, callused fingers grip my jaw, holding me still while his mouth takes mine and our tongues dance a wicked dance.

Each stroke of his tongue takes me higher until I'm teetering on the edge of sanity, not sure how much more I can take. And when he finally pushes his cock inside me—filling me, overwhelming me—I gasp. Agony and ecstasy battle for dominance while I feel like I'm going to break in half in the most sinful way.

He impales me until there's no space between us.

With each achingly slow stroke, his lips worship mine, and my muscles contract around him. Stretching to take him deeper. Clawing to get closer.

Callused fingers grip my jaw, holding me still while our tongues move in savage harmony. And when he finally pushes all the way inside me until there's nothing more left, I'm utterly consumed by him.

"Coop . . ."

His thumb slips down the length of my throat, pressing down on my rapid pulse, and he licks the shell of my ear, whispering, "Tell me how it feels, baby."

"So fucking good," I gasp and then grasp at his ass,

silently begging him to move as I grind my hips against him.

Coop drags his tongue down my neck and pulls out slowly, then sets a punishing rhythm with every hard thrust of his hips. His big body dominates mine. Fucking me harder. Fanning the flames higher. Destroying me.

One strong hand wraps powerfully around my throat, but I want more.

I close my hand around his wrist and whisper, "Tighter."

Coop's blue eyes burn molten hot as the fire between us soars. "You like this, baby?"

"So much," I plead as I buck against him. "So close."

The connection between us is more intense than anything I've ever experienced. It's a white-hot flame licking across my skin as Coop's hand tightens, cutting off the tiniest bit of my oxygen, and my muscles immediately contract around him. Red-hot pleasure flows through my veins, feeding the inferno inside my body.

Cooper's lips capture mine, swallowing my moan as my walls clamp down on his cock, milking him.

A warmth washes over me as he fills me, jerking and groaning against my lips.

We collapse into a mess of sweaty bodies and tangled limbs.

My head presses against his chest, resting over his heart.

He runs his fingers through my hair, and I shiver in his arms. "Jesus, Carys. That was . . . I don't have the words."

My lips tip up as a smile stretches across my face. "Yeah, it was," I tell him softly. "Why did we wait so long to do that?" I try to hold back the giggle that's building inside me. "We could have been doing that for years."

Cooper kisses the top of my head, then rolls me over on

top of him. "Then I guess we better start making up for lost time."

"Baby." Cooper kisses my bare shoulder, then sits up. "I'm going to my room before anyone wakes up."

"Don't go." I tug him down until he's lying alongside me. His warm breath fans my face, and I tuck my body against his. The storm still rages outside, and I want nothing more than to spend every last second of it in bed with him. "Just a few more minutes before we have to go back to reality. How much longer until we're both back in California?"

Cooper runs the tips of his fingers down my spine. "A few more weeks," he growls. "And I swear to God, Carys, I hope you don't have classes for a few fucking days when we get there because I'm not letting you out of bed for a month."

"Promise?" I drag my nails down his naked chest, then play with the waistband of his boxers. "What if I said I don't want to let you out of bed *now*?" I slip my hand inside his boxers and wrap my fist around his hardening cock, stroking it once . . . twice.

"You're not playing fair, Carys," Cooper groans, and I slowly shake my head no and press my lips to his neck.

"Who says I'm playing, Coop?" I lick lazy lines down his neck and along each indent of his chest and abs as I push him back down flat on the bed and get comfortable between his legs.

"No more playing. No more hiding. At least not with each other. Now, it's all about taking what I want." I grip his boxer briefs and push them down his legs, then toss them to the floor. I flatten my tongue and slowly lick my way up the length of his velvety smooth cock, like he's the most decadent thing I've ever had in my mouth . . . because he is.

"Jesus, baby." His rough voice is enough to soak my already wet panties.

"Shh," I order as I take him in my mouth and hollow my cheeks.

The noise Coop makes in his chest is deep and gravelly and, no doubt, the best sound I've ever heard.

I take him deeper.

"That's it, baby. Take me down your throat, just like that."

I gag when I take him into the back of my throat, and Coop runs his rough hand lovingly down my body, cupping my ass. "That's it, baby. Now, sit that needy pussy on my face and let me taste you."

I look up at him through my lashes with wide eyes, both incredibly turned-on and yet nervous about the logistics.

"Carys . . . Come here." Coop's pale blue eyes glow with need in the dark room. His words, whispered and commanding, are just loud enough over the hard rain lashing against the French doors.

I crawl up the bed hesitantly, not sure how this is going to work.

"Sit on my face, Carys." I never knew I'd like being bossed around in bed, but when Cooper growls the words, I nearly melt. He tugs my hips, his fingers biting into my soft skin until I give in and swing one leg carefully over his face.

Before I even get myself settled, he tugs me down against his mouth, and my panties are pushed aside as

Coop's tongue slides inside my wet pussy, sending shock waves through my core.

"Ohmygod," I moan at the first lash of his tongue. "How am I . . . ?" Coop's fingers open me to him while he sucks my clit into his mouth, and I ride his face. "Oh . . . God."

"Suck, Carys. Or this stops," he growls, and I try to concentrate.

I take him back in my mouth and try to focus on not biting off his dick while he works me into a fucking frenzy. I swallow him down into the back of my throat and hum around his dick. Tears pool in my eyes as I try to get him to come, because holy hell, I'm already there.

"So close," I pant around him as I add my hand to work his cock faster and feel the first thrum of my orgasm threatening to tear through me without my permission.

I try to hold still, to not rock back against his face. But there's no stopping the growing wave from breaking when he sucks my clit into his mouth. I come on his face with his cock in my mouth, moaning and panting and praying no one else in the house is awake.

My release pushes Coop over the edge, and I swallow the hot streams of come down my throat before I collapse next to him, boneless.

"Jesus, baby. We should start every day that way." He runs his hand up and down my bare calf, and I purr like a blissed-out kitten at the heavenly touch.

"Yeah, we should." I smile while I lie there like a limp noodle, not able to move. "Now, you can go."

Coop tickles the back of my knee, making me laugh louder than I should. "Oh, I see how it's gonna be. Use me, then discard me." He stands up and slides on his shorts from last night, then smacks my ass, no doubt leaving a handprint. "I'll see you at breakfast."

The smile in his voice is as beautiful as the one on his face.

And both do warm and gooey things to my already warm and gooey insides.

I'm not sure how much time has passed when I feel the weight of another person on my bed and crack open one eye. Chloe's lying next to me on top of the covers, her hair damp from the rain and a mischievous grin on her face. I yank the sheet up to cover my bare chest.

"What the hell, Chloe?"

She reaches down to the floor and grabs a t-shirt to throw at me, then sits up. "Like I haven't seen your tits before. Come on, now."

I slide my arms through the soft shirt and realize my mistake before Chloe's wide eyes double in size. "Oh. My. God. I fucking knew it."

His scent surrounds me.

There's absolutely no mistaking whose shirt I just threw on, considering *Navy* is written across the front of it in black.

"You two avoided each other all night last night, but I caught you staring at him a few times during dinner." She smacks my thigh, then crosses her arms over her chest. "Holy. Shit. You and Coop?" Uncontrollable laughter bubbles up her chest, and I whack her as hard as I can with a pillow.

"Shut up." That just makes her laugh harder. "I'm serious, Chloe. Please lower your voice."

She jumps from the bed and starts pacing my room. "Okay, okay. But I have so many questions . . . Like how long has this been going on? Does anyone else know?" She bites down on her long purple nail, then starts laughing like a loon. "Your brother is going to shit a solid gold brick, Carys."

I stand, and Cooper's shirt falls down to my knees. "This is brand new, Chloe. It started . . . like, just started the night before he left for his last mission. Then he came home and turned right around to go to training. Yesterday was the first time we've seen each other in over a month."

She nods her head as she follows along. "Okay, so it's new. Who knows?"

"Our friends in California, and now you. That's it. And it needs to stay that way. At least for now, Chloe. You can't say anything—to anyone. Please. Give us time to figure this out," I beg her, not sure if I should cry or laugh at the tortured look on her face.

"This is the juiciest piece of gossip we've seen since your brother walked in on your mom and Coach banging on the kitchen table, and you want me to keep it to myself?" She kicks that around for another moment, and I grab a pair of sweats out of my suitcase and drag them up my legs. "Fine. But what do I get out of it?"

My head whips around to hers. "My undying love?" It shouldn't be a question, but it absolutely is.

"Not good enough," she cackles like an evil queen.

"Not good enough?" I pick up my brush from the dresser and throw it at her, missing her by at least a foot. *So not the athlete in the family.* "What the hell do you want? A bigger stake in Le Désir?"

Chloe snags the brush from the floor and waves it in front of my face. "Nope. But you better name your first baby Chloe." She offers me the brush, and I just stare in shock. "Now change your damn shirt and use the brush on the rat's nest sitting on your head. Murphy made a breakfast feast since Coop has to head back tonight, and I'm supposed to be dragging you over there."

If Aiden hadn't been blessed by the football gods, he'd have been a chef. I wouldn't be surprised if that's what he does after his football career ends someday.

I take the brush back and look at myself in the mirror. "I need to shower."

I smell like sex and Cooper.

"Nope. You need to come with me now, or there won't be any food left."

"Fine." I grab a tank with a built-in bra from my suitcase and change out of Cooper's shirt, then throw on a hoodie. "Did you let Coop know?"

"He's over there, having coffee now. He, Brady, and Bash went sunrise surfing."

"In the rain?" I look outside and see that it's let up to a steady drizzle.

Guess he went there when he left me.

She nods her head. "Yup. Now come on."

Breakfast was a whole new experience in awkward, and as much as I love my family, I'm definitely ready to be back in California, without the worry of hiding something from the people I love. That, by itself, should be raising red flags about this thing between Cooper and me, but it doesn't. Instead, I concentrate on not paying any more attention to him than I do to anyone else.

The second round of the storm kicks in, and as we all clean up the ridiculous number of pots, pans, and dishes my brother used to cook his feast, my head starts to bother me. I pour myself a cup of tea and take it into the family room after the last dish is put away, then sit next to my brother and lay my now-aching head on his shoulder.

The guys are deciding what everyone feels like doing during our rainout. No beach today. Mom, Coach, Dec, and Belles are taking the kiddos to the movies to see the newest Disney flick, and Nattie offered to watch Nixon for them, so they didn't have to bring a baby along. The other girls are talking about manis, pedis, and *Avengers*—our version of chick flicks. But I don't join in. Instead, I close my eyes and feel myself drifting off.

COOPER

"NOPE. UH-UH. BRADY WILL ALWAYS BE CAPTAIN AMERICA," Nattie insists, and I hide my grin behind my coffee mug.

Chloe grabs a blanket from the back of the couch and covers Carys with it, then spears Nattie with her eyes. "Sorry to break it to you, Nat. But Coop is the whole Captain America package with a shiny red-white-and-blue bow on top."

We all laugh at Chloe's description and Nat's refusal to listen. She's standing across the room, swaying with Nixon in her arms, trying to keep him happy while Brady makes a bottle. Apparently, she's doing a lousy job, based on the noise that comes out of the tiny human that sounds like a baby pterodactyl.

"I know, Nix," Nat shushes him in her sweet baby voice. "Auntie Chloe is insane. Don't you worry about listening to her."

Carys pulls the blanket tighter around her and burrows deeper against Murphy, who makes an odd face.

He leans his cheek against her forehead like my mom used to do when we were little kids, then rips the blanket away from her.

"Hey . . ." she grumbles, still half asleep. "Give it back. I'm cold."

It's about seventy degrees in here with the air conditioner on, and my girl is in sweats and a hoodie. She shouldn't be cold. I try to control my reaction as I watch the interaction between Murphy and her, but it's not an easy thing for me. She shouldn't be tucked against him. I should be there with her in my arms.

"You're hot, Care Bear. Like, fever hot." He looks over at Chloe. "Do you guys have any ibuprofen?"

Carys's teeth start chattering, and I feel myself getting pissed at Murph. "Give her the damn blanket back. She doesn't feel good, Murph."

He tucks it up around her as Chloe comes in with two pills in her hand and a bottle of water.

Carys sits up with a sigh and swallows the pills, then looks around at all of us. Her tired eyes hold mine for an extra beat before she drags them over Nat, who's feeding a much happier Nixon.

"Sorry, guys. I must have caught a bug. I'm going back to Mom's house. I don't want to get Nix sick."

I stand quickly because fuck this. I'm not going to let her go back by herself. But Chloe moves in front of me. "I'll come with ya, Carys. I could use some time to sketch anyway. Just let me grab my shoes and my pad."

Carys throws the blanket off and pulls her hood up over her head while she waits.

When did she get sick?

She was fine when I left her this morning.

Wasn't she?

My phone vibrates in my pocket just as Chloe comes back into the room.

Chloe: If you're trying to keep this on the down-low, you're doing a shitty job, Coop. I've got your girl for the afternoon.

Holy shit.

How does she know?

Does anyone else?

How do you answer a text like that? Carys asked me specifically not to say anything about us. What's this . . . ? Day two? I can't confirm anything. But there's a big fat fucking difference between not saying anything and lying to someone about how I feel for the woman who no longer looks like the sun-kissed goddess I held all night last night. She feels terrible, and it shows.

And fuck . . . I want to be the one taking care of her.

Later that afternoon, once Dad and Katherine are back from the movies and lunch with Callen, I use that as my excuse to go back to the house. Not that I don't want to get a little time in with my dad. I do, but I also want to check in with Chloe and see how Carys is feeling without it being obvious. I'm a trained operator, and I already blew keeping us under wraps within twenty-four hours of getting here. The team is gonna bust my balls for this one.

I'm finishing up with the goodbyes with my sister, who's crying like she's never going to see me again. She knows exactly how to make me feel worse than anyone else ever can.

"Be safe, Cooper." Nat hugs me close. I don't know if she'll ever forgive me for joining the Navy. "What time do you leave?"

I squeeze her back and press a kiss to the top of her head. "I need to head out around fourteen-hundred if I want to make my flight. Wheels are up at eighteen-hundred, whether I'm on the plane or not. And I need to be on that plane."

Brady holds her back. "Let him go, Nat. We'll see him again soon."

"If you miss my wedding, Cooper Sinclair, I will never forgive you."

Jesus. Don't I know that's the truth.

No pressure or anything.

She squeezes me one more time before stepping back.

"Love you, Nat."

I pound Brady's chest. "Take care of her."

"Always," he answers. And I know he will.

I quickly jog the few yards to my dad's house. The rain has all but stopped, but the day is cold and gray. Overcast skies threaten to dump more rain any minute as I step inside, and Callen comes running.

I pick him up and toss him high into the air.

His floppy hair lifts from his forehead, and a smile stretches across his face as he squeals with glee. "Higher, Cooper."

When he comes down, I tuck him into me like a football and run him over to Dad. "I found something that belongs to you."

Dad laughs. "Pretty sure I'm not missing anything."

Callen pops his head up. "Me, Dad. Me. You're missing me."

Dad takes him from me and sets him on the counter. "We need to wash your face before Mommy finds out I let you have chocolate, Cal. Or you'll get us both in trouble."

Dad washes Cal's face, then hands him off to Katherine for a nap. He leans back against the counter and crosses his arms over his thick chest, looking like an older version of Declan.

"Wanna tell me what's on your mind, son?"

"Just thinking about everything I miss, being on the other side of the country." Best way to lie is to anchor it in the truth. I can't exactly tell him I'm in love with my step-sister. Especially since I haven't told her yet.

Dad eyes me skeptically. "That it?"

I nod. I have no idea how he does that, but he always knows when something is going on with one of us. Always.

"How are things going with this training?"

I have to choose my words carefully. It's easier for him if he doesn't know everything I do. "It's going well. But I'm ready for it to be over. It's weird not being with the team."

"We miss you."

"I miss you too, Dad. I miss all of you. I'm hoping I get a weekend to fly home and see a game in the fall."

"Hey, Coop." Chloe strolls down the hall and joins us in the kitchen. "Coach." Her sketchpad is tucked under her arm, and her hair's thrown up in a messy bun on top of her head with what looks like a charcoal pencil holding the purple tips in place. "Your girl's not feeling too good, Coach."

"Nattie or Carys?" Dad asks, concerned.

Chloe laughs. "Nattie's still riding the engagement high. Carys is asleep in her bed. She's got a pretty high fever. At least, I think it is. I didn't take her temp or anything. But I was coming out here to scavenge for either medicine or Katherine. She's got the chills again." She looks at me, letting me know she's filling me in as much as she can. "I figured Katherine would know best."

"Thanks, Chloe. I'll go get Katie." Dad jogs up the steps, and I head down the hall with Chloe following behind.

"Can you buy me a few minutes?"

She pops her gum, then twirls it around her finger. "I got'cha covered, Coop."

I open the door of Carys's room and sit down on the edge of her bed, brushing my lips over her hot forehead. "Hey, baby."

She moans, "Coop?"

"I'm here." I push the hair away from her face. "Tell me what you need."

"Water, please."

I want to lie next to her. I want to hold her in my arms and let her sleep on me. I want to take care of her. But I can't do any of those things yet. So instead, I stand and tuck the blanket in around her. "I'll be right back."

"No." Her green eyes fly open. "Have Chloe grab it. You can't be in here."

"Carys . . ."

"No," she rasps, then closes her eyes. "We can't get caught, and you can't get sick. Go, Coop. We'll be back in California soon."

"Soon, baby." I brush my lips over hers and force myself to step out of the room. I close the door and walk back to the kitchen in time for Katherine to pass me in the hall on her way to Carys's room.

Chloe's sitting at the counter, sketching something . . . not sure if it's a bathing suit or lingerie. But it looks sexy on the curvy woman she's placed it on. I sit down on the stool next to her and look to see if we're alone.

"How did you figure it out?"

"Oh, please. She couldn't stop looking at you last night with those puppy-dog eyes she's always had for you. The difference was you. She was looking, and you liked it. You looked too, but you were sneakier."

"Seriously?" I didn't think we were that obvious. "Come on . . . we weren't that bad or someone else would have picked up on it."

Chloe taps her pencils to the paper. "Yeah well, no one else walked into Carys's bedroom to find it smelling like sex this morning. She was lying in bed in panties and grabbed your Navy shirt from the floor to cover up." She flips the cover of her sketch book closed with a flourish and smiles. "Be careful, Coop. Murphy's gonna freak if you hide this from him."

Murphy's gonna *try* to kick my ass when he finds this out is more like it.

Hopefully that will be the worst of it.

"We're not even sure what this is yet, Chloe. We just want to take our time before we bring everyone else into it." I regurgitate the words Carys made me swear to.

"Tell yourself that, if you want, but the look you had on your face earlier—when I brought her home instead of you —was not the look of a guy doing casual." She cocks her head to the side and studies me.

"I never said anything about casual, Chloe." I don't even try to hide my annoyance at that inference.

I'm already over this conversation and wishing I was in a different room with a different girl.

"Good. Because she deserves more. And so do you, Coop. You're one of the good ones. One of the best. And if any two people were ever worth dealing with the shitstorm you're going to have to walk through to be together, it's the two of you. Don't fuck it up."

She hops off the stool and kisses me on the cheek. "See you in a few months."

I watch her leave and replay her words.

Carys does deserve more.

She deserves a man who can give her everything.

But she also deserves a man who can honor her wishes.

So for now, we keep the secret.

We take the risk. And damn the consequences.

CARYS

"Okay, well, at least you don't have mono." My best friend, Daphne, sits across from me in a booth at the Busy Bee, our favorite bistro on Main Street in Kroydon Hills.

Her roommate, Maddie, sits quietly next to her with wide eyes, while Chloe hasn't stopped laughing next to me.

I still felt awful as we packed up and drove home from the beach a few days after I had gotten sick, but at least my fever was gone, even if my headache lingered.

I spent most of the next week getting my work done for my online classes or sleeping. When I still wasn't feeling back to normal the following week, Mom insisted I get checked for mono. But thankfully, the results were negative.

"Nope." Chloe steals the cherry right out of the whipped cream that sat on top of my Belgian Waffles and pops it into her mouth. "No mono for our girl. Cooper gets to live another day."

I smack my hand over her mouth and look around. "Could you please lower your voice?"

"Seriously, could you even imagine if he gave you mono? How the hell would you have explained that to your mom?" Daphne looks at me over the rim of her coffee cup with mischief in her eyes.

"No one has mono. I spent all last week with Chloe, and she's still fine," I protest.

Chloe's hands wave around animatedly. "Wait a minute. We were together," she points between the two of us. "But we weren't *together*, together. You know what I mean?" She thinks about that for a moment. "I mean, I love you, but I've seen you naked, and there were no sparks."

Maddie and Daphne giggle, and I slam my hand against the table a little harder than I planned on.

"Touchy, touchy," Chloe mocks, then points at my half-eaten waffles. "You gonna eat that?"

I shake my head and push my plate her way.

I still don't feel great—not sick, just tired.

Chloe and I did some business planning last week. We worked on a few ideas for upcoming designs and figured out what we wanted the second half of the year to look like for Le Désir. We also talked to a graphic designer about branding, met with the two boutiques that have been buying from us in the city, and spoke with someone about outsourcing the manufacturing when we're ready. And I took all three of my second session summer finals.

I'm spent.

"What time is your flight, Carys?" Daphne knows I'm anxious to get back to California, especially now that Cooper's training is over.

"Six-thirty tomorrow morning." I take a nervous breath, wondering what it's going to be like, and my bestie catches it.

"Don't be nervous. It's Cooper," Daphne states like that makes any sense. "Are you really not going to talk to anyone about it before you go?"

Chloe throws an unopened creamer at Daphne. "What are we? She's talking to us."

"You know what I mean. The longer you guys keep this to yourself, the bigger the secret gets. The bigger the secret, the bigger the fallout." Daphne looks at Maddie for support, but she just shakes her head.

"Don't look at me. I don't know the crazy family dynamic you're all talking about." Maddie reaches across the table and squeezes my hand. "You do you, Carys. Everyone else will either get on board, or they won't. But you'll have what you want."

What I want . . . What *do* I want?

I've been asking myself that for months now.

I wanted to go to school in California. I begged my mom to let me go. I wanted the freedom. The independence. And I'm so glad I did it. But while I can't wait to get back, it has nothing to do with school. I thought maybe I'd hate the summer classes less than I hated the previous courses. I was wrong. They were worse. Shortened semesters meant covering so much more during each class. I'm so glad they're over, and I have a few more weeks before the next semester starts.

I keep thinking I've got things figured out, and I keep being proven wrong.

I'm going through the motions, but I'm not sure what the endgame is.

The flight back to San Diego is brutal. The turbulence is enough to make me queasy. I'm not sure if it's because I'm so anxious to get home, but the six hours spent suspended in the air feel more like seventeen. It gives me way too much time to contemplate . . . well, everything. So I do what I always do when I'm trying to make decisions.

I make a list. Writing things down has always helped calm my busy mind.

~ Is school for me?

It really isn't, but can I design and run a successful lingerie line without a degree?

~ Is owning a lingerie company what I definitely want to do with my life, or would I rather design for someone else? No. I want to design for myself. I want to see Le Désir in high-end boutiques around the world.

~ Cooper . . .

There's no question about my feelings for Cooper.

But how do we navigate our nosey family?

I'll give school one more year, then make my decision. I'm lucky my grandparents set up trust funds for Aiden and me years ago. I'm even luckier because my mother is the most financially savvy person I've ever known. And she's spun the money left for us into two small fortunes. I could probably live off that for the next ten years without working a single day if I wanted to. But that's not what I want. Chloe and I have already started to see a small-scale profit that I want to see grow.

I look over my list and realize I don't have that many decisions to make.

I know what I want. Even better, I know *who* I want.

Now, I just need to figure out how to make it happen.

Luckily, the flight lands on time, and everything else moves smoothly. I've retrieved my luggage within an hour of landing, and I'm walking through the revolving door to find my Uber that's in the waiting lane. But I don't see my Uber when I step out onto the sidewalk.

I don't even look for it because Cooper is standing in front of his beat-up old Jeep. His jeans are well-worn and torn at one knee. The faded blue t-shirt he's wearing stretches across his chest and arms, making those eyes I love stand out even more. He looks comfortable in his skin. Confident in a way that's totally Cooper. And maybe . . . just maybe, I'm getting there too.

Coop jogs across the lanes of traffic and scoops me up in his arms, crushing me to him.

I wrap my legs around his waist and my arms around his neck as I breathe him in.

"Jesus. I missed you, Carys." He runs his lips along my jaw and over my lips.

"I missed you too. I'm so sorry I was sick when you left. We barely got to spend any time together." I cling to him like it's been years instead of weeks. Not willing to let go and not caring who's watching, I kiss him with every ounce of pent-up need, frustration . . . and maybe love that I have for this man.

Coop groans deep in his chest, and I love knowing I do that to him. "You can't control getting sick." He puts me down and grabs my suitcase and carry-on. "Let's get out of here."

"Sounds good." I open my Uber app and cancel my ride. Once we're in the Jeep, Coop gets us out of the maze of airport traffic and onto the highway to go home.

"Do you want to grab something to eat first? There's a great food truck a few minutes from here."

I tilt my head toward him and lean back. "That sounds great, but don't you have training or something? What exactly do you do during the day when you're not on a mission?"

"Nah, we're off today. We do a lot of training, though, to make sure we're ready for every situation." Coop stops in front of a taco truck a few minutes later, walks around the Jeep, and opens my door. "What are you in the mood for?"

I look at him, standing next to me, then lean against his chest, suddenly exhausted. "You," I answer honestly. "I just want you."

COOPER

How do you willingly break someone's heart?

When Command asked me yesterday if I could fill in for a brother who'd been injured on Bravo Team, I was hesitant. It means being in Virginia Beach for the next six to eight months. I thought about saying no. I didn't want to leave my team or Carys after just getting back.

I talked to Ford about it.

Not just as my team leader, but as my friend, who's been doing this for a long time. And according to him, it's a great opportunity for me. Especially if I ever want to get back to the East Coast and be closer to home.

I hadn't thought about that before. Right now, Charlie Team is my home.

I don't want to leave them. Although, I might want to be closer to my family one day.

But the bottom line is if the Navy asks, you go. And I'm not ready to push back, possibly fucking with my career by telling them no.

But now, as I haul Carys's suitcase upstairs to her room, I'm not sure how I'm going to tell her or why I even said yes, when it's going to put me on the opposite side of the country from this woman for months.

She drops her carry-on and purse down on her bed and kicks off her mint-green Chuck Taylors, then slides an elastic band off her wrist and ties her hair up on top of her head. She looks like she's preparing for war, but her face softens, and she wraps her arms around my waist.

"Wanna take a bath with me? I can't shake how tired I am lately, and I just want to relax with you. But I need to wash the recycled plane air off my body, and I think I could use some help reaching my back." She tilts her head back, and a slow, soft smile spreads across her pretty face. "Think you can help me with that?"

I lift her in my arms and carry her into the bathroom. "I think I can manage, baby." I sit her down on the bathroom counter and turn on the water in the clawfoot tub. "How do you like the water temperature?"

She hops off the counter and pushes me to sit down on the closed toilet lid, then messes with the old-fashioned black faucet until steam is wafting from the filling tub. "Hope you like grapefruit." Carys grabs a glass canister from the counter and scoops some salts into the water, and a crisp scent fills the air. When she turns toward me, I grab her waist.

"You're far too dressed for that water. Arms up, soldier." Her laughter fills the room as her smile spreads.

I lift my arms into the air and correct her, "It's sailor, not soldier, babe."

"Tsk-tsk." She folds my tee and places it on top of the wicker hamper, then unbuckles my belt. "Shorts off too. You need to get in the tub first."

I do as I'm told and strip down, then watch her eyes dilate as I stand naked in front of her. "Like what you see?"

"Get in the tub before your head gets too big to fit." She presses her palm flat on my chest, and I grab it and bring it to my lips.

"Which head are we talking about?"

She shakes her head, but her smile lights up those green eyes. "Get in the tub."

I step into the tub with a hiss. This water is going to boil my balls. "Damn, baby. It's a little hot."

Carys ignores me and bends over to peel off her black-capri leggings and panties, giving me an unobstructed view of her magnificent ass that's high in the air, before she stands back up and removes her t-shirt and bra.

She stands like a goddess, with the light coming through the leaded-glass window, framing her.

My eyes travel over the exquisite curves of her body. The dip of her hips flaring slightly out and curving into strong, toned thighs. Her high, perfect breasts bring me to my knees, and my mouth waters with want.

Words leave me when she reaches over and takes my hand for balance. She slowly lowers one foot, then the other, into the scalding water until she's sitting between my legs, her back resting against my chest. A perfect fit. I grab the pink puffy thing from the shelf behind the tub and add some of the bodywash sitting next to it, running it slowly down her arms.

Carys hums a sound of approval in the back of her throat, and my cock jumps to attention. "So how was it being back in Kroydon Hills?"

"It was fine. It would have been better if I hadn't gotten sick. Chloe and I got a ton accomplished for Le Désir, but I've got some work to do before classes start, if we're going to stay on track."

After a deep breath, I drag the puffy thing over her chest and down her flat stomach until I reach the apex of her thighs, then run it over her legs and down her calf before repeating it on the other side. Trying to control myself. I haven't seen her in nearly a month, and I really do want to hear all about her trip, even if it's hard to think of anything beyond how badly I want to take her right now.

"And what does staying on track look like?"

She tilts her head to the side and closes her eyes, bringing both knees up to her chest and circling her arms around them. "For this year, staying on track means locking in a manufacturing company who's willing to work with us on a small scale, so we can provide more for the smaller boutiques we're working with. If all goes well, by this time next year, we'd love to be looking into opening up our own shop."

"How will you do that with Chloe and you on two opposite sides of the country? You won't even be done with school yet." Her drive and ambition are sexy as hell.

She shrugs. "Nothing worth it is ever easy."

Then she carefully turns in my arms, with only a tiny bit of water sloshing over the sides of the clawfoot tub. Her fingers curl into my hair, and she rests her knees on either side of my legs. Her pussy teases my cock with every small motion of her body.

"We're never going to be easy, you know that, right?"

I push the damp pieces of hair that have fallen down away from her face. "You're wrong, baby. You and I . . . We're going to be the easiest thing we've ever done. Loving you has come so naturally, I'm not even sure when it happened. I love you, and everyone else can fuck right off if they want to get in the way or have their say about it."

"I've waited years to hear those words from you, Coop. I've loved you for as long as I can remember, and nothing is ever going to change that. But our family isn't going to make it easy on us."

"Yeah. They won't. But as long as you and I are on the same page, they'll come around because they won't have a choice. We won't give them a choice." I slide both hands up her arms and across her smooth shoulders to cup her face. "But Carys, we're going to have to tell them."

"Not yet." She shakes her head. "I just want you to

myself. I just want us to enjoy being us before we deal with them. I want a few months to know what it's like to know you and be loved by you without the added stress of our family." She lifts up and places my cock at her center. "Now show me what that feels like, Coop."

CARYS

I press Cooper's cock against my entrance, then brace my hands against his shoulders as I slide down over him. Pleasure spikes, tinged with pain, as he stretches me so thoroughly my body vibrates around his. I move achingly slowly, my eyes locked on his. Wanting this to last forever but chasing the high I've missed since last month.

"Take your time, Carys. I don't want to hurt you." His hand grips my chin and pulls my face down to his.

Goosebumps cover my skin as I wrap my arms around his broad shoulders and try to move. "God, Coop. I missed you." I press my lips to his. They're firm, warm, and so utterly delicious, I get lost in the perfection of it all for a moment.

When he angles my head and takes control of the kiss, a slow moan spills past my lips, and Coop's tongue slips inside my mouth, deepening our connection. Teasing me. Tasting me. Taking me higher.

Water spills over the edge of the tub, but I don't care.

Can't care.

I just need to get closer.

Take him deeper.

"More, Coop," I pant between kisses, then lean my forehead against his as I finally take him completely inside me, stretched and full. "I need more."

"Good, baby," he murmurs against my lips.

His praise is like a soft, loving stroke against my hypersensitive skin. Then, he finally begins moving in slow lazy strokes, like we have all the time in the world.

And we finally do.

There's no fear of who might hear us.

No timetable where one of us is hopping on a plane. Just us.

Just this.

"Tell me what you want, baby," He groans as his hips pick up speed. He grinds into me, creating the most delicious friction against my clit as his cock hits my g-spot over and over and over again.

I mewl at his words, unable to form a coherent thought.

Lost in my lust.

Chasing my orgasm.

Coop drags a callused thumb over my peaked nipple, then pinches it while capturing my mouth and thrusting his hips. The fire inside me that's slowly building roars to life and threatens to devour me. "Do you want it harder?"

Unable to form words, I nod and lick his lower lip eagerly.

"Words, Carys. Tell me," he growls against my mouth.

"Yes." I inhale and he rewards me by pinching my nipple tighter. My breath catches in my throat. "Just like that."

He drags his tongue over the same nipple, lavishing it with attention, then teases it with his teeth while he fucks me harder. Rougher. With a sweet abandon we didn't get to have at the beach.

I'm lost to the sensations, to the pain and the pleasure. The heat races through me while the flame burns hot against my skin.

One hand slides down to my ass and grips one cheek, opening me, while the other skims my puckered hole, and I jerk with a mixture of fear, anticipation, and desire.

"Not yet, baby. Not in here, and not like this. We've got the rest of our lives." His tongue pushes into my mouth, dancing with mine. "And I'm just getting started with your beautiful body."

Cooper's words take me higher. As I meet him thrust for thrust, my orgasm starts with the slow build I've only ever had with him. My core tightens as my pussy flutters around him, and I realize I'm drowning . . . in him . . . in us.

Drowning in what we are in this moment.

What we could be . . . will be in all the years to come.

I'm overwhelmed by my feelings and his and am still amazed that this man feels the same way I do. The flames lick higher when Coop takes my other nipple into his mouth and bites down. When he runs his tongue over the same spot, my toes curl, and my body weakens. He thrusts up at the same time he pulls my body down against his, and I shatter in his arms, screaming his name without a care for who can hear us.

Cooper follows me over the cliff as he comes on a roar.

He holds me, whispering words that soothe my soul.

"Coop . . ." I lie limp in his arms with my lips pressed to the warm skin of his neck. "I love you."

"You're the only person I've ever said that to, Carys. You're the love of my life. The only one. The only one there will ever be."

We lie there until the water begins to chill. "Don't break my heart, Cooper."

He presses his lips to mine and runs his hand over my hair. "You're the one with all the power, Carys. You always will be."

It's not until later, after we dried off and are lying down on the bed, bathed in the glow of the warm mid-afternoon sun, that Cooper's breath evens out. I realize he's fallen asleep and finally answer him with a whispered plea into the universe as I feel the tug of sleep dragging me under.

"I don't want the power. I just want you."

Bang. Bang. Bang.

"What the fuck?" Coop jackknifes up into a sitting position, essentially throwing me across the bed, as a loud thumping against my bedroom door obnoxiously echoes through my sleepy brain.

"Crown up, buttercup. Get some clothes on and come get dinner with Linc and me," Emerson yells while she continues to beat a horrific rhythm against the door. "You've got ten minutes, then I'm coming in."

Cooper's tired eyes dart to mine. "Is she serious?"

Em answers before I get a chance. "*She's* serious, Sinclair. Get moving."

With the white pin-dot sheet pooling around my naked waist, I sit up, and Cooper's eyes look me over, darkening with need. "We need twenty minutes, Em. And you might want to get away from the door."

He throws the sheet back from the bed and crawls over me.

"I'm hungry," Em whines. "Come on."

"Twenty minutes, Em," I yell as I lock my legs around Coop's waist. "Now, go away." I circle his cock with my hand and pump. "Think we can make twenty minutes work?"

He traces his tongue over the hollow of my neck. "I don't need twenty minutes to make you come."

Cooper did not need twenty minutes to make me come. Nope. He accomplished that feat two times in under ten. Now, we're sitting at a dark booth in Casa De Reyes in old town San Diego, enjoying the absolutely best down-home Mexican food of my life.

"How have we lived here for years and never heard of this place?" Linc asks around a mouthful of pork burrito with pineapple juice dripping down his chin.

Emerson hands him a napkin. "You're just not one of the cool kids, Linc."

He looks hurt for a hot minute before he plants his juicy lips on hers and steals a shrimp right out of her spicy Caesar salad. "Whatever. I can live with that."

"So, how was Kroydon Hills, CC? Was it good to be home, or were you counting down the days until you were back here?" Emerson sips her water and eyes me cautiously, like my answer is significant, though I'm not sure why.

I momentarily lift my eyes to Cooper's, trying to decide how to respond. "I guess a little bit of both." He runs his hand under the hem of my black sundress and squeezes my thigh under the table. I somehow manage to contain my involuntary yelp. "But being home was nice. Getting to spend time with everyone was great."

His callused fingers continue their exploration as they make their way up to my crossed legs and help me uncross them. A cold sweat breaks out over my skin as I realize what he's about to do. But I don't hesitate as I spread my thighs, giving him better access.

He rewards me by lightly stroking over my now-damp panties.

Warmth travels up my face, and I run my teeth over my bottom lip, trying to act natural but failing.

"Being back here feels like a relief too. I don't have to be as guarded here."

Cooper's finger glides under my silk panties, and I squirm in my seat as Emerson looks at me with accusatory eyes.

Damn it. She knows.

But it feels too good to make him stop, and I want more.

He doesn't stop, even with eyes on us. Instead, he pushes his thumb down on my clit and strokes that spot inside me he finds with ease.

My body tightens to a nearly painful point as I cling desperately to any sense of sanity I have while my walls clamp down around Cooper's finger.

"You really didn't tell anyone about . . . Ya know. You two?" Linc's question is directed toward Coop, who silently shakes his head no.

Good. I hope he's as affected as I am right now. But when he adds a second finger, I no longer care and force down a moan, sipping my water as I try to hide the tremor wracking my body. "Not yet," I squeak, covering my face with my napkin and coughing as warmth washes over me and I come.

Right here in a booth inside Casa De Reyes.

Oh. My. God.

Cooper withdraws his fingers, then casually slides one through the guac on his plate and sucks it clean.

Oh holy hell.

"Well, it's not like you're going to have a ton of time together to get caught." Linc shrugs his shoulders and snags another shrimp from Emerson. "Not for the next couple of months, anyway."

"Seriously, chew before you speak, or there will be no blow job tonight."

I don't react to Em's crass words.

Instead, I turn my head slowly toward Cooper, who looks ready to jump over the table and kill Linc.

COOPER

"Cooper?" Carys asks with a tremble to her voice.

Looking for the truth I should have given her earlier.

"You didn't tell her?" Emerson glares at me with daggers in her eyes.

I turn on Linc. "You told *her* before I could tell Carys?"

Before Linc can get any words of defense out of his mouth, Carys grabs her purse and throws a few twenties on the table, then stands.

"I'm obviously not privy to something the three of you know. So I'm just gonna go and let you discuss it amongst yourselves." The look she gives me is glacial before she gracefully walks away.

I sit there for a second, dumbfounded, knowing I fucked up and not sure if there's a way to fix it until Emerson kicks me under the table.

"Get your ass up, Sinclair, and go after her. You've had all afternoon to tell her, and you didn't. Fix it."

Fuck. She's not wrong.

When I stand, she smacks Linc on the chest. "And you're a moron who doesn't know when to keep his mouth shut."

I ignore the two of them and push through the front door to find Carys standing by the curb. Her dark hair is hiding her pretty face, and the warm wind is blowing her black sundress around her knees.

"Carys . . ."

She turns back to look at me, and the tears clinging to her long lashes gut me.

"What do you want, Cooper? To talk?" She blinks and straightens her spine in a move I recognize well.

Shit.

That's not a good sign for me.

"You're leaving again, aren't you?" She moves her hands to her hips and waits me out as I try to figure out how to answer her.

The family sitting on the bench next to the door waiting for their table to be ready seems more invested in this conversation than I'm okay with.

"Can we talk about this in the car?"

"Want to fuck me again first? I'm sure we could find all sorts of fun ways to stall if we get creative." Carys turns away from me as a Toyota Corolla stops at the curb. "Sorry to disappoint, but my Uber's here."

The driver rolls down the passenger side window and says something to her. She steps toward the back door, and I see fucking red.

"Carys, stop."

"Sorry, Coop. I'm not Wanda. I don't like commands." She opens the door, and I push it closed.

I pass the driver a twenty. "Sorry, man. She's going home with me."

"*She* can speak for herself. And she doesn't want to be stuck in a car with you."

A cheer comes from the family behind us, and I drag my hand over my face.

I wrap my hand around the back of her head and hold her still. "Baby, I'm leaving in a few days. I'm sorry I didn't tell you earlier, but I was just so damn happy to see you that I wasn't even thinking about it. I was only thinking about *you*." My thumb caresses her cheekbone. "Now, will you please get in the goddamned Jeep so I can grovel in fucking private? I don't want to waste any of the next few days fighting."

My strong girl breaks down in tears, then buries her face in my neck. "I don't want you to go."

"I don't want to either, baby. But I have to." I hold her in my arms, breathing in the sweet scent of her hair.

"Girl. Don't let him play you like that," comes from the same family as before, and my grip on Carys tightens.

"Can we get in the Jeep now?" I groan.

She lifts her head and runs her fingers along my jaw, then nods.

I press my lips to her forehead and offer up a silent prayer she's going to forgive me. We're quiet as we get in and head back to the house while I try to figure out what to say, but Carys isn't in the mood for quiet.

"When do you leave?" She crosses her legs and angles her body toward mine. "And why doesn't it sound like Linc's going too?"

"First things first. Are we going back to my house or yours?" Not that it makes much difference for the drive home.

"Depends . . . Has Emerson been sleeping at your house or mine? Because I'd rather not continue this fight, knowing Linc and she are in the next room."

"Mine it is then. Linc's been crashing at your place most of this past week." I place my hand, palm up, between us and wait to see if she'll take it. And my girl doesn't disappoint.

She laces her fingers through mine and tugs our joined hands into her lap. "Ready to answer my questions now?"

"I'm being sent to Virginia Beach for six to eight months to help out Bravo Team. I just found out yesterday." I come to a stop at a red light and turn to look at this gorgeous woman who I know I'm hurting. "I'm sorry I didn't say anything earlier today. I was just so damn relieved to see you, baby."

Carys runs the pad of her thumb over our joined hands, sending electricity coursing through my body. Her voice trembles as she asks, "When do you leave?"

"The day after tomorrow."

She exhales a stuttered breath, and I lean into her.

The light changes to green, and the car behind us honks impatiently.

"Take me home, Coop." She grips my hand tighter.

"To *your* house?" I have zero fucking clue how to read this woman right now, but I know I'm treading a fine line.

"No." She squeezes our hands. "To yours."

We drive for the next few minutes in silence.

It's not until we're parked in my driveway that she drops my hand and then climbs into my lap, her legs on either side of mine. She's so small against me, so fragile and yet so strong.

I rest one hand between her shoulder blades and the other possessively on her thigh.

How the fuck am I supposed to go months without her?

Carys's hands grip my shoulders, and her piercing green eyes steal a piece of my soul. "Don't do that to me again, Cooper. Don't fuck me first and then rip my heart to shreds afterward. If we're going to work, you've got to make sure I know exactly what's going on. No hiding. No secrets. I need to know."

Her hands slide up my neck as her thumbs skim my jaw. "I'm not a naïve little girl. I don't need to be protected. I need to be loved. I need to be respected. And hiding something that big from me . . . letting me find out from Linc or Emerson, and in front of our friends instead of in the privacy of my room, wasn't okay."

"I won't always be able to tell you everything." I tilt my head back against the seat and run a hand over her soft hair, tucking it behind her ear. "But I'll tell you everything I can. I promise you, it's you and me. You're my endgame, Carys."

"You and me, Coop. That's all I need." She leans her head down and brushes her lips over mine.

"Me too, baby. Me too."

COOPER

I ROLL OVER THE NEXT MORNING AND REACH OUT FOR Carys, wanting to feel her body against mine, but the other side of the bed is cold and empty. I look around the room, but it's empty too. Her clothes are in the same messy pile on my floor where we left them last night.

So where is she and what the hell is she wearing?

I jump out of bed and throw on a pair of shorts, then make the bed, because . . . well, it's an OCD habit that's been beaten into me by the Navy. When I open the door, the smell of bacon and coffee lingers in the air, and my mouth waters. I make my way down the stairs, toward the kitchen, and stop when I see my girl sitting on a kitchen chair.

One of my gray Navy tees is hanging off her shoulder. She has one leg bent, with that foot planted flat on the seat in front of her and the other dangling down, and Wanda's head is lying on her bare thigh as she scratches behind her ear.

"You're gonna make my dog a pussy, Carys," Trick warns.

Wanda whines when Carys pulls her hand away and whispers, "Sorry," to her.

Then Wanda nudges Carys's hand with her nose until she starts rubbing again.

Yeah, girl. I don't blame you. I love her hands on me too.

217

I walk into the room and drop a kiss on her head. "Mornin, baby."

She tilts her head up and puckers until my lips meet hers. "Good morning."

"Mornin, baby," Trick mocks me. He turns and places a plate of bacon and eggs in front of Carys, then scratches Wanda's butt. "Don't give her any more bacon," He takes two fingers and points them toward his own eyes, then at Carys.

As soon as he turns back to the stove, she sneaks a piece of bacon to Wanda and places a finger against my lips to keep me from laughing. When I lick it instead, she's the one who laughs. And goddammit, what I wouldn't do to bottle that sound.

Trick turns back around and puts two more plates down on the table before he sits. "You heading to base today?"

"Nah." I glance over at Carys, waiting for a reaction that never comes. "I'm free today. I've gotta be there at zero-six-hundred tomorrow for my flight out."

She forces a fake-as-hell smile onto her lips. "What should we do today, then?"

"I can think of a few things." I raise my brows, and she kicks me under the table.

"Cooper . . ." she warns me.

Trick doesn't even bother to hide his laugh. "Guys are coming over tonight for a BBQ. Ford said you need a proper send-off."

Carys forces a smile. "Okay." Having a twin sister means I learned how to speak *girl* years ago, and that "okay" does not actually mean she's good. "What can I bring?"

"Nothing, baby. Just spend the day with me." I drag her from her seat onto my lap.

Trick gags. "Aren't you two just so cute?" he asks with enough sarcasm to almost drown a SEAL.

"Fuck off, man." I give him the finger behind Carys's back.

Trick shovels in the rest of his food, then drops his plate in the sink before he leaves us to get dressed.

Carys turns in my arms and circles hers around my neck. "Are you sure you don't need to go with him? I might not like it, but I'd understand." Her soft eyes hold me hostage, and I wish I didn't have to leave her tomorrow.

"Not today." I capture her lips with mine and lick into her mouth.

She sighs the sweetest sigh, which has my cock twitching in my shorts.

Carys moves away and presses her fingers to her soft lips. "You're mine today?"

My hand runs up her bare leg and under the tee until it's splayed against the soft skin of her back. "I'm yours, period."

"But you won't be here." Her pointer finger runs along my lower lip as she bites down on her own.

"It doesn't matter where we are. I'm yours, Carys. You were made for me."

She leans her forehead against mine. "Really good answer, Coop."

"Come on, future baby momma. Just sing something." Fucking Axel. I kick his leg off the firepit in the backyard as everyone but me laughs. Trick strums the guitar he grabbed from his room earlier, hoping to coax Carys into singing.

We've been out here for hours. Ford's wife, Jess, brought more food than even a SEAL team could eat. Some of the guys have surfed. There's been a cornhole tournament and a lot of ragging on each other, like only brothers can get away with. But now, we're all chillin' in the yard. Relaxed. Carys is sitting next to me with her legs thrown across mine. Her head is tucked under my chin, and my arm is wrapped around her protectively. I don't want to let her go.

Trick strums a familiar chord, and Carys glares at Emerson. "You told him my favorite song?"

Emerson giggles. "Maybe."

She kisses my chin before taking a sip of her water and nodding toward Trick. And when she opens her mouth without ever lifting her head from my shoulder, so many memories come crashing down on me.

How could I have forgotten this song?

This woman sang this song in the car so many times in high school. Whenever Murphy was driving and she was with us, she was singing this old eighties song about living forever young, and damn, if it doesn't make me nostalgic for home and the years before life got so fucking complicated.

The years before I started hiding something this big from my closest friends.

The years before I knew I was sacrificing one relation-ship at the altar of another.

But it only takes one look at my girl to know there's nothing in the world more important than this.

CARYS

Standing off to the side while I watch Cooper's teammates say goodbye is excruciating. My head has throbbed all day already. But between that and the emotions running rampant now, I've got nothing left. My heart feels like it's going to break in two, and I don't know how I'm going to survive.

Okay . . . I realize I'm being overdramatic, but I don't care. This is awful.

Ford's wife, Jessica, walks over to me and laces her fingers through mine before she squeezes. We've only met a few times, but the look on her face tells me everything I need to know before she says a single word.

"You'll get through this. And if you need help, I'm here."

I hold back the first tear that's fighting to fall, knowing if I let it break free, there won't be any stopping the rest for hours.

I refuse to cry until after he leaves.

No matter how much I want to.

Axel throws his arms around me in a big bear hug. "You call me if you need anything, baby momma."

"Fuck off, Axe." Rook shoves him off me, then blocks me from Axel's view. "You need anything, you call any one of us. Even Axe. But know if you call Axe, he's never gonna shut the fuck up about it." It's the most words I've heard him speak since I met him months ago. And his piercing eyes hold me hostage as he leans in and whispers, "Don't let Sinclair see you cry. This is killing him already." He straightens to his full height and puts his hand out. "Give me your phone."

"What?" I look past him and see Cooper smiling at us, then hesitantly pull my phone from my shorts and place it in Rook's palm.

He takes it, holds it in front of my face until it unlocks, then his fingers fly across the screen. After a moment, he does something on his own phone and hands mine back to me. "All our numbers are saved in there, including Jessie's." He smiles warmly at Ford's wife, something I didn't know this scary man was capable of. "I've got your number saved and added you to our tracking app."

"You what?" I must have heard him wrong because who would do that without permission and then tell you it's done? "Tracking app?"

"Don't worry. We won't use it unless we need to, and if we need to, trust me when I say you'll want us to have it." Rook pockets his phone and walks away as if he didn't just add a goddamned tracker to my phone.

"He really won't use it."

I whip my head back to Jessica, not really comforted by her words.

Because if he won't use it unless he needs to, what exactly would make him need to?

"Stop it," the pretty blonde tells me. "Don't go there."

Guess she read my mind.

"Let's grab coffee one day this week. I usually work three twelve-hour shifts at the hospital. So, most of my week is free. You can ask me all the questions I bet you're dying to have answered."

I forgot she was a nurse.

Ford joins us, wrapping one big, beefy arm around his wife, and presses his lips to the top of her head. "Ready to go, Jessie?" His warm brown eyes soften when she tucks herself against him.

"Text me. You've got my number now, Carys. I want you to use it."

"Thank you." I force a smile. "Coffee sounds perfect."

And this is how it goes . . . Cooper says goodbye to his team, and this incredible group of men all offer me their support, their help, and tell me not to hesitate to call for anything. Somehow, I've gained a whole new family, and this one accepts Cooper and me without explanation or interference.

Once everyone is gone, Coop and I stand in the kitchen with Linc, Em, and Trick.

Everyone is quiet.

Hesitant.

Cooper has an arm banded around me as he holds my back to his chest and leans against the counter. "It's just a few months. Then I'll be back." He gets a little choked up. "Don't go getting into any trouble while I'm gone."

Trick gives him the *guy* nod. "Be safe, brother." He slaps Coop on the back and walks out of the room.

"And then there were four . . . that I actually think should be two." Emerson reaches out for my hand and tugs me away from Cooper. "Let's give the boys a minute, CC."

Cooper and Linc have been together since boot camp, all through BUD/S, and now the team. I can't imagine this is easy on either of them.

Em and I walk into the living room, giving the guys a little space. "You're going to be fine. You know that, right?"

I take a deep, stuttering breath. "I think I do. It's just hard. I couldn't wait to get home to him, and he's already leaving."

"You could go with him, you know." Emerson says the

words I've been quietly thinking all day. "Take a few months off and work on your designs in Virginia."

"Drop out of school to follow him across the country? Even if I could come up with a way to explain that to my mother, I don't think it would work. As much as part of me wants to, I've got things to do here. And this isn't permanent." At least, that's what I've been telling myself all day.

"Just remember that, CC. Remember that it's not permanent, and you'll be fine."

Cooper and Linc walk into the room, laughing at something, but as he reaches out for my hand and our skin touches, all laughing stops. "Ready for bed?"

I nod silently and let him lead me down the hall to his room, suddenly nervous. When I walk past him, he pulls me back against his chest, and his warm breath ghosts across my ear, leaving my body humming with anticipation. "You okay, baby?"

I drop my chin down, giving him better access, and let him take my weight. "It's just a few months. We've got this."

Cooper presses his hot mouth to my pulse point, and I melt against him. His lips skim up my neck as his hands gather the hem of my sundress, and he tugs it over my head. He sucks in a quick breath, and I smile triumphantly, knowing he likes what he sees.

Hidden under my plain green-and-white-striped, jersey-cotton tank dress, I'm wearing one of the designs Chloe and I worked on a few weeks ago. It's a dark-green French-lace thong with tiny silk ties on either hip and a matching balconette bra with green silk covering the lower half of my breasts, plumping them up, while matching white lace barely covers the top.

Cooper's callused fingers slide down my sides and under the waist of my panties before stopping abruptly.

I turn my head back to him just as his arm bands

around my waist, and I'm lifted off my feet. "Cooper," I squeal before I'm dropped on the bed.

"I want your ass in the air, baby."

Why do those words make me so wet?

I peek over my shoulder in time to catch him throwing his shirt to the floor as he kicks off his jeans and boxers, and my mouth waters. "Did I tell you to turn around, Carys?"

I turn my head back as my pussy throbs from the rasp in his voice.

Bossy Cooper makes me so hot, my thong is drenched.

The mattress dips under his weight when he climbs on the bed behind me. Heat rolls off his skin, and his hand smooths down my spine before he smacks my ass, sending a power pulse straight to my aching core.

I squirm against him with a moan, desperate to have him filling me.

"You like that, don't you?" His palm rubs over the undoubtedly already red handprint he left in his wake. Then he presses a warm, wet kiss to my skin and rips my panties from my body with a rough snap.

"Cooper . . ." I groan but stop when his skilled lips press against my aching core. I push back against him and drop my head down to the bed while he eats me until I scream. Within seconds, I'm writhing under his touch, shaking as my heart beats faster . . . until it stops.

Cool air hits my hot pussy, and I whine.

Wanting.

Needy.

A protest builds in my throat until Cooper's warmth covers me. His body cradles mine. He grips my face tightly, his lips next to my mouth.

"I don't want to be gentle tonight, Carys. I can't be."

"Don't. I don't want gentle. I won't break." I push back

against him and feel his cock between my legs, teasing me . . . Until he enters me in one forceful stroke, seating himself deeper than I've ever felt. He doesn't wait for me to adjust to his size. One hand wraps around my hip, and his fingers start working my clit as he builds a relentless rhythm with brutal thrusts that push me higher.

Every nerve in my body feels raw and exposed.

A guttural moan rips from my lips with every delicious snap of his hips.

The way his dick drags through my core, over and over, I just can't . . . can't even think . . . until he pulls me back, dragging me up to my knees. That same hand shoves the cup of my bra down and pinches my nipple. Rolling it. Tugging it. Rubbing the soft skin in his rough palm, and I whimper incoherently.

I curl my arm around his neck behind me and tilt my head so I can drag his mouth down to mine. Our tongues duel for control as he fucks me harder. Pounds into me faster. Builds me up to an impossible height, then warns, "Don't come yet, baby. I'm not done with you."

"Coop, I can't . . . I'm there. Please," I beg.

"Not yet." His greedy hands are everywhere as pleasure and pain rain across my body. Fingers dig into my hips in a bruising grip, and I'm slammed back against his hard cock. One hand slips between my legs, running through my soaked sex as he smacks my ass again with the other.

"Jesus," I moan as I drop back down onto the bed for support.

"Not Jesus, baby." He drags his finger, covered in my juices, along the crack of my ass and then, without warning, he pushes it inside me. It burns as he continues to pound my pussy while he fucks my virgin ass. First with one finger, then two, until I explode in a violent orgasm, shaking uncontrollably.

I scream. I writhe. And I keep riding Cooper's cock as he fills me completely.

Telling me I'm his while he fucks me through my orgasm, and I lose every last cord of control.

The stars fucking explode and burn in front of my eyes as I collapse on the bed.

Completely. Destroyed.

Irrevocably in love.

CARYS

3 Months Later

"Carys, honey, are you sure you don't want to fly home for Thanksgiving?"

"Mom, it's tomorrow. Even if I did want to, I doubt we'd be able to get a ticket." I'm not sure why my mom has been so insistent on trying to get me to fly home. Coach and Declan are already in Houston for a game tomorrow, and Aiden has a game in Boston. It's not like we can all be together. Not this year anyway.

I'm FaceTiming with my mom on my balcony because my bed is covered in scraps of lace and silk. A bolt of black jersey cotton is thrown across the foot of it, while I try to figure out a design to make comfort sexier.

I'm over keeping Le Désir quiet.

Chloe and I can barely keep up with our orders as it is.

Not telling her really doesn't make sense anymore.

I'm not sure it ever truly did.

But my plan for this conversation is getting hijacked.

"I really can't," I say. "I've got so much work to get through, I just can't get away. Plus, I scheduled that doctor's appointment you've been bugging me to make, and it's Friday afternoon. I don't want to have to reschedule."

"Honey, don't you have a holiday break or something? A few days? You've been working so hard. Every time I call, you're telling me how busy you are. I understand you not being able to come home, but I feel like you're working yourself too hard."

I take a deep breath and close my eyes for a moment, willing away the headache building at the back of my skull. Then I open them and look at my beautiful mother. She'll support me. She has to. *I think*.

"Here's the thing, Mom." I step into my bedroom and look at the stunning blue set I'm currently working on that's resting on my dress form. I've got to do this. "School work keeps me pretty busy, but Chloe and I kinda started a business last year, and we've doubled in size over the past twelve months. Actually, I'm pretty sure it's more than doubled, but she's the numbers girl. I'm so busy that even if I could clone myself, I'd still be busy."

Okay, so that was the chickenshit way of tearing off the Band-Aid, but it was better than nothing.

"A business?" Mom's big green eyes tear up as a giant smile stretches across her face. "Honey . . . I'm so proud of you. What kind of business? Why didn't you tell me?" Her face transforms, and she gasps, "Carys Catrina Murphy, you're not selling drugs, are you? I mean, you've lost so much weight. You can't be doing drugs." Her face contorts. "Or stripping? Carys, please tell me you're not stripping."

"Mom." I come by my slightly overdramatic nature honestly. My mother is the queen. And she's spiraling. "Mom . . . I'm not stripping or dealing drugs. And what the hell? Did you actually just ask me if I was doing drugs too? It's a business, Mom. We're designing and selling beautiful, luxury lingerie."

Her jaw unhinges so much, it looks unnatural. "Why the hell would you keep that from me?"

"I don't know. I just wanted to see what happened with it, and if we were going to keep going before I told you about it. I mean, I pushed to come out here and major in vocal performance, and then I changed my major before the end of my first semester." I sit down on my bed and run my hand through the silk swatches. "I think I was worried you'd think it was stupid and tell me I shouldn't give up singing."

"Carys, only you can decide what you want to do with your life. As long as you're not hurting yourself or anyone else, I'll always support you." I hate that I doubted her. "You don't ever have to keep anything from me."

Guilt tugs at me because I have no intention of telling her everything.

This is the only thing I'm willing to share for now.

"Now, show me some of your designs," Mom orders, as if it were nothing at all, and I relax, knowing that's one less thing to worry about.

I must have dozed off because my bedroom is dark when Theo's voice drags me out of my dream. And damn, it was a good dream. Cooper's shampoo still lingers in my mind, but that's all it is. A memory.

Theo pushes through my mostly open door, then leans against the frame. "CC, you coming down for dinner? I picked up Chinese food." Jack, Emerson and Linc drove up the coast to spend Thanksgiving with Stone. They asked if Theo and I wanted to go to, but we passed. I completely forgot he was grabbing us dinner tonight.

I sit up quickly but immediately lie back down as the room spins around me, suddenly feeling nauseous. "Whoa . . ."

Theo runs in. "Hey, you okay?"

"No." I close my eyes and breathe through the nausea. "I'm not okay."

"What's wrong? What can I do?"

The poor guy has concern washing off him in fat waves, but I can't worry about that as I run to the bathroom and throw up what little I've had to eat today, then dry heave when my body decides it's not done, even though there's nothing left.

Theo follows behind me and gathers my hair, holding it back from my face and out of the way while my body retches. Eventually, when I finally feel like I have nothing left, I lie down on the floor and thank God for my obsessive need to clean when I'm stressed because my bathroom is spotless. Definitely clean enough to lie down in. And right now, the cold tile floor against my overheated face is the only thing that feels good.

"Hey, Carys." Theo places a cool, damp rag on my forehead, then gently pushes my hair back. "You feel really hot."

"Can you get me some ibuprofen and a bottle of water?" I whisper, not wanting to jostle any part of me by trying to do it myself. "And my phone."

Theo's big, warm whiskey eyes skim over me. "At least let me help you to bed. Come on. You can't stay here."

"Yes, I can." I tuck my legs up so I'm in the fetal position. "Please. Just some ibuprofen, water, and my phone."

"Carys, I need you to wake up for me." The soft voice sounds familiar, but I refuse to open my eyes. "Carys."

When I ignore the voice for a second time, she sounds annoyed. "Pick her up and put her in her bed, babe. Theo, can you get me a bowl or trash can in case she gets sick again?"

I'm gently lifted from the ground, forcing me to finally open my eyes. "Ford?" I croak. My voice is strained and hoarse from heaving for so long. "What are you doing here?"

"Theo answered the phone when Sinclair called. He told him you were sick. Coop called me to see if Jessie could swing by." The giant of a man tucks me in bed, then drags my comforter over me and hands me a bottle of water. "Drink. You need to replenish your fluids."

Jessie scans a thermometer over my head, then sticks it back in a bag at the foot of my bed. She touches two of her fingers to my pulse and stands quietly for a minute. I assume she's counting my heart rate.

"Okay, I need you to take two of these." She hands me two small white pills that I swallow with a sip of water, all the while praying they don't come right back up.

Theo places a trash can next to my bed and looks at me with that same look of worry from earlier. "What can I do for you, CC?"

"I need you guys to give us ladies a few minutes of privacy, please." Jessie looks from Ford to Theo, then makes a shooing motion with her hands. "And shut the door behind you."

"Thanks," I whisper.

"No problem. You don't need an audience when you don't feel good. And I need to ask you a few questions that aren't anyone else's business but yours." She sits down next to me on the bed and runs her fingers softly through my hair. "Are you pregnant, Carys?"

I swing my head her way so quickly, I think I might hurl again. "What? No. I had my period last week. And every month since Cooper left. Definitely not pregnant."

Sweet baby Jesus, no. We don't even have our own shit together yet. We cannot add a baby to this messed-up mix.

"Okay. Thank God. Not that you and Cooper wouldn't make beautiful babies, but girl . . . this life takes a hell of a lot out of you. And I want you two to have more time together before you start having to worry about a third."

"Me too." I take a small sip of my water, hoping it stays down.

"Next uncomfortable question. Are you taking any drugs? Prescribed, over the counter, or recreational?" Jessie seems so calm as she asks these questions, although I'm feeling anything but calm.

"No. Well, none other than birth control. I have PCOS, and the pill helps with everything." I think I'd be squirming if I felt like I could move without throwing up. Not exactly conversations you have with a new friend.

"Cooper told Ford you were going to the doctor soon because you've been sick a lot lately."

"Yeah. I've been really tired too. And this has got to be the third or fourth fever I've had since July." I pull the blanket up higher and feel the weight of sleep already tugging me under. "My appointment is Friday."

I know Jessie says something else, but I'm already asleep before it registers.

COOPER

THERE'S NOTHING LIKE CALLING YOUR GIRL AND HAVING HER roommate answer and tell you she's sick . . . again. Carys has been sick a handful of times since I left her at Dad and Katherine's last summer. And I've had to bug the hell out of her to finally get her to schedule a doctor's appointment.

My girl is stubborn.

I may have threatened to tell Murphy so he could torture her. She gave in after that. Now I'm sitting here on the other side of the country, waiting for my team leader to call me back and let me know how she's doing.

This fucking sucks. I shouldn't be here. I should be home with Carys.

With my team.

Instead, I've got at least two more months before I'm done. And that's two months too damn long. My phone rings in my hand, and I swipe to answer as soon as I see it's Jessie.

"Jess, what's going on?"

"Good to hear your voice, Coop. How are you holding up over there?"

I've never been so fucking happy to have someone mother-hen me as much as Jess likes to, but I don't want to talk about me.

"I'm good, Jess. How's Carys?"

"Sinclair." Jessie points her phone toward Ford's face. "Get your goddamned mind in the game. And get the fuck home. We need you back here."

"Will do, Master Chief. Two months to go. Now tell me, how's Carys?" I know he means well, but it's twenty-one-hundred hours here. Nothing's happening. And he'd be freaking out if Jessie was the one sick . . . again.

"She's okay, Coop. She's running a fever. Really fatigued." Jessie sighs. "She's not pregnant, so you get to live another day."

Holy shit. I didn't even know that was a concern.

"Theo mentioned she's stopped running, but if anything, she looks thinner to me now than she did when we had lunch a few weeks ago." Jessie keeps talking, and everything she says fucks with my mind even more. "Her doctor's appointment is Friday. I told her I'd go with her, but she may have been asleep by then."

Christ, I feel like an ass. I should be there, taking care of her, instead of asking Ford and Jessie to do it. "Seriously, Jessie. Thank you. I wish I was there."

"Don't worry about it, Coop. That's what families are for. Listen, don't call her tonight. She needs to rest. Call tomorrow. But don't worry if she doesn't answer. She may just sleep through the day. Theo's there if she needs anything."

I can't hide my answering groan.

I guess little drummer boy isn't so bad after all.

"And Ford and I are just a call away. Most of the guys are coming to our house for turkey tomorrow, so we won't be far."

A smile stretches across my face, thinking about the Thanksgiving Day football game we played at Ford's last year and the amazing dinner Jessie and Rook made.

"Wish I was gonna be there, guys."

"Go to bed, Sinclair," Ford groans. "Check in with your girl tomorrow. We'll see you in a few months."

Yeah . . . a few more months.

Before I can go to bed, I shoot Carys a text.

Coop: Hey baby. When you feel up to it, let me know how you're doing, okay? Love you.

I don't hear back from Carys until halfway through the next day.

Carys: Hey hot stuff. I feel like I've been run over by a tractor trailer. Everything hurts. I just got out of the shower, and I'm going back to bed. I'll call you tomorrow.

The call never comes on Friday because I'm forty thousand feet in the air by mid-day on my way to South Africa for an op that lasts fifteen fucked up days.

It's not until day three that I can finally call Carys. The phone rings for so long, I'm sure her voice mail is about to pick up until it clicks over, and her angelic voice echoes through the phone.

"Cooper? Are you there?"

God, it's so fucking good to hear her voice. Relief literally makes my knees weak.

"Yeah, baby. I'm here. How are you feeling?"

"Better." She breathes out a sigh of, I'm guessing, relief. "Where are you?"

"Out of the country." My answer is short. I don't want

to talk about me. "Did you go to the doctor? What did he say?" I adjust the phone and walk away from my team. "I don't know how long we've got to talk, and I want to hear about you, Carys."

"They ran a ton of tests. I'm a little amazed I have any blood left in my body, they took so much of it. Jessie said that's normal for something like this. They don't have any good starting point. So, they start everywhere." I can just imagine her worrying her bottom lip while she's talking so fast. "They made me pee in a cup. That was fun. Oh, and I have to keep a journal. I need to document what I'm doing and what I'm eating, in case it's something environmental bothering me."

"Like an allergy?" How the fuck could an allergy give her a fever?

"I guess. I go back in a week for the results. I'll know more then. But I feel better now. How are you?"

"Missing you, baby. How are classes? How's things with Chloe?" Jesus, I just want to see her face. To touch her.

"Classes suck ass. I'm done. I swear, I don't want to take any more. I'm thinking about taking a semester off. Things with Chloe are amazing. We've sold an entire line to two different boutiques in Philadelphia, and I just sold one here in San Diego too." The excitement in her voice settles deep in my soul.

"I'm so proud of you, baby." I lie down on the makeshift bed in this hole-in-the-wall safe house and listen to her tell me all about the designs and boutiques for the next ten minutes. Then I realize it's time to get off the phone.

"Sing me something, Carys. If I can't be home, at least I can feel like it."

Chills run down my body as she sings an old favorite of mine, "Crazy Love." And when she's done, with my body relaxed, I close my eyes and picture home, imagining us together.

"I'll be home soon."

"I love you, Cooper."

"Always, baby."

COOPER

DAD LEFT A PASS FOR ME AT THE WILL-CALL BOX FOR TODAY'S Kings game. If they win this game, they win the division. I promised I'd do my best to be here. But I asked him to keep it quiet, in case something came up. He understood. Once he got over the initial fear and hesitance when I told him I was joining the Navy, he's been supportive, like he always is.

He was upset I wasn't going to college. I think he was disappointed he wouldn't have another son following in his professional footsteps, but he never said it out loud. My older brother, Declan, the all-pro quarterback, will have to be enough for both of us.

After I grab my lanyard, I walk around the stadium and take in everything that's changed since we first moved here years ago. Dad's won two championship trophies for this team in the past five years. A huge picture of Declan throwing the winning pass last year takes up an entire wall now. I smile and wave to one of the team owners as I pass her.

My buddy Sebastian is marrying her sister at some point. When I'm here, I feel like I'm home in a weird way.

Maybe I should consider switching to Bravo Team permanently.

It would mean we'd be closer to the family.

If the family knew there was a *we* to start with.

I quietly let myself into the box suite, full of my family and friends, and watch them for a minute before they realize I'm here. We're already ten minutes into the first quarter, and everyone is scattered throughout the room and in the seats that sit on the other side of the glass. It's a room full of the people I love.

All but one.

I can picture her standing on the fifty-yard line a few years ago, belting out the National Anthem to the sold-out stadium. She was incredible. I remember wondering how that big voice could come from such a small body.

"Cooper?" Nattie's voice brings me back to the present as she throws her arms around my waist. "Oh my God. What are you doing here?"

Her blonde hair tickles my face, and I inhale her familiar vanilla scent.

"Hey, Nat." I squeeze her back. "I had the day free, so I drove up. I wanted to see Declan and Bash kick some Denver ass."

I spend the rest of the first quarter catching up with everyone. But my twin doesn't leave my side. A bit later, when I sit at the table with Brady and her, she asks the question I knew was coming. Call it *twintuition*.

"Okay, so what are the chances of you staying with the team in Virginia? I mean, they wouldn't have asked you to fill in if they weren't interested, would they?" She looks so damn hopeful that I feel like a fucking ass for leaving in the first place. It was the right decision for me, but she always knows how to make me feel bad.

"Leave him alone, sweetheart." Brady rests his arm across the back of her seat and winds his fingers through her hair. "We don't even know where we're going to end up next year if I get drafted."

"Listen here, Brady Ryan. You're a finalist for the Heisman. There's got to be a team on the East Coast that wants you. I don't want to raise our babies on the other side of the country from our families." If Nat was standing, she'd be stomping her foot with her hands on her hips. And judging by the smirk on Brady's face, he knows it too.

"Hey now," I laugh. "You two just got engaged. How about you give it a few months before you make me an uncle?" I'm kidding. I mean, yes, I don't think my sister is ready to be a mom, but are any of us ready to be a parent until it happens?

Nattie glares at me even as her eyes sparkle with mischief. "Don't change the subject, Coop. Don't you want to move home? Maybe find a girl you want to see for more than a night?"

"Drop it, Nat." I blow out a deep breath, knowing I need to tread lightly.

Apparently, that was the wrong thing to say. I just added fuel to the fire, according to the devious look on my sister's face. "Come on, Cooper. You've got to settle down at some point."

"Natalie Grace." Brady stops her in a way no one else can contain what is Hurricane Nattie. "Leave him alone. If I didn't have you, I'd be—"

"You'd be what, QB?" Nattie's attention turns from me to her fiancé, a new fire on her face.

I take my cue to get the hell away from the two of them before she explodes. When I cross the room, my niece Gracie lifts her arms up to me, and I toss her in the air. Her blonde ringlets fly high around her head before she comes down, and two chubby little arms cling to me.

"I missed you, Uncle Cooper."

I bury my face in her hair. "Me too, princess. Me too."

At my sister-in-law, Annabelle's, insistence, I follow her and my brother home for dinner after the game ends later that afternoon. My nephew, Tommy, shows me his room and all the changes he's made since the last time I was here a year ago when Bash's dad died. It's hard to believe it's been a year already. Dinosaurs still invade so much of the space, but so do his trophies from his buddy sports league. He shows me everything, tells me all about his games, his wins, and the few losses he says sucked.

Tommy has autism. And when this kid—this teenager— opens his world to you, it's a beautiful thing.

Later that night, after dinner and once the twins have been put to bed, Annabelle goes upstairs to nurse a cranky Nixon, and Declan and I sit in the family room, talking, like we don't usually get a chance to do.

"It was a great game, Dec. I'm so fucking proud of you." I look around the open room at all the pictures. All the toys. The mess. "You've got it all. You've got the dream."

He puts his beer down on the coffee table and leans back, like he's about to impart some older brotherly wisdom on me. There's only a four-year age difference between us, but when I look around this house, it feels like a lifetime. He's settled in this homey place with a family.

"What's on your mind, Coop? Something's bugging you."

"Am I that easy to read? The Navy's spent a shit ton of money making sure I'm better than that," I laugh.

"Yeah well, the Navy hasn't been watching you work through your shit your entire life. So, what's up?"

"I can't really talk about it, man." No matter how much I wish I could.

Declan groans. "That's bullshit, Coop. If you need to talk about something, talk about it. It won't leave this room. I won't tell a soul."

"Not even Annabelle?" I shoot back.

"I tell Belles everything. But if I ask her not to say anything, she won't."

I eye him skeptically.

"Bullshit. Our family sucks at keeping things quiet." I say it lovingly, but I say it all the same. It's the truth.

Annabelle glides down the stairs, in one of Declan's old tees and a pair of shorts, with knit knee socks pulled up her legs. "Cooper." She sits on Declan's lap and faces me. "Can I ask you something?"

I drag my hand over my face and grunt. "You're gonna ask even if I say no, so go ahead."

"Are you hesitant to talk about work . . . or about Carys?" My sister-in-law drops that bomb, then sits quietly while Declan tries to figure out what she's talking about.

"What the hell are you talking about, Belles? What about Carys?"

I stand from the couch and walk away anxiously, then turn back. "How?" One word that carries so much weight.

"It was the beach. I had a feeling something was going on while we were on the beach. It was the way she looked at you. The way you two tried to avoid each other. But at dinner . . . her reaction to Murphy. The look on her face when she yelled at him, and the look she gave you before she went inside. I just knew."

"Carys?" Declan asks, still in shock. But Belles and I ignore him.

"Does anyone else know?" Fuck, she's gonna hate this. "She doesn't want anyone to know yet."

Belles's face softens with her words. "No one else knows. I don't think anyone was paying attention. I was next to her that night, and I was in the room with her after dinner."

"You didn't say anything." Declan sounds hurt.

She turns in his arms. "I wasn't sure. I just had a feeling, and it was none of my business."

"You're gonna pay for that later, baby." Declan tightens his grip on Belle, who squirms in his lap.

"Promise?" she asks with a saucy wink.

Then Nixon cries out over the baby monitor.

"Damn it, he must have thrown his pacifier out of the crib again." Belles stands from Declan's lap and hugs me. "Be careful, Cooper. I don't know what's going on between you guys, but you have the power to destroy this family. If this goes bad, and you can't be in a room together, you're going to split us right down the middle. The longer you wait to tell everyone, the harder it's going to be." She kisses my cheek. "Be safe driving home."

Declan watches his wife walk back up the steps, and then he turns on me. "You and Carys?"

I nod, not sure what to say.

"How long?" There's a hard edge to Declan's voice.

"Since this past spring. But I've been gone most of the time. We just want to get time together before we bring everyone else into it. We deserve that." I try to defend myself, but my words sound like a childish excuse now.

Declan stands, and I follow him into the kitchen where he pours two shots of tequila. "Do you love her?" He downs the first shot.

"Yes," I answer without hesitation, then push my shot his way too.

I've got a five-hour drive home tonight. Tequila won't help.

"Fuck, Cooper," he draws my name out, and I cringe. "You've got to be careful. Belles is right. If this goes badly, it could really fuck up the family. But if you love her, you need to figure your shit out. Put her first and show everyone that you're both in this for the long haul. I think they'll come around." He throws back the second shot. "Eventually. But the longer you take to tell them, the harder it's gonna be."

Tell me something I don't know.

CARYS

Why are doctor's offices so damn cold?

A December day in California is different from one back home in Kroydon Hills. Today, I'm wearing a hoodie I stole from Cooper's closet a few weeks ago, paired with black leggings, and I'm fine. Or I would be if this office wasn't set to a temperature equivalent to an arctic freeze.

I don't have much time to focus on it, though, because luckily Dr. Cruz doesn't keep me waiting long. She strolls through the door to her office in a beautiful cream silk suit. Her dark hair is styled to perfection, and her crisp white coat, with her name embroidered in it in blue, looks like it's been perfectly pressed.

This woman looks badass.

My fingers are crossed that she can help me.

"Hello, Miss Murphy. How are you feeling today?" She takes a seat behind a large oak desk and opens a file before looking back up at me.

Oops. Guess she's waiting for an answer. "Nice to meet you, Dr. Cruz. I'm good. How are you?"

My primary out here referred me to Dr. Cruz when she ran out of options last month, and Jessie may have called in a few favors at the hospital to get me to the front of her very long waitlist.

"Good?" she asks, clearly not believing me as she skims through my file.

"Sorry." I blush. "Force of habit. Generally, people don't

want to hear that you're twenty years old with a constant headache and bone-deep exhaustion. I feel a little like I'm going crazy."

Her warm smile calms my nerves—*slightly*.

"Well, I do. I want to hear every single detail. Don't leave anything out."

"I go through bursts of feeling fine, then feeling like I have the flu. The bad symptoms—like the headaches, body aches, fever, and vomiting—can last for a few days and sometimes up to a week. But I feel the lingering effects for a few weeks at a time. I used to be a runner. I've run marathons, but now I barely have the energy to walk to class half the time."

By the time I've regurgitated everything from the last six months of my life, I realize I must sound like a hypochondriac. I stuff my hands inside the pockets of the warm hoodie and sit back. Suddenly tired.

Dr. Cruz lays down the tablet she's been using to take notes and takes out a form. She fills it out quickly and checks more boxes than one person should ever need. But when she's done with that one, she grabs two more forms and fills them out as well.

"You're not going crazy, Miss Murphy. We're going to get to the bottom of this." She hands me the papers. "I'd like you to have these scans and labs run here at the hospital, so I can get access to the results faster. Do you think you could get them scheduled for some time this week?"

"Sure."

"Good. I'd like to see you back here in two weeks. We're going to figure this out. In the meantime, keep doing what you're doing, and call the office if you need anything." She stands from her desk, then opens the office door. "Happy New Year, Miss Murphy."

"Happy New Year, Dr. Cruz."

I leave her office and head to the parking garage. Cooper gave me his Jeep while he was gone, so I didn't have to ask for a ride or grab an Uber today. Once I'm heading home, I call my mom and fill her in. I cut my trip home for the holidays short, in part, because I didn't want to miss the appointment. At least that's what I shared with her. I didn't want her to know that being there without Cooper was making me miserable.

Once we end our call, I message Coop.

Carys: Just got out of my doctor's appointment. More tests. Then a follow-up with her.
Carys: Call me when you can.

I wait a minute to see if he responds, but nothing comes.

Twenty minutes later, I walk into my house and see the band sitting around the table, going over a playlist. They've had a few different singers front for them since September, but none have worked out. Jack's done the past few weeks himself. I think he's fantastic. But it's not the sound he wants.

"Hey, CC. Come help us pick out the opener." Theo twirls his drumsticks between his fingers with an easy smile.

I appreciate that he doesn't ask me about my appointment.

Jack's also definitely become a better friend since we all moved in here.

I move between Jack and Theo while Lucas sits there, strumming his guitar.

"What are your options?"

"What would you want to sing?" Jack asks me.

I shake my head, but he cuts me off before I can get any

words out. "Just this once, CC. It's New Year's Eve. It's a huge night for us. Come on, it'll be fun."

"Jack . . . seriously. I just want to hang out here and watch the ball drop. I'm exhausted."

"Leave her be, man." Theo drags the sheet of paper across the table with the tip of his stick. "We've got this, CC."

Jack wraps an arm around my waist and tugs me over to him. "Sorry, CC. Promise me one day you'll sing with us again, and I'll shut up."

"I promise." Then I grab the sheet back from Theo and help them figure out their set.

"Are you sure you don't want to come with us, CC?" Emerson reapplies her red lipstick, then rolls her lips together with a pop. "Linc should be here any minute, and I think most of the team is going to be there. At least for a few hours."

I tug my comfy blanket up around me on our couch and pick up the remote. "I've got Ryan Seacrest, popcorn, and sweet tea. I'm good. I promise." She doesn't need to know I've already popped two pain relievers because I feel a nasty headache coming on.

"Okay. Call me if you need anything." She turns to leave but stops to lean down and kiss my cheek. "Love you, CC."

"Happy New Year, Emerson."

Finally, my phone rings with the incoming FaceTime from Cooper I've been waiting for.

"Hi." My heart skips a beat at his handsome face. He's let his usual scruff grow out a little longer, and I itch to run my fingers over it.

"Hey, baby. Happy New Year."

Relief mixes with heartache. I want him next to me so damn badly, but I refuse to show him that. I can be strong for a few more months. "Happy New Year."

A knock at the door makes me frown. I hold the phone steady as I get up.

Em must have forgotten something.

"Has the ball dropped yet?" I guess that's a stupid question. It's after ten p.m. here, so it's after midnight there.

"Answer the door, Carys."

"What?"

I yank open the door and then burst into tears as I drop my phone and throw my arms around Cooper. "How? Why?"

He wraps his arms around me and kicks the door shut behind him, then carries me to the couch. When he sits down, he holds me impossibly closer. My legs are locked behind his back, and my face is buried in his neck.

"I requested leave. It's just for two days, and I flew commercial, not military. So I have to be on a red-eye tomorrow night. But baby, I needed to see you. To feel you."

I finally pull back and look deep into those blue eyes I love to get lost in. "I love you."

Eventually, we make our way upstairs and drag blankets and pillows outside to my balcony, nestling together under the moonlight. Filling each other in on everything and anything we haven't had a chance to discuss. The mundane, everyday things that aren't a big deal but you just want to share with your best friend.

"How much longer, Cooper? When are you coming home?"

"You are my home, Carys." The words are everything I've ever wanted to hear, but the small crack in my heart that started when he left grows a little deeper.

I press my lips gently to his. "When are you coming back to me?"

"I'm not sure, yet. It could be next week. It could be the beginning of March." He cradles me to him. "They've talked about offering me the position permanently."

A million what ifs race through my mind. "You'd leave Charlie Team?"

"I'm not sure. But if I did, we could be closer to home." His fingers lace with mine as he lifts them to his lips. "Once you're done with school, we could live in Virginia. We'd only be a few hours from home. If Murphy moves to DC to be with Sabrina, you'd be just a few hours from him too."

I sit up in shock. "But what about the guys? Your team? You love them. Why would you leave?"

"I love you more."

COOPER

"COOPER . . . ?" SHE REACHES OUT LIKE SHE'S GOING TO touch me but pulls her hand back unexpectedly. Carys stands as the first fireworks explode over the ocean, signaling the start of the new year. "You want me to move to Virginia with you?"

"I want to at least know what you think about it. We haven't talked about where you see your life. Is it here in California? Or is in it Kroydon Hills? Hell . . . Do you want to move somewhere else?"

"I hadn't really thought about it. I guess I thought if we wanted to be together, we had to stay here."

"No, babe. Your options are endless. But mine are San Diego or Virginia Beach. I don't think that's changing any time soon." It would kill me if she doesn't want to live in either place, but we'd figure something out.

I think.

Bright colors burst in the distance behind her, and her hands white-knuckle the railing. "You know, a year ago I was just barely hanging on. I had no idea who I was. Did I want to be a singer? An actress on a Broadway stage? I'd been groomed my entire life for that because it's what I always thought I wanted. But that dream changed. Le Désir became my new dream. And one by one, things started falling into place."

Carys spins around to face me but doesn't let go of her hold on the railing.

"Baby . . ." she says slowly, like she's scared of my reaction to whatever she's about to say.

I think I'm about to have my heart ripped out.

"I love designing. I love creating. Chloe and I make one hell of a partnership, and I want to see where that goes. I'm stronger now than I was a year ago. I finally like the person I am. I like that I've figured out how to speak up for myself. I like me."

She crosses back to me and sits down in my lap. "And I love the me I am when I'm with you. I don't really care where I live. I think Chloe and I can work together wherever we are. And I want to be wherever you are, Cooper. If that's on the East Coast, then that's where we'll go."

"Are you ready to talk to the family? Because I don't want to hide us anymore." I run my hand over her soft hair and wrap it around my fist. "I'm tired of hiding, Carys."

"Cooper, if you add up all the days we've actually spent together since we started this, it doesn't even total two weeks. I refuse to bring our family into this until we've gotten to enjoy us. I love you. I'd do almost anything for you. But I'm not willing to do *that* yet."

I tug her face down to mine, but she tugs away. "Carys, we're making this harder on ourselves than it needs to be. How can we talk about living together . . . about moving across the country to be together and closer to our family, but not tell them?"

"I'm not ready yet. I'm yours, Coop. But I'm not willing to share us with the world yet. What happens if Mom and Coach freak out? Our families are big news back home. I don't think we'll be able to stay under the radar without anyone finding out that we're together for very long. How's that going to look? We're stepsiblings. Not to mention, Aiden's going to lose his mind. What happens if he hates you? If he won't speak to either of us?"

I kiss her quickly to calm her down. "One step at a time, Carys."

"I won't be able to move anywhere until after this semester," she sighs against my lips. "Just give me until then. Give me until May. Please, Coop. Can you do that?" Her eyes search mine for an answer, like I could ever deny her anything.

"We can't hide it from them forever, Carys."

"I know. We'll tell them eventually. Maybe when we're married—with a kid or two already." She quickly looks away, like she just realized what she said.

I cup her jaw and turn her face back to me. "Babies. Plural, huh?"

"Don't you want babies, Cooper Sinclair?" She asks with a cheeky smile. "You'd make beautiful babies."

I tickle her sides. "Oh, I want babies with you, Carys. I want so many babies with you that we give Dec and Belles a run for their money. I want a life filled with love. But the key to all of that is you."

Carys's hands push my shirt over my head, and then she places a kiss on my chest, the warmth of her lips traveling down my body. "You have the most beautiful heart, Coop." She tugs her sweater off and tosses it down with my shirt. Then she stands and shimmies out of her leggings and panties.

I drag her to me and bury my face in her pussy.

Kissing her. Licking her. Devouring her. Until she jerks away.

"Take your pants off, Cooper, and fuck me. I need you. Show me what it feels like to be loved by you."

Once she's in my arms, her legs straddling my hips, Carys drops her warm, wet pussy down onto my cock and starts rocking slowly. Without the bulky sweater, I can see how much weight she's lost, and my girl didn't have any extra to lose. Her collarbones stand out above her chest, and as my fingers graze her hips, I'm worried I'm going to break her.

I wrap my arms around her tiny frame and hold her to me.

Guiding her as she sets a slow, relaxed pace.

The fireworks continue their dance above us.

A thousand colors light the night's sky while I worship this woman in my arms. She arches her back, and I take her breast in my mouth. First one, then the other as Carys moans loud and long.

"I'm not going to last long, Coop," she pants.

"You feel so fucking good." I grip her hips harder and rock into her. "I love watching you take my cock like a good girl." I draw her hips down hard against me, impaling her as a surge of electricity courses through me in a spiral, sucking me in. "Come now, baby."

She throws her head back, and a raw, beautiful moan pours from her lips as her pussy milks me for every last drop.

"God, I love you." I take her lips in a bruising kiss.

"Until the end of time, Cooper."

Until the end of time.

CARYS

I'VE BEEN POKED AND PRODDED MORE TIMES THAN I CAN count over the past two months. Dr. Cruz has been a woman on a mission, determined to figure out what's wrong with me. And it has become increasingly obvious that something is definitely wrong. Her office is in the building attached to the hospital where Jessie works, so she met me here today as soon as I called.

Dr. Cruz's receptionist called this morning to let me know there was a cancellation and said the doctor would like to see if I could come in. Something about that made me nervous. I've been waiting for an answer. For a diagnosis. Until now, it hasn't come, but I think that's about to change. And I guess I'm a big baby who's scared to face that alone.

When Dr. Cruz walks in today, she looks as stylish as ever, but her normally warm eyes are a few degrees cooler. Jessie sits next to me in front of the big wooden desk, and I reach for her hand.

"Rip the Band-Aid off, Dr. Cruz. I can tell you have news. And you wouldn't have been in a rush to see me if it was good news. So just tell me what it is."

Her chocolate-brown eyes look between Jessie and me before she sits down in her chair opposite us. "Carys, I need to refer you to another doctor."

My stomach drops, and I can't breathe for a moment before her words crash down on me. I let go of Jessie's hand, then stand and start pacing. "Please don't do this. I've spent the last three months seeing you. I spent a month before that seeing my primary."

"Carys," she says in a calm, soothing voice. "I need you to see a rheumatologist. I believe you have lupus."

I drop down into my chair.

"What?"

Jessie's hand grabs mine. "Really? Lupus?" she asks.

"Understand that I am not a rheumatologist, and there are a few more tests I believe they will run to confirm my diagnosis. But yes. I believe you have lupus."

"I don't even know what that means," I admit in a fog. "What is lupus?"

"It's an autoimmune disease that's most common in women and is typically diagnosed between the ages of fifteen and forty-five. It's not an easy disease to diagnose, but it can be treated. If I'm right, and this is what has been causing you to get sick, you need to understand that it isn't something that's curable, Carys. But it's treatable. You'll live with lupus for the rest of your life, but with proper treatment, you'll live." She picks up a card from her desk and places it inside a white folder. "This is the name of my colleague here at the hospital. I've already made a call, and they're waiting to hear from you."

She closes the folder and hands it to me. "Call them today, Carys. Don't wait."

I stand to thank her, noticing the folder is heavy in my hands as the room starts to spin around me. Jessie steadies me as we say our goodbyes. She doesn't leave my side as we walk to the elevator with our fingers laced together while silent tears rack my body.

"I don't even know why I'm crying. I have no idea what lupus is or what it does," I admit, feeling ignorant.

"Give me your keys," she demands.

When I don't move fast enough for her, she places her palm in front of me. "Give 'em. I'm driving you home."

"What about work?" I don't want her to get in trouble.

"I'm done for the day. Now, keys please."

I give her the keys and get in the passenger side of the Jeep. "What about your car?"

"Don't worry about it. Ford and the guys will grab it for me later."

I lay my head back against the seat and close my eyes, not sure what to do first.

"Carys, take your phone out. Get the card and call the rheumatologist. Make your appointment."

She's right. But it doesn't make any of this feel real.

Hours later, I've devoured everything I could find online about lupus.

Some of it gave me hope. Apparently, you can manage what they call your *flare-ups*. For me, those flare-ups have been the fevers I've been getting, coupled with the fatigue and headaches. I haven't really experienced the joint pain or swelling, but I have had the occasional shortness of breath and a little chest pain. I hadn't exactly mentioned that to anyone though. But that was why I stopped running. It was getting harder.

From what I can tell, lupus can cause complications with most of the major organs in your body. I stopped reading that part because it was too scary to keep going down that road, and fear is already a driving factor in all of this. The list of complications is long. And there at the bottom . . . was potential pregnancy.

As if it wasn't already going to be hard enough for me

to conceive and carry a baby with my PCOS, complications of lupus can be dangerous for the baby and me. I slam my laptop closed and throw it across my bed as I read those words.

Increased risk of miscarriage.

Increased risk of preterm birth.

Consult your doctor before getting pregnant.

I'm twenty years old. I'm not ready to have a baby now. But I want to know it's an option when I'm ready. A baby with Cooper's blue eyes and blond hair.

My phone rings with an incoming call from Coop, but I decline it instead and curl up in a ball, not ready to talk to him or anyone else.

Maybe Dr. Cruz was wrong.

Dr. Cruz wasn't wrong.

One week later, Jessie came with me to my appointment with Dr. Gaither, my new doctor. I made her promise not to tell Ford anything until after today's appointment. I haven't told anyone yet. Not my family or my roommates. Not even Chloe or Daphne. And definitely not Cooper. None of them can do anything to help me. So until there's something definite to tell them, it's easier not to say anything.

Dr. Gaither is an older man with stark white hair and small glasses, who reminds me of someone you'd cast as a wise old grandpa on a TV show. He seems warm and understanding, and the awards on his walls make me think he's at the top of his field, which I find extremely comforting.

"Do you have any questions for me, Carys?"

We've been in here for nearly an hour already. I have lupus, but it's not a death sentence.

"I have so many, but I can't think of a single one right now." Brutal honesty is about all I have the energy for at this point.

"Continue tracking everything in your journal, but I do think the prolonged exposure to the sun seems to be a trigger for you."

A single tear tracks down my cheek. "Will I be able to have kids?" I'm trying so hard to hold myself together but failing.

"There's no way I can give you a qualified answer to that question right now, Carys. Quite a few factors will come into play when it's time to consider that." He's dancing around the answer, and I don't appreciate it.

I look over to Jessie, who has a notebook resting in her lap where she's been taking notes during the entire appointment. Her watery eyes force me to push harder. She's a nurse practitioner. She understands all of this on a level I don't yet. If she's upset, there's a reason to be upset.

"Dr. Gaither, if I wanted to get pregnant right now. Today. What would you tell me?"

"Carys, I don't like to play what if games." The look he sees on my face must change his mind. "But if you need an answer today, based on the flare-up you've been in on and off for months now, as well as your medical history, yes, you could possibly get pregnant. But whether you could carry to term is uncertain. And it could be extremely dangerous for you. I don't know how your body would physically handle a pregnancy. I wouldn't suggest it. In fact, I'd warn against it."

With a small nod, I stand. "Thank you, Dr. Gaither. I'll schedule my follow-up for next month on my way out."

"Please do, Carys. I need to see you monthly until we

have this under control." He rises from his desk and watches us leave his office.

I make my appointment and add it to my calendar, then look at Jessie. "Ready to go home?"

"Yeah. Want me to drive?" She's been such a good friend throughout this. Some people come into your life at the exact moment you need them most, and Jessie is definitely that person.

"No, I'm good. At least now I know what I'm dealing with. That's a start." I'm pretty impressed with the front I'm able to put on right now.

She doesn't need to know that my heart is breaking.

COOPER

WHEN MY PLANE LANDED ON BASE IN CORONADO THIS morning, I had a plan. I needed to speak with Command, then with Ford. Command was easy, but when I find Ford in the cages where we keep our gear, I feel like a fucking asshole.

It's a big room where each member of the team has his own cage. We keep our weapons, gear, and basically everything we need for our missions in here.

He's sitting in his cage, and judging by the look on his face, he's waiting for me. "Sinclair." He stands up when I enter the room. "I heard you were getting back today."

I unlock my cage and drop my bag inside. "Is that all you heard?"

Ford smiles in a way that answers my question.

"Am I making the right decision?" I sound like a kid asking for permission. "Leaving you guys feels wrong, man."

Ford crosses his arms over his chest and stands silently for a moment. "This was a trial run, Cooper. You passed. Bravo Team wants you, and Lou's leaving at the end of the year. He just needs to finish his time. You're good. You know it. We know it, and now, they know it too. Do I want to see you go? Fuck no. But if you go there, you can be close to that crazy fucking family of yours, and I know you want that." He rocks back on the heels of his boots. "Most of us don't come from the kind of family you've got, Sinclair. I get it. I'd want to be there too. Plus, it gets your girl closer to home, if you take her with you. Jessie and she have gotten tight. Don't fuck it up. She's a good girl."

"Yeah well, nothing is final. Looks like you're stuck with me for the rest of this year." I lock my cage back up and face my team leader. My friend. "Damn, leaving you guys is gonna suck."

"You want your own Alpha Team someday, Sinclair. And I think that's gonna happen for you with Bravo Team. Just don't go getting lazy on me in the meantime." He pulls me in for a back pound. "Come on. Carys has your Jeep, right? I'll give you a ride home."

Part of me doesn't want to leave this team.

But the bigger part of me knows that for the longevity of my career, this is the move I need to make.

This will get us closer to our family, and even if Carys isn't ready to tell them about us yet, she'll want too soon.

I hope.

I call Carys on my way to her house, but it goes to voice mail, so I shoot her a text.

Cooper: Hey baby. I'm home and I'm dying to see you. You home?

She doesn't answer my call or text. But worst-case scenario, if she's not there, I'll just walk down the street to my place. When Ford stops in front of the house, my Jeep is sitting in the driveway, so I'm hoping that means she's home.

"Thanks for the ride, man." I climb out of Ford's truck and lean in the door.

"Be at the beach at zero-eight-hundred. Let's see if you can still keep up." The asshole pulls away, laughing. Joke's on him. I cut time off my personal record, and I'm closing the gap between us. Ford may have been the fastest fucker on the team when I left, but we'll see if he still is.

I walk up to the front door and knock once, then wait. When the door swings open, drummer boy's on the other side of it. He eyes me carefully, and I can't quite figure out what he's thinking.

"Hey, man. Is Carys home?"

"Yeah." He steps aside to let me in. "She's not feeling well, so she's lying down. Jack and I are downstairs, if you need anything. You know where her room is." He shuts the door and heads toward the basement.

"Hey, Theo." He turns around. "Thanks for taking care of her. I appreciate it."

Where a minute ago he was open and easy, now he bristles at my words. "I didn't do it for you. I did it for her." He takes a step closer. "She's too good for you, you know that, right?"

My blood boils at every word. "Yeah? And you're good enough for her?"

He pulls a drumstick out of his back pocket and flips it through his fingers. "No. We're friends. That's it. But at least I'm here. Remember that."

The motherfucker walks away.

Smug. Because he knows he's right.

It's mid-March. I'll be here until July, then I'm gone again until the end of the year.

I take the stairs two at a time, then knock lightly on Carys's door. When there's no answer after a moment, I crack it open and whisper her name into the dark room.

She's asleep on the center of the bed. Her hands are tucked under her face, her dark hair spread out behind her on her pillow, and her legs are tucked up against her.

I close the door and kick off my boots, then lie down behind her, gently pulling her against me and holding her.

Carys whimpers in her sleep, then settles in my arms.

She sleeps soundly for another hour, and I lie here and watch her.

Thinking about all the things we've got going against us and all the ways I'd fight to keep her.

Eventually, she rolls over in my arms, and her lips press against my jaw. Her eyes remain closed, and her breathing is even, but she knows I'm here. "Love you, Cooper."

"Until the end of time, Carys."

CARYS

Dr. Gaither told me not to push it when I felt a headache coming on. I'm supposed to take two ibuprofen and relax. Sleep. This was his advice a few days ago. Sleep has been hard to come by since he confirmed I have lupus. My mind has had a hard time settling. But today, before I even open my eyes, my body tells me I've been in my bed for hours. I dream of Cooper every night, but now, his clean, masculine scent still lingers in my nose as if he's here with me. Clinging to the remnants of my dream, I bask in the feel of the weight of his arms around me and the warmth of his body against mine.

I refuse to open my eyes, wanting so badly to go back to my dream, where this is real.

Where he's here.

"Wake up, sleeping beauty."

I snuggle in deeper, not wanting this to end. "No." My voice is hoarse.

Warm lips press against my skin. "Baby . . ."

My eyes fly open when I realize the voice saying that word isn't just a dream. "You're here?" I tremble as Cooper holds me against his chest. "How are you here?"

"I told you I was coming home this week. I came right here." He pushes my hair away from my face and peppers kisses along my forehead and down my cheek and jaw until he finally presses his beautiful lips on mine. "I missed you."

We fit together like pieces of a puzzle.

All his hard angles press against my soft curves, and I luxuriate in the moment—until my headache from earlier pushes back against my moment. I sit up slowly and grab my water and pill bottle from the nightstand, then swallow two pills.

Cooper sits up behind me and holds my back against his chest. "Are you okay?"

Shit.

We haven't talked much this week, and I haven't told him what's going on yet.

I know he's gonna be pissed I didn't tell him sooner.

This is not how I envisioned our reunion.

I pull my knees up to my chest and rest my head back against his arm and the headboard. "So . . . You know how I told you that Dr. Cruz referred me to another doctor?"

"Yeah. Did you make the appointment?" Shit. I guess I didn't tell him that either. Our communication has sucked the past few weeks. It's 100 percent my fault, but I didn't want to talk about this. That would have made it real. And until I saw Dr. Gaither the other day, I refused to accept this as my reality.

"I did. Jessie went with me, and I saw Dr. Gaither earlier this week." I think about all the things we discussed. All the possible complications. And I really don't want to get into this with Cooper now. But he deserves to know.

"What did he say, Carys?"

"Coop." I drag myself away and turn myself to face him, then grab his hands in mine. "They finally figured out what's wrong with me. I have lupus."

"What?" I feel his shock and fear reverberate through both of us. "Are you okay?"

"I'm going to be okay, but I have to take care of myself.

There are a ton of possible complications. Most of them, I can't even fathom yet. But for now, it's fatigue, fever, loss of appetite, and the damn headaches."

He drops my hand and cups my face. "Why didn't you tell me?"

I grip his wrists. "It was just the other day, and I knew you were coming home. I wanted to tell you when you were here. I told Mom over the phone, and it was awful. I didn't want to do that again."

"What do you need from me?"

His breathtaking blue eyes are already pleading with me to let him fix this, and the truth is, he can't.

"I don't know yet, Coop. I have another appointment with Dr. Gaither in April, but Mom wants me to fly home for spring break next week to see a specialist in Philly." His face drops, and I realize I kept that from him too. "I'm sorry. I know you just got here, but I already told her I'd go."

He tugs me against him. "You've got to go. We'll do whatever we have to, baby."

We will. Even if it breaks us.

A week later, I'm sitting in my favorite coffee shop back in Kroydon Hills with my best friend, Daphne. "Is Momma Murphy still treating you like you need to be put in a bubble?"

"She sure is. I think she'd be 100 percent onboard if I told her I wanted to drop out of school, move home, and live with her and Coach again. She's upset I'm leaving tonight. She's asked me at least three times if I want her to reschedule my flight." I sip my coffee and drag my finger through the frosting on the cupcake in front of me.

Daphne shrugs her shoulders. "You've been considering it. Maybe this is a sign. Didn't you say Cooper wants to come back too?"

Damn it, that shouldn't hurt so bad.

"He does. It's already in the works for the end of this year. I just don't know, D. I freaking hate this feeling of doom that's been hanging over me."

"What do you hate? Having your man want to rearrange his whole life so you can be closer to your family?" She sips her coffee. "It must really suck being in love."

"Shut up, brat." I look out the window and watch the traffic drive by. The trees are just starting to come back to life after a cold winter. Signs of life are beginning to pop up everywhere. "I do want to come back here. I love what being in California gave me, but I don't think I'm supposed to stay there permanently. I just don't know if I'm supposed to do it with Cooper."

"What?" She practically yells across the table. "What the fuck are you talking about? You have loved that man for years. *Years*, Carys. And you've finally got him. What would make you ever consider throwing that away? Did he do something?"

"No, he's perfect. He's everything, D. That's why I don't think this is going to work. He deserves someone who can give him everything. That's not me. Not anymore." It's the first time I've said any of this out loud, and it feels worse than I thought it would.

Daphne grabs my hand across the table and laces our fingers together like we used to do when we were kids. "You said yourself both doctors said this is manageable, Carys. This isn't a death sentence."

"They both said it doesn't have to be, not that it won't

be. They also both said that between lupus and my PCOS, having babies could be very complicated." I force back the tears threatening to break free.

"Complicated doesn't mean can't. And even if you can't carry your own babies, there are so many other ways to have kids, Carys. Don't give Cooper up before you've given him a chance to prove himself to you."

I rip my hand away from her and place it in my lap. "He shouldn't have to prove anything, D. He loves his life. He loves his team in California. He shouldn't have to give any of that up for me."

"This isn't about the teams. This is about you getting scared. You're running away, Carys, and you're using Cooper as an excuse."

"I'm not. In a lot of ways, I'm in such a better place now than I was last year. I know who I am. I know what I want to do with my life, and Chloe and I are already taking steps to make it happen. I know I'm not going back to school after this semester, and that decision was made before I was diagnosed with lupus. Before Cooper ever mentioned Virginia. I made it myself because I know what I want. I like this person I've become, and I don't want someone to feel like they have to take care of me for the rest of my life. That's not fair to Cooper, and it's not fair to me."

I take a big bite of my chocolate cupcake and shut up. Verbal diarrhea isn't a good look for me.

Daphne throws her napkin on the table, disgusted with me.

Yeah, me too, D.

"So that's it? Decision made?" Daphne and I have known each other for over ten years, and I think this is the first time I've ever seen pity in her eyes.

"Decision made," I say with a forced bravado I'm not feeling.

"I love you like a sister, so keep that in mind when I say you're fucking this up. You're throwing it away, and you don't have to. But I'll be here when you need me to pick up the pieces."

I laugh through my tears. "Love you too."

COOPER

GETTING BACK INTO THE ROUTINE WITH CHARLIE TEAM IS like breathing to me. You don't even realize you're doing it. It requires no effort. No thought. The guys and I work together like a well-oiled machine. And when Trick, Wanda, and I walk in the house Saturday morning from a five-mile run on the beach, Linc and Emerson are sitting in the kitchen, staring at something on the table.

"Hey Em, have you heard from Carys?" She's been distant since she left for Kroydon Hills. She's barely responded to my texts, and we've only spoken once. That's not like her.

"Yeah." She doesn't lift her head. Doesn't so much as look my way. "She came home late last night. I think Theo picked her up from the airport.

I still while blood roars in my ears. "What?" Why the hell would she ask him to do that?

She doesn't say anything.

Linc doesn't say anything.

"What the hell is up with these two?" Trick asks as he throws me a bottle of Gatorade.

"Em." I move in front of her.

Linc shoves me away with a hand to the center of my chest. "Back off, brother. You're not the only one dealing with something right fucking now."

I take a step back and look at my friend. He's pale as a ghost with a freaked the fuck out expression on his face.

Trick stands next to me, and we both look down at what they're staring at on the table.

"Holy shit."

Linc looks up. "You can say that again."

"I'm gonna be sick." Emerson bolts for the bathroom with the three of us watching in shock.

Linc picks up the pregnancy test with two pink lines displayed brightly on the screen. "She's pregnant."

Trick and I stay with Linc until he gets his shit together enough to go to Emerson. Then we try to give them some space as they work this out.

"Dude, what do you think they're going to do?"

I shrug and chug my Gatorade. "No clue."

"What would you do if this were you and Carys?" He sits down at the table, looking at the pregnancy test like it's a disease he can catch.

"Pretty sure I'd marry Carys tomorrow if she'd say yes. But to get to that point, I need her to agree to telling the family. She's not there yet. So, I don't have a fucking clue what we'd do." The thought makes my head spin. "I didn't even know she came home last night."

"You gonna head over there? Try to catch up with her?"

I stand to head to my room. I need to shower and change. "Yeah. I'll head over before I go to base. See you in a few."

Thirty minutes later, Carys opens her front door to me, and her face drops—a reaction that's diametrically opposite to the one I usually get from her. She looks good in ripped jeans, cuffed at her ankles, and a pair of bright-red Chuck Taylors on her feet that match a slouchy sweater, which is falling off one shoulder. Her black lace bra strap is teasing me, and my mouth aches to taste her skin.

"Cooper. Hi. I meant to call you . . ."

Her formal greeting reminds me that I'm frustrated, even if just seeing her eases some of that. I push inside the door and look around. "Where is everyone?"

"Umm . . . I think Em's at your place, and Theo and Jack have something at the school. Are you okay?" She reaches her hand out and fixes the collar of my camo polo shirt, then pulls it back quickly. "Are you on your way to base?" She closes the door and walks into the kitchen.

I follow her like a moth to the flame. "What's going on, Carys? You haven't returned my calls or my texts. You've been avoiding me. And you asked Theo to pick you up from the airport." I stalk behind her and circle my arms around her waist, drawing her back to me. "What's changed, baby? Talk to me."

She tugs free and takes a few steps away. "I . . . Cooper . . ." Carys runs her fingers through her hair, then laughs.

"What the hell, Carys?" I force myself to stand still, even if it goes against every fucking fiber of my being to do it. "Talk to me. It's you and me, baby."

Carys spins on her heels and exhales a stuttered breath. "Cooper," she sobs. "I can't do this right now."

"Can't do what?" Fuck this. I take two steps forward and grab her shoulders. "What can't you do?"

She shoves back against my chest. "I can't do *this*." She shoves me again, but I refuse to let go. "I can't do *us*. Not right now, Coop. I just can't."

"Why? I need you to explain to me what's going on in that beautiful brain of yours, baby. Because this doesn't make sense. I'm yours, remember? I'm not going anywhere. I know you're going through hell right now, but let me carry some of the load for you. Let me be there."

"I don't want you here, Coop. I don't want you to carry the load." She shrugs herself free, and I let her go, feeling like I've been sucker-punched. "I need some space. I think . . . I just . . ." Her lip trembles as she tries not to cry, and I'm at a complete fucking loss.

I take a step closer, needing to fix this, but she takes one step back. "Carys, you were in my arms a week ago. What's changed?"

"Everything," she whispers. "Please, Cooper. My head is throbbing. I just want to lie down. Just go."

"Carys . . ."

"Just go, Coop." Her words are soft but deliver more weight than any words I've ever heard.

"I love you, Carys Murphy. I love you, and I know you love me." I'm practically begging her to say the words because I can't imagine my life without this woman who's falling apart in front of me.

"It's not enough, Cooper. Not now. Please just go."

Those words break me in a way that I didn't realize a man could break.

On a level I didn't know existed before.

"Carys . . ." I have no words of wisdom. Nothing left to say to fight for us because I'm so fucking confused. What just happened?

She turns and walks away without looking back, and I just stand there, dumbstruck, watching her. Trying to figure out where we went wrong.

CARYS

I shut my bedroom door and slide down it until I'm sitting on the floor in a sobbing heap.

I just tore his heart out and decimated mine in the process.

And I don't know if I'll ever recover.

I'm not sure how long I sit like that, but eventually a knock yanks me out of my desperation. "Go away," I tell whoever is dumb enough to be bothering me right now.

"CC, I need you," Emerson cries.

I immediately stand up and open the door to find Em on the other side, looking an awful lot like I must at the moment. "Em, what happened?"

"What happened to you?" she laughs out on a scary sob, then drops down on my bed and wipes her tears. "You wanna go first?"

I shake my head. "Nope. Your turn." I sit down next to Em, then lie back to mirror her.

She turns her head to the side, close enough that I can smell the minty mouthwash on her breath. "I'm pregnant."

"What?" Nothing else comes to me. No words of comfort. Just complete shock.

She nods. "We found out this morning. I've missed my last two periods, so Linc ran out and got me a test today. He actually bought several of them. And they all said the same damn thing. Two pink lines or one pink word—*Pregnant*." She sits up and smacks the bed. "And why the fuck are they all pink? Do they think that's a soothing color? Seriously? What the fuck?"

I sit up and stare at her, still shocked. "Pregnant?"

"Yeah, you're gonna need to get past that word because it gets worse." She grabs a scrap of green lace from my nightstand and wipes her face with it. "Linc asked me to marry him."

"Oh, holy shit." Yup. That's all I got.

She nods again.

"Did you say yes?" I just blew up my relationship with the love of my life, and one of my best friends is getting to live out my dream. Karma is a fucking bitch, and so am I for thinking about myself instead of Emerson.

She blinks the tears away from her lashes. "I think I did."

Oh wow. This just keeps getting worse. "Oh, honey. You think? What does that mean?" I hug her to me, and she leans her head against mine.

"He had all these good points. Like I'd be on his medical plan. And I could get his benefits if something happened to him. Which I yelled at him for even thinking. Like what the fuck, CC? I told him he isn't even allowed to put that thought into the universe. I can't handle that too." The tears come back, followed by the snot. "I told him yes."

Oh. My. God.

"Umm . . . okay. Did you mean to say yes?"

"Maybe?" She laughs. Okay. Good. Laughing, I can handle.

"Well, I think you need to decide that pretty soon, babe. That's a big answer if you're not sure." I have no idea if this is good advice. What would Daphne tell me?

"I think Linc loves me more than I love him, CC. But I do love him. I mean, that's okay, right? My mom always says she loved my dad more than he loved her, so she wasn't surprised when he left. If he loves me more, he'll never leave me like that." Her navy-blue eyes are so heavy . . . so sad. I don't know how to answer her.

"Em, do you want to marry him? Can you imagine your life without him in it?" And now, my first tear falls because I can't imagine my life without Cooper in it. Not after months of having him, even if he was a country away. Sometimes more than a country . . . But my choice is for him. He deserves more.

"Right?"

I look at Emerson, who obviously just asked a question that I completely missed.

Shit.

"Have you made an appointment with an OB/GYN yet?"

She shakes her head, and my head spins. "Emerson, we need to make an appointment with your doctor. Until she tells you you're pregnant, this could all be for nothing. Just a false positive."

She holds four fingers in front of my face. "*Four* false positives, CC? I'm pregnant. There's no wishing this away. And I'm not terminating. But I'll schedule the appointment." She grabs her phone. "Will you come with me?"

"Anywhere you need."

A week later, Emerson is officially pregnant, and my heart is officially broken.

Linc and she are getting married. I think it's a mistake, but she's a big girl, and this is her decision. They don't want to wait to do it. Linc wants to be sure, if something happens to him, she's protected. I kind of want to shake him.

First, for putting those thoughts into the universe.

And second, because she's the daughter of one of the biggest rock stars of all time.

She's protected.

But she's also happy. And that's all I want for my friend. Especially since I don't know if I'll ever have what she has.

I haven't heard from Cooper, which is what I wanted. Even if ending things was the hardest thing I've ever done. And it was. It is. I don't know that it'll ever stop being hard.

But here I sit at the kitchen table, going over all the last-minute things we still need to do for Emerson's wedding tomorrow at the house. Her dad is on tour, and her mom is on a twenty-five-year-old, according to Jack. So Em just wants to do something small here and have a party afterward.

Emerson throws her arms around my neck and chokes back a cry as Linc, Jack, and Theo look around uncomfortably. Em has turned into quite the crier over the past few days. But better her than me.

"Thank you so much for everything, CC. I love you."

I pat her back and look around at the guys. "We've got this, Em. You're going to be a beautiful bride, and it's going to be a perfect day."

COOPER

"You good, brother?" Linc and I stand in our dress whites at the end of the makeshift aisle in Emerson's backyard next to Ford, who's newly certified with the authority to perform the marriage, thanks to the internet. Jessie's fussing over all three of us, making sure everything is in its place. A friend of Emerson's from the photography department at school is taking pictures, and Theo is strumming a guitar, a skill I didn't know he had. Now, we're just waiting for the bride—and in my case, the maid of honor—to walk down the aisle.

I haven't seen Carys in over two weeks.

I haven't called. I haven't texted. And I haven't stopped by.

I talked to Declan and Ford. The two guys in the healthiest relationships I know who I can actually talk to, and they both told me to give her space but not too much space. She needed time, so I needed to give it to her. But it fucking sucks.

Truth be told, I think they both asked their wives what I should do.

It doesn't really matter. I'm fucking miserable either way.

Jessie kisses Ford quickly on the cheek, then wipes her lipstick away with her thumb, and a pang of jealousy hits me right in the solar plexus. I try to push it aside. She leans in and kisses Linc, then does the same to me.

Only instead of a kiss, she whispers in my ear, "Don't give up on our girl yet, Cooper. She's scared, and she's pushing you away. She might not be ready to talk now, but don't give up on her." She kisses my cheek, then walks away as Theo starts to play "Here Comes the Sun" by The Beatles.

And there she is. The love of my life. Walking down the aisle in a soft pale-blue dress that ties around her neck with a long soft ribbon and skims down over her curves. Her hair is done up in a million curls, piled high on her head. And her smile . . . it takes my breath away. I'd do anything to be the reason that smile is on her pretty face.

She looks everywhere but at me as she walks slowly down the aisle, until she does . . . Until her eyes finally lock on mine, and I watch her breath catch in her delicate throat. I see the tremble of her lip. And then her eyes are gone. Focusing on Linc. Smiling at him. Happy for her friends.

This is bullshit.

The ceremony is fast. It's only ten minutes before Emerson is in Linc's arms and Ford has pronounced them man and wife. Everything happens pretty quickly from there on out. The photographer sets us all up for pictures. So many pictures. And I can't keep my eyes off Carys. She's laughing with everyone. Jack and Theo haven't left her alone. But not in a way that makes me worry there's something going on. They seem protective, like they're making sure she's okay. And I'm suddenly glad she has them, even if I should be the one taking care of her.

Servers appear with trays of hors d'oeuvres, and people

move around the yard to mingle as Jack, Theo, and Carys take their places where their instruments are already set up. Jack taps on the mic a few times.

"Hey everyone. I'd like to thank you for coming today to celebrate my baby sister and her new husband. We're all so happy for the two of you. Welcome to the family, Linc." Jack gets a little choked up, looking at Emerson. "Emmie picked this song for Linc's and her first dance, under one condition." He looks over at Carys, who's lovingly stroking the mic in her hand. "The only present she wanted from our beautiful roommate was this song. So, could we please get the new Mr. and Mrs. out onto the dance floor for their very first dance as a married couple?"

Rook stands next to me and hands me a bottle of beer as Jack plays the first few chords of "Iris" by the Goo Goo Dolls before Carys joins in.

"She's fucking incredible."

I agree, never taking my eyes off her. "She really is."

"You gonna fight for her or just let her go?" He sips his beer, watching me.

"It's not that easy."

"Man up, Sinclair. What have you got to lose?"

Both our phones ring, and mine is the ringtone I assigned to messages from Command. Rook and I both look at them, then look around for the rest of the team. Looks like we're heading out.

The song ends, and we all say our goodbyes to Emerson and Linc, who's on leave for the next few days and won't be coming with us.

When I turn around, Carys is no longer standing with the band, and I don't see her anywhere, even after I scan the yard.

Emerson reaches out for a hug, stopping my search for Carys. "She just went into the house, Coop. She's been miserable without you, but if you tell her I said that, I'll break you."

"Thanks, Em. I owe you."

She smacks my shoulder. "Don't forget it, Sinclair."

I step into the house, full of servers and guests, and I catch a glimpse of her blue gown as the front door closes behind her. Walking quickly through the crowd, I open the door and nearly steamroll over her.

I grab Carys's bare shoulders and hold her back against me. "Sorry, baby" leaves my lips without any thought.

"You're leaving." It's not a question, so I'm not sure what she wants to hear, especially since I haven't heard from her in over a week.

"Do you care?" I know it's a shitty thing to ask, but I'm like a fucking bear with a splinter in his paw. And even knowing that doesn't help.

Carys turns slowly in my arms. "I'll always care, Cooper. I need you to be safe."

"Will you be here waiting for me when I get home?" I grip the back of her neck and squeeze. "We need to talk."

"I'll be here. That's all I can promise, Coop."

"That's not an answer, Carys. Your brother's wedding is next month. I was hoping we could talk to the family about us before then."

She closes her eyes, and her shoulders deflate in front of me. "There's nothing to talk about. There is no us." She reaches up and presses her lips to mine. "Be safe, Cooper."

And then, she's gone.

CARYS

"The universe really is a fickle bitch with a fucked up sense of humor. You and I both know that." Chloe's FaceTiming me to make sure I like the new idea she came up with for a swimwear line she wants to get into production next week.

"Physically, I feel great. It's just my heart that hurts." I haven't had a flare-up in a few weeks. No fever. No headache. I've even started running again. Okay, so I'm not pushing myself as hard as I used to when I was training for a marathon, but a few miles a day a few times a week has me feeling more like myself than I have in months.

My career is starting to explode in front of me. The path is wide-open and blue-skied. Stone's girlfriend bought a few shirts from me a few months ago and wore them during the filming of her show. A realtor asked where she got one of them, and she dropped Le Désir's name. And holy moly, Chloe and I blew up. We were trending online the other day. *Trending*. All of a sudden, our little two-person company has more business than we can handle. Chloe started looking for a company to partner with to outsource our manufacturing, so we can increase production and continue to meet our demand. It's insane and so exciting.

"Have you made a decision about the fall semester yet?" She picks up a swatch of bright-red fabric and pairs it with another one that's hot pink, and I shake my head no.

"Yeah, I have. I'm going to take the fall semester off and stay in Kroydon Hills. Any chance I can crash with you? I really don't want to move back in with Mom and Coach." My eyes go wide, and I smile when she pairs the red with a black accent. "That one. That's perfect."

Chloe drapes them both over her dress form and pushes the others to the side. "Of course you can stay with me. I've got an extra room."

"Love you, Chloe. Thank you."

"Stop. If you want emotions, talk to Nattie or Belles. If you want brutal honesty, I'm your girl." She sits down at her sewing machine and props the phone up. "And in the vein of brutal honesty . . . are you seriously not going to talk to him before Murphy's wedding?"

I lie back on my bed and hold the phone above my face. "Talk to who?"

"Don't play dumb, Carys. I'm better at it than you. You still haven't talked to Cooper, have you?" Chloe has already told me she doesn't agree with my decisions. She understands them but thinks it's the wrong move.

"Nope. They got home from their op last week. I haven't seen him yet." I don't mention that he texted me, telling me he was home and safe. I didn't answer, but I did add a little heart to his message. "I'm not ready, Chloe. If I talk to him now, I'll give in. I know I will."

"Maybe you *should* give in."

I groan. "I can't." There's a knock on my door, then Em's head pops in. "I gotta go, Chloe. I'll see you in Hawaii in a week."

"Yup. See you soon." We end our Facetime, and I sit up as Emerson walks in. Her tiny baby bump is on display in her tight-black tank top and yoga pants, and her skin is glowing, actually glowing as the late day sun streams in through my windows.

"Jack's ordering dinner. Are you in the mood for pizza?" She sits down next to me.

"I can always do pizza. Pineapple, please," I lean my head on her shoulder and plead.

She scrunches her face up in disgust. "You're gross." She shoulders me away, then adds, "But of course, we'll order your pizza."

"Thank you." I smile, knowing how much I'm going to miss her. "How did the apartment hunt go earlier? Did you and Linc find anything yet?"

"Ugh. He's driving me crazy. They're leaving in July for six months, so he wants me to stay here with Jack and Theo until they come home. He hates the idea of me being alone when the baby comes." I wonder if she even realizes the way her hand possessively moves to her belly while she's talking.

"He's not wrong, Em. They could be helpful." The look Emerson gives me leaves no doubt how stupid I sound. "Okay, so maybe not really helpful. But to at least have another set of hands. I mean, it couldn't hurt."

"I want my own place, CC. I don't want to bring a new baby home from the hospital to a house I share with my brother's band."

"Has Lucas agreed to take my room?" She nods. "Well, that didn't take long." I only told them a few days ago I wasn't coming back for the fall.

She stands and offers me her hands, then tugs me up. "I'm going to miss you, CC."

I hug her tightly. "You could always come stay in Kroydon Hills. At least until Linc comes home."

"Or you could just not leave."

We've been over this already, and all it does is make us both sad.

"Come on. Let's go make Jack order your gross pizza. I

think I want a greasy sandwich. Like a cheesesteak." She rubs her belly again. "What do you think, my little bean? Does that sound good?"

I lay my hand over hers. "One day, beanie, you're going to visit Auntie Carys in Philadelphia, and I'll show you what a cheese steak really is."

"I'm losing you to a sandwich."

We walk through my door and stop at the top of the steps. "You're not losing me, Em. But I need to do this."

"I know. Just don't forget about us." She walks downstairs.

I whisper, "Never."

COOPER

When I met Aiden Murphy my junior year of high school, I never would have guessed that he'd marry the president's daughter. Sabrina's dad was a senator back then, and Murphy ended up campaigning for him when it came time. So this isn't a new thing, but it's still hard to get my head around it. When I get to the resort on the island of Kauai, Secret Service agents stop and check me over to make sure I'm not a threat and am on the approved list.

They've rented out the entire resort for two weeks. Most of our friends and family have been here for a week already, but I wasn't able to do that, even if I wished I could have flown out when Carys did. If only to have a few hours with her, stuck next to me on a plane where she couldn't run for the first time in two months.

Once I'm checked out by security and checked in at the front desk, I walk around the quiet resort to find my room. The white-sand beach is dotted with individual huts looking out over the clear blue ocean. A few huts stand on stilts over the water, and a large boutique hotel sits behind it all, practically empty except for employees and security.

Chloe is the first person I see as I get closer to the huts. She's closing the door to one of them with a black-and-white bag in her hands.

"Coop." She jogs over to me and throws her arms around my neck. "Thank God, you made it. Murphy's been stressing out. Seriously. He's more of a bridezilla than Sabrina could ever be."

"You look good, Chloe. I like the hair." She's cut her normally long, blonde hair to just below her chin, removing the purple strands she had the last time I saw her.

"Thanks." She runs her fingers through it. "I promised my mom I'd keep it blonde for the weddings, but I might go rainbow as soon as Brady and Nat say 'I do.'"

"Well, if anyone can pull it off, it's you, Chloe." I glance around the empty beach. "Where is everyone?"

"You just missed the guys. They're deep-sea fishing. And the girls are having a spa day." She looks up at me with a coy expression. "Are you going to ask me about her?"

I really wasn't going to. Not because I didn't want to, but because I didn't think she'd tell me. "Are you going to tell me anything if I do, or is there a girl code you can't break?"

"Fuck the girl code. She's miserable, Cooper. She's pushing you away because she thinks you'll be better off without her, not because she doesn't love you." This girl I've known forever stares me down with a sad look in her eyes. "Don't let her do it, Coop. Fight for her. She's worth it, even if she doesn't think she is."

"What the hell do you mean she doesn't think she's worth it?" Anger licks across my skin like a red-hot flame.

Chloe looks at me like I'm the biggest idiot she's ever met. "Why do you think she's pushing you away, Cooper? Jesus. You two are the densest smart people I've ever known. If you want answers, talk to Carys. Her hut is down there." She points to the opposite end of the beach. "Number 10. She should be back there soon. But I swear to God, if you tell her I told you any of this, I'll tell the world you have a micropenis, Sinclair." She smacks my ass as she walks away, and I'm left sorting through everything she just said.

How the hell could this woman ever think she wasn't worth it?

Coop: At the resort.
Murphy: Nice of you to finally join us, fuckhead.
Bash: We'll be back in an hour.
Brady: Girls are at the spa, if you want to find your sister before she hunts you down.
Declan: Can't control your woman?
Brady: Fuck off, Dec. Like Belles doesn't have you wrapped around her pinky.
Murphy: I'll bet Brady likes it when Nattie is wrapped around his little thing.
Brady: It's not little.
Bash: That's not what she said.
Coop: Dude. Stop.
Declan: Want to watch the kids tonight so Belles and I can have a few hours to ourselves?
Bash: Give it up, Dec. You've literally asked everyone.
Murphy: He asked the Secret Service.
Declan: I was drunk.
Coop: Sorry Dec. I get two nights and I'm not spending them with the kids. Love ya, but no.
Declan: Whatever. Dad's reeling in a fish. See ya soon.

We all gather at the beach later that night to walk through the rehearsal for tomorrow. The wedding coordinator lines us all up at the back of the aisle and laughs. "Well, I'd normally encourage the bride and groom to put you all together according to height, but I believe most of you are coupled up already, and you boys are giants. So how about if you're married or engaged, go stand next to your significant other?"

Belles and Declan, Brady and Nattie, and Lenny and Bash all move, leaving Carys, Chloe, Belles's younger brother, Tommy, and me all standing alone. Chloe moves next to Tommy and puts her arm through his.

"What do you say, Tommy boy? You and me?" she asks brightly.

He looks to Belles for permission, then nods, and I offer a silent thank-you to Chloe. I really do owe her one.

I look Carys over and try not to smile too big. "Guess that leaves you and me, mini-Murphy."

She rolls her eyes at the use of the old nickname and probably at Chloe's blatant manipulation. "Guess so."

We're lined up from there and told to wait for our cue to begin our walk down the aisle. It's the closest we've been in months, and my skin feels like it's stretched too thin against my body as I ache to reach out and hold her in my arms.

Carys stands next to me, behind Nattie and Brady. Her soft brown hair is held back by a thin white ribbon, and a white lace sundress brushes her knees. All the girls are in different white dresses except for Sabrina, who's wearing an emerald-green one. Carys's skin is warm against mine, and I ache for so much more. More of her. More of us.

I don't think she even realizes her body is leaning toward mine.

Of course, it fucking is because we're supposed to be

together. She might be holding back, but this woman is mine, and she knows it on a subconscious level.

Brady and Nattie are told to walk, leaving the two of us momentarily alone.

"You look pretty tonight, baby."

The smile she gives me is sad.

"You look nice too, Coop," she whispers. We're told it's our turn and walk slowly down the aisle.

"Can we talk later?" I ask.

"Everyone's watching us, Coop." Her words are clipped, and her lips barely move.

"You better say yes then."

We come to the end of the aisle, and she whispers, "We'll see."

What seems like minutes later, we're done, and everyone is walking to the main resort for a formal sit-down dinner and drinks. And as we make our way there, my girl makes sure she's as far away from me as possible. She does the same damn thing when we take our seats, and for one of the first times in my life . . . I wish my friends and family weren't around.

I need to get her alone.

It's time to end this game.

CARYS

I picked a seat at the long table set up in the stunning dining room as far away from Cooper as possible. Sabrina's parents spared no expense for this event. It really is a shame that she and Aiden refused to let it be photographed for a magazine. They all asked, but my brother and soon to be sister-in-law wanted it kept small, intimate, and completely private.

Once dinner is over and dessert has been served, everyone gets up to mingle, and controlled chaos ensues. Chloe sits down next to me with an evil glint in her eye. She's having way too much fun torturing me today. When she came back from grabbing the special lingerie she and I created for Sabrina earlier, she couldn't wait to tell me that Cooper was here and that he looked hot as hell. *Lickable* was the word she used.

Brat.

She wasn't wrong though. He looks devastatingly handsome in his khaki pants and white linen shirt, but the understated clothes barely contain the raw power Cooper wears like a second skin.

And that smell… Clean, citrusy, and earthy. My stomach somersaults as memories assault me, and the familiar flare crackles to life at the thought of when his skin touched mine . . . God, I ache for him.

I feel like that kid at the table, longing to be a part of the cool kids again as I watch my brother and him

297

laughing with their friends. He tucks Sabrina against him and whispers something in her ear before they both look at Aiden and burst into hysterics over whatever he just said.

I miss that easygoing laugh.

But I did this to myself.

I chose this.

"You're drooling, Carys." Chloe hands me my napkin, and I snap it out of her hands. "Why are you doing this to yourself?"

Twisting the napkin in my hands, I look around the room, full of the people I love . . . The people who have no idea that I'm in love with him . . . That I'll always love him, and I cringe. "Lower your voice."

Aiden comes over and drops his hands on the backs of both our seats. "You ladies having fun?"

"Murph, who's single? I mean . . . somebody here has to be down for some fun?" Leave it to Chloe to be blunt.

The wedding is small, just the way Aiden and Sabrina wanted it. But with some extended family from both of our sides and the few people Sabrina's father had to invite. Small is a relative thing. There's still probably about ninety people who have flown in over the course of the week.

Aiden leans down between us and starts giving Chloe the lowdown on a few cousins from both sides of the family, and I'm pretty sure I'm about to lose her for the rest of the night.

I stand, and then he and I are engulfed by our mother. "I love when all my babies are under one roof." Callen's on her hip, wrapping his arms around me. "You'll understand when you're a parent one day. We take this for granted. All those years of running you guys from one thing to another. All the late-night dinners. All those family movie nights . . ."

She fights back tears.

"Don't cry, Momma." Callen looks at Mom with big, concerned eyes, and Aiden mimics him.

He tugs Mom and me into a big hug as his eyes water. "Don't cry, Momma. We love you."

"Oh my God. If you cry, I'm going to cry." I laugh at them, but in reality, I'm on the verge too. It was the three of us for so long.

"Life goes by fast." Mom's green eyes scan over the three of us. "Enjoy every minute." She kisses us each on the cheek, and then exaggeratedly kisses both of Callen's cheeks as Coach joins us and takes Cal from her. He rests an arm on her shoulder, and she leans her head against him.

"And love hard, my babies. Love hard and don't let go."

My eyes find Cooper, who's watching me with brooding intensity from across the room, and my heart fractures a little more. Loving hard is easy. Not letting go is a whole other thing.

The party is still going late into the night, but one of the things I've learned over the past few months since I've been diagnosed is to watch out for my triggers and to know my limits. Too much sun is definitely a trigger for me, so I use an abundance of sunscreen and never walk out of the house without it on now. Another trigger is lack of sleep. I'm much more likely to feel run-down now than I've ever been. So, knowing that tomorrow is the big event and it will probably be a long day and longer night, I decide to call it a night a little earlier than everyone else.

I hug my brother and say goodnight to everyone, then make my way down the stone path from the main hotel winding through the garden. A thousand stars light up the humid night's sky. The sweet scent of tropical flowers surrounds me as I walk toward my hut. I'm paying more attention to them than to what's around me when a hand clamps down over my lips, blocking the scream that tries to escape.

Cooper comes into view, and I relax as he takes his hand away. "What are you doing out here?"

"We need to talk, Carys. We've needed to talk for months, and you're avoiding me. That ends tonight." He takes my hand and tugs me behind him. "Come with me."

"Where are you taking me?" I don't put up a fight. I probably should, but I'm tired of fighting. "Cooper . . ."

He doesn't answer and instead, just guides me down the path away from the huts to a stone grotto surrounding one of the pools. When he finally stops, he spins me so my back is against the stones and his hands are caging me in on either side of my head.

"Are you done yet?" His baby-blue eyes beg me to give him the answer he wants, but I can't.

"Done with what, Cooper?" My blood starts to warm at his insinuation. "Do you think this is a game for me?"

He crowds me with his big body, but I don't back down. "We were making plans for our life together. I went back to Virginia Beach after New Year's and talked to my commanding officer about switching teams when their sniper retires." His jaw clenches, and I fight an internal battle.

Do I want to soothe him or scream at him?

Anger wins because it's an easier emotion to deal with right now.

"My whole life has changed since then." My voice raises as my muscles shake. "What my future looks like and how I live my life are completely different now than they were six goddamned months ago, Coop."

"And what, Carys? You got sick, so you don't love me anymore?"

He could have slapped me and it would have hurt less.

Everyone has tiptoed around my diagnosis. My mom, my friends, our family . . . all of them have treated me like glass, but none of them have come out and admitted that I'm sick. But not this man. He never treated me like I was someone who needed to be protected. He treated me like an equal who needed to be cherished.

"What the hell is wrong with you?" I whisper, allowing my anger to build from deep inside me. I know it's not fair, but anger is easier to deal with than pain, so I embrace it.

"What's wrong with me?" He slams his palm against the rock next to my face, and I jerk away. "I love you. I want to spend my life with you. I want to tell everyone here this weekend that you're mine and they can get on board or get over it because you're worth everything. And you threw me away."

He drops his hands and takes a step back. "You threw us away like we were nothing. I was ready to give up every-thing for you." Then Cooper turns away from me, his broad shoulders tight with rigid muscles.

"I never asked you to." I take two steps toward him and shove his back with both hands. "I never asked you to give up anything. Anything," I scream, shaking.

"No. You liked us being a dirty fucking secret, didn't you, Carys? Was I just a fun fuck?"

I swing my hand to slap him across the face, but he grabs my wrist mid-air and stops me.

"Tell me, baby." Venom drips from his lips as he snarls the word *baby*. It used to envelop me like a caress. Now, it stings my skin in a brutal punishment. Calm now, but his eyes are boiling with fire . . . with hurt and anger mixed with want and need. "Was that all you wanted? To be fucked by a man?"

My pussy clenches at his harsh words as my nipples tighten to hard peaks.

He backs us up a step, bringing his body closer to mine. "Did you just want my cock, Carys? Do you miss the way I fill your cunt? The way your body hums for me?"

I take a step away from him but bump into the cool rock against my bare back. He closes the gap between us, his hard body pressing against mine. And there's no hiding how much he wants me, even if he wishes he didn't.

I squirm as my pussy drips for him, and Cooper's eyes flare in recognition.

"Is that what you want, Carys? Do you want my cock?" He drops my hand and runs his up under my skirt, along the inside of my thighs, lighting my skin on fire.

I tremble at his touch, knowing he's going to destroy me, but I don't care.

I need him.

"Your cock was never the problem, Coop." Brave words spill from my lips. I'm desperate. I don't have the strength to stop him.

Not when every molecule in my body lights up with insatiable need.

His finger runs over the lace covering my pussy. "Is your pussy wet for me, Carys?"

I whimper when his finger slides under my panties, then traces the seam of my sex. "Fucking drenched."

I pant. Trembling. Not able to form words.

He slaps my pussy, and I cry out, "Oh my God." Then two fingers slide inside me.

"Tell me to stop, Carys." Cooper's tongue licks up the

length of my neck. "Tell me to stop now, and I'll walk away."

My hands go to the belt on his pants. "Don't stop, Coop."

He hoists me up in his arms, both of his hands grabbing the cheeks of my ass. "I'm not going to be gentle, and you need to be silent."

I shove his pants down, and in one swift move, Cooper pushes my panties aside and impales me. He spins us, so his back is against the stone. Protecting me. Always protecting me.

His grip on my ass tightens as he slams his lips against mine while violently pounding into me.

When I cry out again, he stills. "You need to be quiet or this ends."

I close my eyes and nod my head.

"Good girl." He lifts me, dragging his dick along every sensitive inch of my pussy, and fireworks explode behind the lids of my eyes before he impales me again and again.

I claw at his back, needing to be closer. Wanting to feel his skin but being denied by the layers of clothes between us.

"Coop," I plead.

His tongue lashes against my lips until I open for him.

He takes my mouth in a brutal rhythm. His hips piston, and my toes curl.

That familiar fire ignites inside me.

My heels dig into Cooper's ass, and he groans. The sound spurs me on, and I bring my lips to his neck. Sucking. Scraping my teeth against his skin. Pleasure ripples through my veins, warming me.

One of Cooper's hands slides down my ass until his fingers bite into my skin.

"Jesus, I'm close," I breathe.

"Come on my cock," he orders with one final thrust.

I detonate on a whisper while Coop works me through my orgasm silently, then sets me carefully on my feet.

Come drips down my leg as Cooper tucks himself back inside his pants.

When he looks up, it's with a mixture of apprehension and regret on his face. "Did I hurt you?" He doesn't reach for me. Doesn't touch me. He never once called me baby when he was fucking me, and that realization steals my breath from my lungs.

"Carys . . ."

Oh. I didn't answer him. "No. I'm fine. I just . . ."

"Let me walk you to your room." Worried blue eyes meet mine.

"There's Secret Service all over the resort, Coop. I'm okay. I don't need you to walk me back."

"We need to talk." An unreadable mask slides over Cooper's face. "I leave the day after the wedding, Carys." His words are a warning as he turns and walks away, and I'm left watching him go.

Wondering if I made a mistake tonight, or if the mistake was made two months ago.

COOPER

I SPENT THE NIGHT STARING AT THE WOODEN PALM-LEAF ceiling fan spinning and feeling like I'm doing the same damn thing. I know I fucked up last night. She's running away, and instead of forcing her to stay, forcing her to talk, I gave her another way to avoid me. Sex wasn't the answer. It was a Band-Aid, a fucking phenomenal stalling tactic that solved nothing.

Just before sunrise, I give up on getting any decent sleep and decide to go for a run. But on my loop around the resort, I slow as I come up to Carys's hut, and without overthinking it, I knock on her door. I stand there, leaning against the door frame, waiting. Muffled noise comes from the other side, so I know she definitely heard me.

When she cracks open the door, I realize just how early it is and remember Carys is *not* a morning person. Too late now.

"What do you want, Cooper? It's six a.m." She's dressed in black lace boy-cut panties and a matching black lace-bra thing that kinda looks like a tank top but shorter. And way sexier. Damn. Her hair's a mess around her face, and those emerald-green eyes of hers are glaring daggers at me for waking me up. All I want to do is kiss her, but she'd probably break a lamp over my head if I did.

"We need to talk, Carys, and I'm not giving you a chance to run away this time." I take a step forward, and she begrudgingly opens the door further to let me in.

"Fine." She grabs a tee out of her suitcase and throws it over her beautiful body, which certainly helps me concentrate. I'm strong, but I don't know if I'm strong enough to have this conversation with a half-naked Carys. Although, when she turns around, I force back the groan caught in my throat. One of the few things better than a half-naked Carys is her half-naked in my shirt. My inner caveman roars to life at the vision in front of me, seeing her in one of my old Kroydon Hills Prep football tees with *Sinclair* and my number across the back.

"Nice shirt."

Her delicate hands grip the hem, tugging it down while she looks to see what she's wearing and then blushes. "It's comfortable," she shrugs. "What do you want, Cooper? What do we have left to talk about?" She crosses her hands over her chest, and the five-year-old shirt lifts with her, grazing the tops of her thighs.

I mimic her stance. "How about we start with why you pushed me away?"

"I told you—"

"You didn't tell me anything. Just said you needed space. I need more than that, Carys. I deserve more. We deserve more, and you know it." I force myself to stay put and not cross the room. To not go to her the way I want to. "What happened to us?"

"Cooper . . ." The way my name leaves her lips . . . It's a sigh of exhaustion. She drops down onto the small sofa and tucks her feet up under herself. "Can't you please just accept that it's over and leave it at that?"

"No, I can't. I refuse to. We were fine. We were making plans, and everything was fine. I know I said I wanted to talk to the family about us. I wanted us to be open with everyone. But when you pushed back that you weren't ready, I promised to give you time. What the fuck happened after that to cause this? Because I love you, and I'm pretty damn sure you still love me too, baby."

Her eyes flare on my last word as they shoot up to meet mine. "It doesn't matter, Cooper. None of it matters anymore."

"Why?" I push, needing better answers than she's giving me. "Why doesn't it matter? Because you're sick? What kind of man would I be if I backed away because of that?"

Her hands fly up into the air, pissed off. "I'm not sick right now, Coop. I'm living with lupus. I have good days and bad days. Sometimes bad weeks, but I'm not always sick." Some of her anger subsides as she lowers her voice. "But that doesn't mean there aren't complications that I don't want you to deal with. This is for me to live with. Not you."

"Who are you to decide what I live with? I love you. I want to live with you. I want to spend my life with you. I don't care about the rest. Who better to lean on when you need support than the man who loves you?" I stand my ground, staring down at this beautiful woman who must have no idea what she means to me. "Where the hell did I fuck up? Why don't you believe that I love you enough for us to get through anything?"

Carys stands up and pushes at my chest. "Because I don't want you to have to get through this, Coop." She turns her back to me for a moment, gathering her composure. Her finger tightens into fists at her side before she spins back to me.

"I love you, Cooper. Part of me always will. But I can't give you what you want. I can't give you what you'll need, and I'd never forgive myself for robbing you of that." Her green eyes fill with unshed tears. "We have no idea what the next twenty years are going to look like for me. I could have issues neither of us has even considered. But it's almost guaranteed that I'm going to have issues having a baby. I was going to have complications before this diagnosis. And now . . ." The first tear falls. "Now, it could be catastrophic for me or the baby."

I step into her and gather her in my arms as she cries, pressing my lips against the top of her head. She grips my shirt with her fists and sobs. Long, deep, gut-wrenching sobs. "Let it go, baby. Let it all out." I hold her tighter and let her cry, rubbing her back . . . her hair. Soothing her any way I can. Then I pick her up and sit down with her small body tucked against me.

We sit there for a long time as she calms down.

The two of us holding each other.

"Baby, why didn't you tell me earlier? I don't care. We can adopt. There're tons of kids out there who need good homes. I don't care if we can't do it the traditional way. And I'm not even thinking about kids right now. I just want you. I'll stand with you every step of the way, Carys. We'll get through this together." I lift her face to mine and gently press my lips to hers.

"You'll care one day, Coop. What if I'm sick and they won't give us a baby? I've read horror stories online. It's not as easy as you're making it sound. There are so many possible complications." She runs her thumb over my cheek, and I know before she speaks what she's going to say. It's plain as day in her eyes. "I can't do that to you, Cooper. I won't. I refuse to let you make those decisions now for the both of us, only to regret it later. I don't want to live like that. I can't."

Carys climbs off my lap and tugs her shirt down. "You deserve more than that, and so do I."

"Fuck that." I stand in front of her and grab her hand. "You hate when people make decisions for you. You fucking hate when people treat you like they know what's best. That's what you're doing now. You're not listening to me." I lift her hand and lay it over my heart. "I don't care about any of that if it means I don't have you. You're it, Carys. You're everything."

Her face softens. "I wish I could believe that."

"But why can't you? When have I ever given you any reason to doubt that? To doubt me?"

"You haven't," she whispers. "But I'm scared. I don't know what to do, Coop. I don't know what to think or how to feel. Just as so much of my life is coming together, a whole different piece of it is falling apart."

"Let me help you. We'll deal with it together." It's crazy how much a year can change things. I can't imagine my life without this woman standing next to me. I'd fight any battle, wage any war if it meant I got to keep her.

"I'm moving home, Coop. I'm taking a year off of school and moving back to Kroydon Hills so Chloe and I can concentrate on the business. My doctor in Philly is the best in the country, and I'll be close to Mom if I need her."

"That doesn't change anything. None of that does." I lift her hand to my lips and kiss her fingers. "I'm home for Nattie's wedding and have to fly back to Coronado the next day. We leave for our six-month deployment right after that. When I come back, I'm transferring to Virginia Beach and Bravo Team. I did that for us, baby. So we could be closer to our family. To our friends. It can all work out."

She closes her eyes. "I don't know, Cooper. I want to believe it can all work out, but I'm just not there yet."

"Yet. You're not there *yet*. But you can get there. Don't doubt me. Don't doubt us. We're worth it, Carys. We're worth the risks. We're worth the hell. Together. You and Me. We're worth it all."

She walks willingly into my arms and rests her cheek

against my chest. "Just give me time, Cooper. I'm not making any promises, but I need time."

"Don't shut me out, and I'll give you whatever you want, baby."

I'll fight forever for this woman, whether she wants me to or not.

CARYS

I'm not sure how I accumulated so much stuff over the past twelve months, but as I tape up the last of my boxes to be shipped back to Philly, I wonder, yet again, where it all came from. When we moved into this place last year, I only had two bins, my suitcases, and a few canvas bags full of stuff. I lost count of the boxes the guys have taken from my room. They've been great, carrying it all downstairs for me.

I look around my now-bare room and run my hand over the box I've carefully packed my sewing machine in. I can't believe I'm saying goodbye to California. And as Cooper knocks on my door, it's even harder to believe I'm saying goodbye to *him*.

"Hey, you almost ready to head to the airport?" We've texted a few times in the three weeks since my brother's wedding, but it's been awkward. Stilted. He's trying to give me the space and time I need to figure out where my head's at, but I'm no closer now than I was a month ago. I did agree to let him drive me to the airport today.

I take a look around the room and appreciate what living in this house gave me one last time. This past year showed me how strong I am and how fragile life is. I'm done hiding. I'm done holding back. I'm living my life. I wish it could be with this man at my side, but I don't think that's how this is all going to work out.

I take a deep breath. "Yeah, I'm ready."

Cooper pushes the door open, and I walk past him and down the steps.

Emerson's waiting in the kitchen with a bag of oil and vinegar chips in her hands. This kid is going to come out with a cholesterol issue from the way Em's been going to town on junk food. Her tiny bump popped and no longer looks like a food baby. Linc and she decided not to find out what they're having, so we're still referring to the baby as whatever fruit the books compare it to each month. I think this week it's an eggplant.

She hugs me with her greasy fingers, crushing the bag against my back. "I can't believe you're really leaving me."

"I'm just a plane ride away. And your dad has a private jet. You can come to Kroydon Hills whenever you want."

Em starts crying. "I'm going to miss you so much."

"Love you, Em." I hold back my own tears, not wanting to make this worse, and the way she's been emotional lately, it would definitely turn into a sob-fest.

Linc circles his arms around his wife. "You've got to let her go, babe. You'll see her again soon." He looks at me for support.

"Absolutely," I agree.

Linc hugs me to him with his free arm and kisses my cheek. "Stay in touch, Carys."

"Come here, CC." Jack tugs me from Linc and hands me a notebook.

I turn it over in my hand. "Jack," I gasp. "This is your notebook." I run my thumb along the worn pages. "You can't give this to me. Your songs are all in here."

"They are. But you promised you'd help fine-tune them. I still need your help, and we can work it out over Face-Time or Zoom." He hugs me, whispering, "Don't be a stranger, okay?"

I know what this means to him and can't believe he'd

give it to me. "One day, I'm going to say I knew you two when." I look over at Theo and open my arm for him to join us. "Thanks for letting me sing with you guys. I'll never forget it."

Theo chuckles. "We'd never let you stop if we could. Your voice is one in a million, Carys, and so are you. Promise you'll call if you need anything."

"Promise," I push the word out, perilously close to losing it.

Cooper must see that I'm struggling because he clears his throat. "We've got to go, Carys."

I step back and look around at the makeshift family I formed here.

Completely unexpected but absolutely perfect.

"I love you guys."

Cooper places his hand at the small of my back and ushers me through the front door to a chorus of goodbyes and love yous before I climb into the Jeep and let the tears come.

I know this is the right move, but saying goodbye always sucks. And as I watch Coop walk around the Jeep before he gets in, I know saying goodbye to him will be the hardest.

We're quiet on the quick drive to the airport, neither of us talking and instead choosing to sit in the heavy silence surrounding us. Not sure what's left to be said.

When Cooper pulls up to the terminal and shuts off the Jeep, I hop out and grab my carry-on as he picks up my suitcase. We meet on the sidewalk, and I can't help but feel like this is it. "Thanks for the ride, Coop."

Jesus. Could I sound more pathetic? I might as well have told him I carried a goddamned watermelon.

"I'll see you in two weeks at the wedding." His arms circle around me, holding me tight to his chest, and I melt in his embrace, fearing this is the last time I'm ever going to feel this. I'm still so utterly fucked up over all of this.

I kiss his cheek, then look up at those eyes I love. "Two weeks."

Coop grips the back of my head and crashes his lips to mine, and chills break out, covering my body. I hate how much I love him because that's how much I want to protect him from me and my life.

When he pulls away, his fist wraps in my hair and tugs my head back, forcing me to look up at him. "Text me tonight when you land. Let me know you got in okay. And remember, this isn't over. I'll see you at the wedding."

I purse my lips together and nod. "Okay." Then I turn to leave.

"Carys . . ."

I stop and look over my shoulder. "We're worth it, baby. I love you."

I blow him a kiss and walk into the airport. Alone.

Carys: I landed. Flight was fine. Chloe's picking me up from the airport.
Cooper: Thank you. Are you going straight to Chloe's or stopping at home first?
Carys: Just going to Chloe's tonight. I promised Mom I'd come over for lunch tomorrow.
Cooper: See you soon, baby.
Carys: Be safe, Coop.

CARYS

One of the things that I've learned in the two weeks I've been living with Chloe is that nobody knocks on the door. Of course, that's because she never locks it. And when she does, everyone just uses their key because *everyone* has a key to the townhouse. We're leaving for the beach houses later today, so it could be just about anyone who's stopping by now when I hear the front door slam shut behind them.

Not gonna lie. I hate this.

Cooper made me crazy about locking the doors, and now I can't stand knowing anyone could walk in. "Hello . . ." Nattie's voice bounces off the high ceiling downstairs.

"I'm upstairs, Nat. Come on up so I can make sure everything fits." We've been working on a lingerie set for her honeymoon but had to make a few alterations when she tried it on earlier in the week.

"Hey." She pops into what Chloe and I have turned into our workshop. Her shiny blonde hair bounces around her shoulders, and an absolutely glowing smile stretches across her face. "Is Chloe here?"

"Nope. She had to run out and pick something up. She should be back soon though." I hand her the bra and panties first. "Now, try them on, and let's make sure you bring Brady Ryan to his knees."

My stepsister moves behind the screen we have set up

in the corner of the room and changes into the white French-lace set, throwing her clothes over the top of the screen. "Carys, seriously. When you decide to get married, just elope."

She steps out from behind the screen and moves in front of the antique cheval mirror we have set up in here. "Don't get me wrong. Saturday is going to be amazing. But part of me wishes we'd just eloped and I was already his wife."

I step up behind her and adjust the back of the bra slightly. "Nat, have your boobs gotten bigger?"

Her blue eyes, that look so much like her brother's, stare back at me through the mirror, shocked. Fuck. Did I just tell the bride she gained weight?

I ignore her reaction and adjust the panties, noticing they're not fitting right either.

"Carys . . . Can you keep a secret?"

Fuck no, I can't. But I also can't tell her that either, so I nod like a good stepsister and steel myself for whatever bomb she's about to drop.

"I'm pregnant."

Ice water coats my veins. *Pregnant.* My mind spins until I force myself to react. "Oh wow. That's amazing, Nat. Congratulations."

She turns around and hugs me. "It's twins."

I take a beat to collect myself, then force a smile to my face. "Twins. Oh my God. You've got to be thrilled."

She smiles, torn. "We are. I just wish it had happened a year from now. I'm scared. It's barely been two months since Brady was drafted to the Sentinels and we moved to Maryland. And seriously, the fact that Murphy was drafted there too . . . I mean, it's fantastic to be there with him and Sabrina." She tears up. "It's just all so much."

Nattie hugs me again, and I wonder how many pregnant friends I'm going to have to hug before I let go of feeling sorry for myself that this is something I'll never get to experience?

Cooper: Driving down from Dover now. Should be at the house in less than two hours. Am I going to see you tonight?
Carys: Not sure. You guys are going to O'Malley's Bar for Brady's bachelor party. I'll be at Dec & Belles's for a little ladies' night.

Cooper doesn't answer after my text, and I wonder if this is the week he gives up.

This isn't fair to him. I have no idea what I'm doing or if I'm ever going to be able to give him the relationship he wants. The one he deserves. I'm trying so hard to be the strong one and walk away, but I might need it to be him.

When I wondered earlier how many pregnant friends and family I'd have to hug before reality crashed down in a giant, heavy heap on top of my head, I got my answer tonight. Apparently, I'm going to have to hug all my pregnant sisters. Two sisters-in-law and a stepsister. Because that evening at Belle and Dec's house, not only does Nattie announce that she's pregnant, but we find out that Sabrina is too. And so is Annabelle, for the third time in four years. Even Bash's fiancé, Lenny, is pregnant. There's a damn baby boom happening in Kroydon Hills, and Chloe, Mom and I are the only ladies at our little party who haven't been drinking that water.

They're all pregnant.

They're all glowing.

They're all deliriously in love, and I can't decide if I'm jealous or if this pain is just my body's way of finally dealing with the acceptance that I won't be able to have this. To be this person.

I sit outside late that night, thinking about it. Thinking about all of it.

I'm so happy for these incredible women in my life. I am. I love my nieces and nephews, and now there'll be more of them to love. I do accept that. I embrace that. I just won't have it for myself.

And with that thought in mind, I know what I have to do.

COOPER

"You sure you don't want to crash at our house?" My very drunk brother says to me as we pile out of the party bus that drove us home from O'Malley's tonight. Everyone is stumbling in different directions. Murphy, Sabrina, Nattie, Carys, and I are all staying with Dad and Katherine tonight. It's killing Brady not to spend the night before the wedding with my sister, but one night won't kill him.

I'd know.

I pat Declan on the back, drunk, but maybe not as inebriated as him. "Nah, man. I'm good. I dropped my stuff off at Dad's earlier."

"Yeah, you did." Murph throws an arm around me. "I hope you have headphones for tonight because my wife has been horny as hell since she got pregnant, and it's so much fucking fun.

"Dude, more than I need to know." He's gonna fucking kill me one day when I tell him I'm in love with his sister.

Bash and Declan walk in one direction to their houses. Bash bought the one next to Dad's a few months ago, and Brady goes the other way to his, while Murphy and I walk in the front door, trying to be quiet but failing miserably. The lights are off when we walk into the kitchen to get some water, and he opens the fridge door. "I'm fucking starving. You hungry?"

"I could eat."

When Sabrina and Carys walk into the kitchen a few

minutes later, Murph and I are devouring what's left of a tray of mini-sandwiches and fruit. Not the most filling thing I've ever eaten, but it'll work in a pinch.

Sabrina walks into Murphy's arms and kisses him. "You two have to lower your voices. Nattie sleeping in a bedroom upstairs, and you're not allowed to wake up the bride the night before her wedding because you have the munchies."

"We're not stoned, babe, just drunk." He kisses her again but deeper, and I look away, catching Carys's eye, wanting us to have the freedom to be that open.

Fuck. I'd settle for the freedom to touch her like that in private again.

"Okay, you two." Carys walks around the kitchen island and pushes Murph's back. "How about you take this to the bedroom and shut the damn door? Maybe turn on some music. I really don't want to hear you having sex."

We watch them walk down the hall to their room, which is on the opposite side of the hall from the two rooms we're in.

"How was O'Malley's?" Carys picks up one of the little sandwiches and sniffs it before putting it back down and going for a grape instead.

"I miss these guys. It was great to be back there with them."

She lifts herself up to sit on the counter and leans back against the cabinet. "Did you hear the news?" She looks away from me and grabs Murph's half-drunk bottle of water to sip.

"What news?" I watch her throat as she swallows that water. She's wearing white cotton shorts with tiny red hearts embroidered on them and a matching red tank. The tops of her breasts are plumped and pressing against the neckline. Her face is fresh, no traces of makeup, and her hair sits haphazardly on top of her head. And I swear to God, she's the most gorgeous fucking woman I've ever seen.

"Everyone's pregnant." Her voice is flat when she says it, but the fake smile on her face doesn't escape me.

"Yeah." I round the counter and stand between her spread legs. "I heard. You doing okay?" My hands rest on the bare skin of her thighs, and my cock gets bad ideas.

Carys rests her warm hands on top of mine but doesn't push them away. "I'm okay. I'm happy for them. More babies to love can never be a bad thing. It's just a little overwhelming." My hands inch higher, and Carys slides her hands to my shoulders. "This isn't a good idea, Coop."

"Then tell me to stop, Carys." My thumb grazes her bare sex, and we both moan just as the stairs creek. We jump, and I move away from her. She grasps the back of her head where she just slammed it against the cabinet.

Katherine walks into the kitchen, a concerned look on her tired face. "Hey, Cooper." She turns to Carys. "Honey, are you feeling okay? Your face is red."

"I'm fine, Mom. I just got up for water, and Cooper and Aiden had both just gotten home." She hops off the counter and kisses her mom on the cheek. "I'm going to bed now. I'll see you both for brunch tomorrow morning. Good night."

I wait for Katherine to go back upstairs before I quietly make my way down the hall and stop outside of Carys's bedroom. There's a rhythmic creaking coming from the room across the hall that Murphy and Sabrina are in, and I raise my hand to knock on Carys's door before I think better of it and look at the knob.

What's the worst she can do?

Ask me to leave?

I try the knob and get my answer when the door is locked.

Fuck. That's worse.

The next day is the definition of controlled chaos all day. Dad and Katherine insisted on having a brunch for just the family, no friends. They rarely make that request, but it's Nattie's wedding day, and they wanted us all together. The twins and Callen were hopped-up on sugar from the minute the waffles and syrup touched their lips. Nattie spent the morning throwing up, and Sabrina and Belles barely touched any food. People were in and out of the house all day, and there was no privacy at all before Declan, Tommy, Murphy, and I were all kicked out to go over to Brady's house to get ready with the groom.

I did manage to grab Nattie coming out of the bathroom before I left though. "Nat."

She turns and looks at me. She's in short white shorts and a little zipped-up hoodie that says *Future Mrs. Ryan* on the back. Her hair is piled high in rollers on top of her head, and she looks a little green.

"Hey, Coop." She leans her head against my shoulder. "Am I married yet? Because I'm already exhausted."

"You're cooking the next Sinclair twins. It's no wonder you're tired, sis." I kiss her head. "I'm so proud of you, Nat. I remember when Brady talked to me about dating you. Did he ever tell you what I told him?"

She shakes her head—no.

"I told him he was a good guy, and that I trusted him to take care of you. He's a great guy, Nat, and you're the best there is. The two of you deserve to be happy together. You deserve it all. I love you, little sister."

She laughs like I knew she would. "I'm three minutes older than you."

"And an entire foot shorter." I squeeze my sister, my pregnant sister, who's about to get married. "Man, when did we get so fucking old and responsible?"

"Says the guy the military trusts with guns bigger than me." She rolls her eyes.

"Go get ready, Nat. Is there anything you want me to tell Brady?"

The smile that graces her face is incredible. "Yes, please. Tell him I can't wait to be his wife." She lifts up on her toes and kisses my cheek. "Thank you so much for being here, Cooper. I don't know what I would have done if you couldn't be."

"Love you, Nat."

She beams up at me. "Love you too, Cooper. Now, go before I cry."

I stand there for a moment as she goes upstairs, watching Carys chase Callen around the kitchen, laughing. And I know without a doubt, I'll never stop fighting for her.

I'm going to marry that woman one day, and we're going to get our happy life the way my sister and Brady are.

.

CARYS

Tommy and I are dancing to Otis Redding halfway through the reception when Cooper cuts in. "Hey, Tommy. You think I could dance with Carys for a few minutes?"

Tommy looks at me, and I smile and nod. "Save one for me later, okay?"

"Okay, Carys." He starts to walk away when Chloe grabs him to dance with her.

The band's horn section hits their part beautifully, and Cooper spins me around the dance floor. "Have I told you that you're the most gorgeous woman in this room?"

I blush, and the band switches to "When I Fall In Love." It's like the freaking universe is conspiring against me. "No, you haven't. But no one here tonight holds a candle to your sister."

My skin lights up with heat at the touch of his hand against my bare shoulder blade.

"My eyes have only seen you all day, Carys." The hand on my waist tugs me closer to him.

"Coop . . . Be careful. What if someone is watching?" I glance around, but no one seems to be paying any attention to us. This wedding is gigantic compared to Aiden's. There are at least four hundred people here, and that does make it easier to blend in.

"What if I told you I don't care if anyone is watching?" He's got that stubborn look in his eyes that I know well.

"I'd say even if we were at that point, your sister's

wedding isn't the place to make an announcement like that." I slowly slide my hands up his arms, taking in the feel of his muscles under his jacket, and savor every second in his hold. "You smell good."

Cooper chuckles. "Soap and water, baby."

"It smells really good on you." I take a risk and lay my head against his shoulder for a moment, inhaling his uniquely clean scent, then step back. "We can't do this. Not here. Not now." The band switches to an older song I've heard before. "True Companion." I think it was originally by Marc Cohn. And it's like they're trying to rip my heart out.

I turn and grab a glass of wine from a passing server and walk outside. The country club where the reception is being held is on the beach, one town over from the houses. I walk away from the man I'll always love, down the stone path through the grass, planning to go sit on the beach for a while until I'm called over to where everyone is sitting on crisp white, Adirondack chairs around a beautiful stone firepit. Nattie is in Brady's lap, glowing. Sabrina sits on my brother, as does Lenny on Bash. My heart hurts for a minute that I'm not allowing myself to have this. If I wanted it, it would be mine. If I was willing to do that to Cooper.

Chloe sits by herself and yells over to me. "Come on, Carys. You can sit on my lap."

I join the group and sit down on the arm of Chloe's chair just before I spot Cooper walking outside, looking for me. I clock the minute he finds me with our family, and his entire body changes.

Loosens somehow.

Relaxes.

And maybe that's what I was looking for.

He's relaxed with them, but what I'm doing isn't fair. I'm hurting him.

The chatter around me continues as music pumps out from the open doors.

Nat smiles from her place on Brady's lap, her long white dress covering both their legs. "Pretty sure I need to thank Chloe and Bash," she laughs. "If it hadn't been for the two of you, I may never have gotten Brady's attention."

"Oh, sweetheart. You had my attention the first second you walked into that kitchen." He kisses her, and we all groan and then turn as one to look at Cooper, waiting for him to say something the way he's always teased the two of them. But how does he do that, now that he's been hiding what we've done from his best friends? As that thought crashes down around me like a violent wave, I hear him.

"What?" Coop asks. "I can't yell at him for kissing her anymore. He married her."

I've done this to him. I've asked him to lie to his friends and our family.

I've ruined so many things, but I can fix it.

Chloe grabs my hand in hers and squeezes it reassuringly.

She knows how much this hurts.

Nattie's head pops up. "Do you have to go back tomorrow, Cooper?"

"You know I do, Nat," Coop tells her solemnly.

I need to get out of here. Standing up, I turn to the group. "I'm going to check on Mom. See if she needs help with Callen." I feel Cooper's eyes burning into me as I hear him.

"I don't fly out until tomorrow night. Who wants to sunrise surf in the morning?"

They all groan.

The singer announces the last dance of the night, and I

peek over my shoulder to see them all lift their glasses in a toast. "To the new Mr. and Mrs. Ryan."

"To the Ryans" is echoed back before Nattie adds, "To family."

Journey's "Don't Stop Believin'" drifts through the open doors, and I hold in the sob that catches in my throat.

I leave my room unlocked when I go to bed.

Knowing I shouldn't but praying he checks.

Like he did last night.

I lie on top of my bed in his old t-shirt, wishing it still smelled like him, knowing this is it and trying not to cry as my heart fractures further.

It's not long before the door cracks open and his eyes lock with mine. I nod my head and Coop slips inside. His gray suit coat is thrown on the chair, and we don't speak. We don't need to. We both know what this is.

Cooper's hands skate over my skin as he lifts my shirt gently over my head, and I fumble with the buttons on his shirt. I'm not as gentle when I rip his white dress shirt from his muscled chest, desperate to feel his skin against mine.

He lifts me from my feet, and my legs lock around his waist. "Coop . . ."

"Shh, baby. I've got you." His lips graze mine, and my skin pulses at the electricity coursing through it. "I've always got you, Carys. Always."

I yank his belt from his pants, then shove them and his boxers down his legs.

His big body covers mine until our hearts beat in sync, and I fall a little deeper. I take him in my hand and rub the thick head of his dick against my soaking wet entrance. We both moan as he pushes inside me, and pleasure courses through my veins.

"I need you," I cry against his mouth as my hips cradle him to me. "Oh, God."

He drives his hips against mine in slow, deep, loving strokes.

Worshipping me.

Whispering every word I ever needed to hear. And breaking any final remnant of my heart that was still intact before tonight.

His lips are a velvety caress against the skin of my throat as his hands wrap around me, and he sits us both up, never losing our connection.

My legs stay circled around his waist as he holds me impossibly close.

We move as one.

So different from all the other times I've been with this man, and I lose myself in him.

I crest on a silent sob as hot come fills me and shatters my soul.

We don't talk afterward.

Cooper holds me in his arms and doesn't act like he knows I cry myself silently to sleep.

I know I'm alone before I open my eyes. My hand smooths over the cool sheets in search of Cooper, but he's not here.

Why would he be? We both knew what last night was, didn't we?

A quick glance at the clock on the bedside table tells me just how early it is.

I didn't want to close my eyes last night. I tried to stay awake, to savor the moment in his arms. My last time with the man who's owned my heart since I was fifteen.

I knew the morning would bring an end to us.

To everything.

But I don't see any other way, and I've tried.

He's catching a flight back to Coronado today, so he can fly out for his deployment this week. This will be the last time I see him like this. The last time I'll have any claim to him.

I gaze through the window at the dark ocean and know exactly where he is.

And as much as the guys love him, no one was waking up for sunrise surfing today but Cooper.

I slip a soft black Kings sweatshirt over my head that I picked up yesterday from a chair, and instead of putting it away in Cooper's room like I should have, I left it in here. Wanting something that still carried his scent, that would envelop me like the man himself has so many times, letting it wrap around me and kiss my skin.

I force myself to remember I'm doing this for a reason.

I'm breaking us on purpose now, so I don't destroy us later.

Don't destroy him.

I've never been the strong one. It's always been him. He'll never let me go if I don't force him, and I can't let him do that.

I can't take his full, beautiful life from him.

I can't handle the resentment that would eventually come with it.

It's easy to slip through the sliding-glass doors of my room undetected since everyone else in the house is sound asleep. I follow the well-worn path through the sand dunes and beach grass down to the hard sand and look out at the edge of the stormy ocean. The sky is gray with no sun in sight. But there he is, his bronzed body sitting atop his surfboard, waiting for the perfect wave. He's got the patience of a freaking saint. Always has.

So I do what I do best.

I watch. Always on the outside looking in.

At least until he's beside me. Then I finally fit.

If only for a little while.

Coop lies down on his board and starts to paddle as a wave builds in the distance behind him. Thunder crashes overhead, and I watch him one more time.

He's a golden god out there on his board, a frogman perfectly at home in the ocean.

He's gorgeous.

He's everything.

And I got to have his heart for a little while. That has to be enough.

He rides to the shore, unstraps his board from his ankle, and digs it into the sand. His blue eyes sparkle even brighter against the gray clouds overhead as another boom of thunder warns the skies are going to open soon. A relieved grin overtakes his handsome face as he makes his way to me.

"You came." Never stopping, he grabs my face with both hands and crushes his lips to mine. His tongue licks into my mouth, and my hands grip his biceps with all the strength I have.

Peace is a fleeting sentiment. And peace is what I've always felt in his arms.

Tears burn the back of my eyelids as I turn my head away. "I had to say goodbye without everyone around us."

Cooper stands stock-still, like I just stole his breath. "Don't do this, Carys. Don't do this to us." He grabs my hand and flattens it against his heart. "Feel that, baby. It beats for you. Feel me. I'm yours. We can figure everything else out if you give us a chance. You're it for me." He presses his lips to mine again, but I just can't.

"Cooper." The tears fall as soon as his name leaves my lips. "I can't," I sob. "I just can't do this anymore. It's not fair to either one of us. You deserve everything, and I can't give that to you."

"Baby." He wipes the tears from my face just as the first fat raindrop falls. "I can live without everything else. But I can't live without you. How can you even question that?"

I push him back with the hand resting against his chest, my tears coming hard and fast, mixing with the cool rain. "I love you, Cooper Sinclair. I always will. But last night doesn't change anything. We're over. We have to be."

"You're wrong. Don't do this to us, Carys . . ."

I take a step back. Then another. "I have to because you never will. You're too good, Coop. You'd never hurt me, and that would end up wrecking us."

"Baby, please . . . We can work through this." Fat raindrops cling to those long lashes I love, and the heavens open up with a vengeance as the rain pounds down against the sand, making it hard to see.

I shake my head no because I can't force the words to come out. "Be safe, Cooper."

"Don't do this, Carys." He drops to his knees, and I know he'll never forgive me, and I'll never forget this moment.

It's already done.

I turn my back on him and walk away for the last time.

My heart shatters completely in the process.

"Carys . . ." I don't look back. "This isn't the end of us."

He's wrong.

Cooper Sinclair is the strongest man I know. But he can't fix this.

CARYS

In the month since Nattie and Brady's wedding, I've become really good at acting like I'm okay. Maybe I *should* have been a Broadway actress, after all. I've cracked a few times, but for the most part, I've done a pretty good job of hiding my pain.

I've noticed I now *eat* my feelings.

Not the best move, but I'm still running in the mornings, so it's not effecting my health or the size of my ass just yet.

I haven't heard from Cooper since that morning in the rain.

It's what I wanted. What I knew we needed. But I fucking hate myself a little more each day. Chloe, Daphne, her roommate, Maddie, and I have been trying to do regular brunch dates at the Busy Bee. Everyone's lives have gone a little crazy this summer, so it's been a good time each week to sit down and laugh at our problems, instead of crying over them.

With our food mostly eaten, we're just bullshitting at this point when Maddie looks at Chloe. "So, Chloe . . ." She waits dramatically for Chloe to stop running her finger through the syrup and look up. "Did Daphne tell you Watkins asked for your number?"

Oh holy shit. Watkins plays on the Philadelphia Kings team with Declan and Maddie's brother, Brandon.

"Um, no." Chloe eyes me with a smile. "But I'm pretty

sure that's a big old no. Our inner circles are already a little too incestuous, if you ask me. I will not be dating your brother's work wife, Mads."

I slap a hand over my face to hide the obnoxious laugh threatening to break free. "Oh my God. His work wife. That's great."

Chloe's phone vibrates against the table, and she silences it. "It's Nattie. I'll call her back. She probably just wants to make sure I'm going to watch the game. Like I haven't seen enough of our brothers playing football to last a lifetime." Brady and Aiden were both drafted to the Maryland Sentinels last spring.

The phone vibrates again, and Chloe blows out a breath, then slides her finger over it. "Nat, I'm out at breakfast with the girls. Can I call you after?" Whatever she just said has Chloe's face going terrifyingly white as she looks over at me. "Breathe, Nattie. I need you to breathe. Where's Brady?"

My heart skips a beat. "What's happening?"

Chloe ignores me and looks across the table toward Daphne.

"Well, call his coach, Nat. Call Murph." She sits quietly for a minute, refusing to meet my eyes. "Hang up the phone, Nat. I'm calling Sabrina to come over until we can get Brady. Give me a few minutes, and I'll call you back." She sucks in a sharp breath. "I love you too, Nat. Call his coach. I'll get Brina there as soon as I can."

She ends the call and refuses to meet my eyes.

It's as if a vacuum has sucked all the oxygen from the room, and I can't breathe.

"Chloe . . ." My body starts shaking as the tears pool in my eyes. This can't be . . . "What happened?" I push the question past my lips.

Chloe takes a handful of money from her purse and

334

throws it on the table. "We've got to go." She pushes me out of the booth, and I vaguely hear her say something to Daphne.

I turn around once we're outside the Busy Bee and grab hold of her arm with shaking hands and whisper, "What. Happened?" Terrified of her answer in a way nothing has ever scared me before in my life.

"Let's go to your mom's, Care Bear." Chloe looks over my head toward Daphne and Maddie, and I snap. My entire body is strung tight when I claw at her.

"Chloe," I beg through the tears that are pouring down my face. "Please, just tell me. I need to know." When Chloe doesn't answer, a guttural scream scratches up my throat. "Tell me!"

Chloe grabs my hands while Maddie and Daphne gather around me. "It's Cooper."

No.

It hurts to breathe.

"Is he dead?" The words are barely above a whisper as I shake uncontrollably.

Chloe tilts her head to the side, and a tear leaks down her cheek. "We don't know. His unit . . . They were captured."

There's a gut-wrenching cry ringing in my ears as my legs give out, and I fall to the sidewalk.

The sound is horrific.

Like a dying animal.

Someone make it stop.

Please.

It isn't until Chloe grabs my face in both of her hands and yells my name that I realize the sound is coming from me.

Time is a funny thing. It plays with your brain.

I'm not sure how long I've been sitting on Coach's couch, waiting for a breadcrumb of information from whoever called Coach with the news in the first place when it dawns on me I have my own people to call.

When I stand, Chloe stands with me, but I shake my head. Declan and Belles watch from the other side of the sectional couch.

"I can call my old roommate," I announce. "She's married to Linc. Or Cooper's team leader's wife. Either one of them might have more information."

Declan stands and presses his hand to the small of my back like his brother's done so many times. "Come on, Carys. Let's go to the other room."

We walk into the dining room, and I grab my cell phone from my pocket with shaking hands, then look up at Declan. "What if we don't want to hear what she says?"

"He's fine, Carys. Cooper's too fucking stubborn not to be fine. And I think you know that." He holds me against him, supporting my shaking body, and I call Emerson and hit the speakerphone so Declan can hear.

It rings three times, and I think I'm about to be sent to voice mail when Jack answers, "Carys. Jesus Christ, Carys, are you okay?"

The sobs I've been trying to control since we got here push from my lungs. "No. I'm not okay, Jack. Is Em okay? What does she know? So far, all anyone has told us is that they've been captured."

"We're at Jessie and Ford's house. Emmie just wanted to be with Jessie." The strain is audible in Jack's voice.

"Can I talk to one of them, Jack? I need to know if they

have more information than we do." I force my legs not to give out from beneath me as I push away thoughts of never seeing him again.

"Carys?" Jessie's hoarse voice comes through the phone.

"Jessie . . ." We both cry. "Please tell me someone gave you more than they're giving us."

"It's not good, Carys. I'm waiting to hear back from one of the guys who called me earlier. He wasn't supposed to, but he did. They're hurt, Carys."

Declan's fingers tighten against my shoulders, and I look up to see everyone standing in the doorway. Nattie and Brady must have gotten here at some point because she's standing in his arms, shaking, while Coach and Mom push into the room.

"What do you mean, Jessie? Who's hurt? What happened? Do they know where they are?" Everyone in the room starts talking at once, and I yell at them all, "Stop! I can't hear her." I move out of Declan's arms and pace the room. "What the hell's happening, Jess?"

"I'm not sure, but I got a call from one of the guys from a different team who I know. He said they're hurt but not captured. They couldn't find them in the rubble, so they thought . . . But they're not . . ." She tries to stay calm, but I don't think any of us are capable of that right now. "He wasn't sure of anything yet, Carys. But I can call you back the second I get word from him, or the official call. But I'll get it from him before that."

"I love you, Jess." A tear hits my phone, and I wipe my face.

"Love you too, Carys. Stay strong. That's what they'd want."

We end the call, and I turn to look at the entire family staring at me. "You heard what she said. According to her guy, they're not captured, but they might be hurt."

They look at me curiously until Coach gives me a strong hug. "Alright, everyone. We have no idea how long it's going to be before we know anything. So, we might as well all get comfortable."

The doorbell rings, and we all jump, then Mom rushes to answer it.

I hold my breath, praying it's not the military on the other side.

She opens it slowly and exhales loudly when a delivery man is there with a huge tray of food. Declan crosses the room and takes it from the man, then lays it down on the kitchen table. "It's from Max Kingston."

Max's family owns the Philadelphia Kings football team that Coach coaches and Declan plays for. He's also Daphne's boyfriend.

Coach walks into the room. "Max had the team jet fly the kids in from Maryland earlier, and he told me it's ours if we need it."

My heart swells at the kindness of this man, and I fight back more tears, then walk outside to sit in the backyard. I lower myself to sit with my feet in the pool and remember the first time I saw him here at a party the summer after he moved to Kroydon Hills.

He was gorgeous.

There were so many guys from our high school, tanned and toned and showing off, but he was all I could see.

I slowly swing my foot around in the water and picture his face appearing in the ripple.

It's amazing how nothing seems like it's important anymore. Nothing but him being safe and whole. I'd make a deal with the devil himself if it meant Cooper would be okay.

I'm not sure how long I'm alone before Annabelle joins

me. She lowers herself carefully to the cement, her pregnant belly throwing her balance off.

"How are you doing, Carys?"

I look at her. If you didn't know her, you'd think she had everything she ever wanted. A dream life. An easy life. But she had to fight her way there. Her parents died, leaving her as the sole guardian of her little brother. A crazy stalker tried to kill her and the twins while she was still pregnant with them. Declan and she have an incredible life, but she had to go through hell for it.

Was I not willing to fight for what I wanted?

Was I being weak when I thought I was being strong for both of us?

"Carys . . ." she pushes.

"Sorry, what?" I guess I got lost in my own thoughts. "Where are the kids, Belles?"

She runs a finger through my hair. "We gave in and got a nanny a while ago. I needed help, and she's amazing."

"That's good," I tell her absently.

"Carys . . . are you—"

The back door opens, and Murphy yells for us to come inside. "They found Cooper."

CARYS

When Belle and I stand to go back into the house, I realize the sun has already set, and I have no idea what time it is or how much time has passed since we got that first call this morning.

Time is like a shape-shifter.

It takes many forms.

In the year we were together, we were hardly ever in the same place, but it didn't matter. We had each other. I spent the days we were apart, counting down until I got to see him again, each day moving slower than the last. The more I wanted to see him, the slower the days seem to pass. But the time we spent together was over before it started.

Today is different. Time moves slowly around me now as I take each step but not slow enough. The fear of what Coach is being told from the other end of that phone is enough to cripple me in fear.

And somehow, Annabelle must sense it, too, because she laces her fingers through mine. "The fear is the worst part."

I try to push it aside and put one heavy foot in front of the other, but my feet feel like they're stuck in cement.

I'll never be able to unhear whatever we're about to be told, once it's been said, and I'm not ready to accept that yet.

We walk into the kitchen where everyone's gathered

341

around Coach, who has his phone pressed to his ear. Declan tucks Annabelle against him protectively holding her pregnant bump, and I catch myself wondering if depriving Cooper of that was as big a deal as I made it out to be.

Did I waste these past few months?

Were they the last few months . . . Jesus, I can't even finish the thought.

Whatever they're telling Coach causes his shoulders to sag, and tears stream down his face as he drops into the kitchen chair.

Nattie sobs hysterically next to him before Coach ends the call.

I don't know if I can do this.

I take a step back. I don't think I can be here for this.

Coach opens his mouth to speak, and it seems like minutes pass before the words slip past his lips. "They've got them. They're in bad shape. But they've got them."

My phone vibrates in my hand.

I've been holding it for hours in case Jessie calls, but I can't answer it now. Not when Coach is still speaking. Only I'm not sure I'm processing his words.

"What?"

Everyone's eyes swing to me in slow motion. "They're hurt, Carys." Coach repeats himself. "They're being taken to a military hospital in Germany."

"He's alive?" I whisper, scared to believe it.

Nattie turns with rage shining from her eyes. "Yes, he's alive! Of course, he's alive. What the hell is wrong with you, thinking he might not be?" she screams as if possessed.

Brady holds her in his arms, murmuring soft words the rest of us can't hear while she cries.

I look at the phone in my hand, then back up at Nat. "I

just got a message from Jessie." I look at her and watch the anger rising in her cheeks. "She's at her house with my roommate Emerson." My words are slow, as if stuck in molasses.

"What the hell is wrong with you, Carys?" Nat yells.

I get it. She needs someone to yell at right now.

Some way to exercise the fear that's been building to impossible heights all day.

That continues to threaten us with the idea that he's safe but hurt.

Cooper is *her* twin. They have a bond, one that everyone in this room knows and understands and expects.

And because I wouldn't let him tell our family when he wanted to, they have no idea what this man means to me.

I look at my phone again, then at Nattie before fear and regret claw their way up my throat. "I'm going to call Jessie to see if she heard anything we haven't." I step toward the door, but Mom stops me.

"Why don't you call from in here, honey? That way, we'll all know what's happening." She's looking at me in a funny way, like she doesn't understand what's going on with me, but then again, I guess she wouldn't.

I hit Jessie's name on the screen, then wait as it rings once before Theo answers, "Carys . . ."

"Theo." My voice shakes. "Why are you answering Jessie's phone?"

He ignores my confusion. "Carys . . . Did you hear about Cooper? Have they found him?"

Someone behind me says something, but I tune them out. "All we've been told is that they found the guys, but they're in bad shape." The phone shakes in my hands, and it takes me a moment to realize it's because I'm shaking.

"Two guys dressed in full uniform came to the house.

343

They were here to ask Jessie if she could come with them. They were about to go to Emerson's house before they realized she was already here."

I lean back against the wall for support.

"Why were they going to Em's?"

"It's Linc." I hear Emerson wail in the background and slide down the wall to my butt.

"Theo . . ."

"Linc's gone, Carys. He didn't make it. Jess is trying to get Em to calm down, and one of the dudes called a doctor to come over for her."

My eyes fly to my mom's when she sits down next to me, and I grab her hand and hold it close. "Can you let me know how she is? I wish I could be there for her, but . . ."

"We all know, CC. Let us know how Coop is when you find out, okay? I'll have Jess call you when she can."

The sound of Emerson's wails breaks me, and I end the call and throw my arms around my mom as I cry. "Linc's gone. He's dead. Emerson is eight-months pregnant, and he's dead. Oh my God, Mom."

My mom runs her hand over my hair as she holds me while we both cry for the sweet man with the southern twang who will never get to see his baby born.

Eventually, I realize everyone in the room is staring at us.

Waiting.

Mom and I climb to our feet, and Coach tugs us both into his strong arms.

"I need to go with you to Germany, Coach."

My mom runs her hand down my back. "Honey, I don't think we'll all be able to get into the hospital."

"Your mom's right, Carys. Only two of us are allowed in." He steps back with sad eyes, having no idea how badly I need to be there.

I guess it's time to strike the match and burn my world to the ground.

"I need to be one of those two people, Coach."

"I don't understand, Carys." His kind eyes hold an ache and confusion within them.

Nattie steps forward. "What the hell is going on, Carys? It needs to be me. Or it needs to be Declan. Why would you go with Dad?" She's trying to understand, but anger and accusation lace every word.

"Natalie. Stop." Declan's words are strong and clipped. "You're scared. We all are, but you need to stay here. Let Carys go with Dad." The room quiets, and my eyes lock with Declan's, offering him a silent thank-you.

"How long have you known?" It's the first time all day that I don't shake when I speak.

"Since he came up for the game last December." His red, tired eyes never waiver. "He'd want you to be the first person he sees."

And that's when I lose every ounce of strength I'd summoned. My entire body trembles as I fight back the tears.

"What the hell are you talking about, Declan?" Murphy's face is slowly morphing from ghostly white to a furious red. "Why would Carys be the first person Cooper would want to see?"

Sabrina gasps, and Mom's breath catches in her throat.

Time to watch it burn.

"Cooper and I have been together for over a year." I don't tell them about the past few months.

They don't get to know that.

Not yet.

Maybe not ever.

None of it seems important now.

"What?" Nattie shrieks. "No way. He'd never keep that from me."

"Nat," Declan warns, and her head spins like the possessed woman in *The Exorcist*.

"No, Dec. You don't get to *Nat* me." She looks back at me with venom dripping in her tone. "The two of you were together and kept it from us?"

"Yes." I take the anger that's pouring off her in violent, heavy waves and let it lap at my skin. I deserve it, and it won't change anything. "We wanted to figure things out for ourselves before we brought the whole family into it."

Nattie finally snaps.

She's still angry, but hurt and fear are overpowering her anger. "Why wouldn't he tell me?" Her voice shakes as she glares over at Declan. "He told you, but not me. Why?"

"I'm going to fucking kill him," Aiden growls, and without a thought, I slap him across the face.

"How dare you utter those words right now. You're the reason." I look between him and Nattie. "You both are. We knew you would get involved and have opinions. And we wanted time to figure us out without you." My voice cracks on the last word.

We wanted time, and I still threw us away.

"Did you figure it out?" my mother asks.

I soften my tone. "I love him." I look at Nattie but ignore my brother. "In Cooper's defense, he wanted to tell you all months ago. He didn't care what anyone thought. He didn't want to hide what we had. We were worth more than that to him."

"Then why didn't you?" she asks, angry again.

"Do you think we could table the discussion on all the ways I fucked up until after we come back from Germany?" I turn to Coach, ready to beg if I have to. "I'm getting on that plane with you, Coach, if I have to fly it myself."

"Go grab some clothes from your old room. I want to be out of here in thirty minutes."

I lit the match.

I watched it burn.

Now it's time to deal with the pain.

CARYS

It's late in the night by the time Declan drives Coach and me to the small private airport just outside the city, where the Kingston family's personal jet is fueled and waiting to take us to Saarbrücken Airport, which is about twenty-five miles from Landstuhl, the military hospital where Cooper and his team have been airlifted. Coach and Declan sit in the front seat of the SUV, talking quietly while I stare out the window behind them. Thinking.

We say goodbye to Declan, and Coach and I sit on opposite sides of the jet as we settle in for the eight-hour flight ahead of us. I take out the Kroydon football hoodie I stole from Cooper's old bedroom at Coach's house and slide it over my head, then tuck a blanket around my legs and close my eyes.

That's how Coach and I spend the first few hours of the long flight.

Quiet and on opposite sides of the jet.

At some point over the Atlantic Ocean, my phone vibrates, and my heart skips a beat at the incoming call from Jessie. I slide my thumb across the screen, and my voice cracks. "Jessie . . ."

"Carys, I just heard from Ford." She sounds as tired as I feel.

"How is he? What did he tell you?" Coach stands and crosses the aisle to sit next to me. He takes my empty hand in his, and I put the phone on speaker between us. "Jess, I put you on speaker. Cooper's dad is next to me."

"Ford couldn't tell me everything. He didn't have much time or much information, but he wanted me to hear it from him. Something happened, and an op went really wrong. A building they were in was blown up and collapsed. But there had to be more to it than that. Ford took two shots to his leg. The guys are all hurt. Cooper's in surgery now, and so is Trick. He didn't know everything, but Cooper was shot. He doesn't think Trick was. He told me to tell you that Coop was awake during the flight to Landstuhl, and he was asking about you."

Tears flood my eyes, imagining him hurt and asking for me.

Please let this man forgive me.

"Did he say anything else, Jess? Does he know anything else?" I'm grasping, desperate for information to cling to.

"No." She sighs, exhaustion no doubt trying to yank her under. "But I'll call you back as soon as I hear anything else."

"Okay. Coach and I are flying to Germany now. We should be there in a few hours." I swallow my fear and try to put on a brave face. "How's Emerson?"

"The doctor gave her a sedative earlier, and she went home with Jack and Theo. They didn't want her staying at her place alone, so they took her to your old house." Another piece of my heart breaks for my friend, and it's hard to believe there are any solid pieces left.

"Thank you, Jessie."

"Love you, Carys. Stay strong. That's what he needs from you now. Give him all the strength you have and call me after you see him. We'll cry together when no one else is around."

I look up at the ceiling of the jet and blow out a breath,

trying to control my emotions. "I'll call you as soon as I can, Jess." When I end the call, I look over at Coach, who's staring at me.

"Are you ready to talk to me, kiddo?" His soft voice relaxes me slightly, but I'm all too aware that this is Cooper's father and I just admitted to hiding something from him for a year.

"I love him, Coach. I have for years. But I knew I wasn't supposed to. I knew everyone would think it was wrong." I knew in my heart it wasn't, but everyone else would have tried to push us apart.

"Love is never wrong, Carys. It's complicated." He sighs. "Between the two of you, more so than most. But it's not wrong."

"It seems easy to say that now that it's out there, but that's not what it felt like in the beginning, Coach. We were already figuring things out long-distance. In the first six months, I don't think we spent an entire week together. It felt insurmountable as it was, and yet, falling in love with him—real love, not a teenage crush—that was the easiest thing I've ever done."

Coach's deep-blue eyes crinkle in the corners as he smiles a small, soft smile for the first time since we got the news earlier. "According to Declan, Cooper is very much in love with you too. He told Dec he'd give the rest of us up before he gave you up, if he had to."

I bite down on my bottom lip, holding back the sob that catches in my throat. "I messed it up though."

"I'm sure whatever happened can be fixed." Coach always exudes strength and confidence, just like his sons.

"I pushed him away. After my diagnosis, I was scared. I didn't want to force him into taking care of me for the rest of my life, knowing I wouldn't even be able to give him kids. Knowing that my life could be shorter than his." I wipe my eyes and shake my head. "It sounds so stupid after today. He begged me not to. He told me it wasn't the end of us."

Please, God, let him be right.

"My son is the strongest man I've ever known, Carys. He's going to pull through. He's going to be fine. And you're going to be by his side while he does it. Leave your brother and Nattie to me."

I lean my head on Coach's shoulder and offer up a silent prayer, begging for him to be right.

Hours later, we land in Germany and are taken directly to the hospital, where we wait for another two hours in a freezing-cold waiting room before the doctor finally comes out to talk to us.

"Mr. Sinclair?" a man in blue scrubs asks as he enters the waiting room.

Coach stands. "I'm Joe Sinclair."

The doctor joins us in the quiet corner of the room. "Petty Officer Sinclair is out of surgery and awake. He sustained a grade-three concussion from the blast as well as a gunshot wound to his abdomen. He lost a lot of blood but is doing as well as can be expected now. A nurse will be out shortly to take you back to see him."

The doctor stands as if to leave, and I jump in front of him.

"Is he going to be okay?" I move in front of him while I try to get control of my shaking hands. "You didn't say he'd be okay."

"The next twenty-four to seventy-two hours should tell us more." He nods his head and walks away.

Before I sit back down, a nurse in green scrubs with her hair back in a low bun joins Coach and me. "I can take you back to see Petty Officer Sinclair now."

"Thank you," we both say as we follow her down a stark white hall.

The hum of the fluorescent lighting gets louder with each smack of my sneakers against the dark linoleum floor.

I'm not sure how I got to this moment.

A year ago, I was in his arms. We were happy. He loved me.

And I suddenly fear what's waiting on the other side of that door.

Coach knocks once and steps in ahead of me while I linger in the hall, steadying my nerves before I follow him in. My breath wooshes out of me when I see Cooper in the hospital bed. Bruised, battered, cut, and stitched. His skin is a pale gray instead of his normal golden glow. There are stitches by his brow and a bandage taped around his wrist.

But he's here.

He's alive.

He's breathing.

The rest can be fixed.

We can be fixed.

Tears stream down my face as I walk around to the other side of his hospital bed and lay my hand on top of his before he violently yanks his away.

His eyes pinch as he looks at me in a way he's never done before. "What are you doing here?"

His voice is full of anger.

His eyes and the way he's said the words leave no room for discussion.

But I still don't move.

My feet are stuck in place as I stand, frozen, staring at him. "Cooper . . ."

He pushes a button on his bed, and within seconds, a different nurse appears in the doorway, and Cooper looks at me for just a moment before moving his attention to her.

"I want this woman removed from my approved list. I don't want her here." He looks at me one last time. "Get out."

The sensational conclusion to The Risks We Take Duet is available to read here.

ACKNOWLEDGMENTS

M ~ Thank you for your unwavering love and belief in me. Every hero has a piece of you in them.

To my very own Coop ~ I hope your namesake's book lived up to your expectations! Thank you for everything.

Hannah ~ Thank you for all of your notes, tweaks and all of our late night plotting sessions! And a big HUGE thank you for lending me Rook.

Savannah ~ Thank you for every you do.

Heather ~ I'm so incredibly thankful that you helped me with this book.

Vicki ~ I am so grateful to have you in my corner! Cheers to full cups.

Sarah ~ Thank you so much for putting up with me.

To my Betas ~ Nichole, Hannah, Meagan, Shawna & Heather. Thank you for helping me make Coop & Carys everything they deserved to be. I appreciate each and every one of you!

My Street Team, Kelly, Shawna, Vicki, Ashley, Heather, Oriana, Shannon, Nichole, Nicole, Hannah, Meghan, Amy,

Christy, Adanna, Jennifer, Lissete, Poppy, Jacqueline, Laura, Kathleen, Diane, Jenna, Keeza, Carissa, Kat, Kira, Kristina, Terri, Javelyn, Morgan, Victoria, Jackie, Andrea, Marni ~ Thank you, ladies, for loving these characters and this world. Our group is my safe place, and I'm so thankful for every one of you in it. Family Meetings Rock!

My editors, Jess & Dena. You both take such good care of my words. Thank you for pushing me harder, and making me better.

Gemma – Thanks for giving it that finishing touch.

Shannon ~ you are so talented! Thank you for bringing these covers to life.

To all of the Indie authors out there who have helped me along the way – you are amazing! This community is so incredibly supportive, and I am so lucky to be a part of it!

Thank you to all of the bloggers who took the time to read, review, and promote Changing The Game.

And finally, the biggest thank you to you, the reader. I hope you enjoyed reading Cooper & Carys as much as I loved being lost in their world.

ABOUT THE AUTHOR

Bella Matthews is a Jersey girl at heart. She is married to her very own Alpha Male and raising three little ones. You can typically find her running from one sporting event to another. When she is home, she is usually hiding in her home office with the only other female in her house, her rescue dog Tinker Bell by her side. She likes to write swoon-worthy heroes and sassy, smart heroines with a healthy dose of laughter and all the feels.

STAY CONNECTED

Amazon Author Page: https://amzn.to/2UWU7Xs
Facebook Page: https://www.facebook.com/bella.
matthews.3511
Reader Group: https://www.facebook.com/
groups/599671387345008/
Instagram: https://www.instagram.com/bella.matthews.
author/
Bookbub: https://www.bookbub.com/authors/bella-
matthews
Goodreads: https://www.goodreads.com/.../show/
20795160.Bella_Matthews
TikTok: https://vm.tiktok.com/ZMdfNfbQD/
Newsletter: https://bit.ly/BMNLsingups
Patreon: https://www.patreon.com/BellaMatthews

ALSO BY BELLA MATTHEWS

Kings of Kroydon Hills

All In

More Than A Game

Always Earned, Never Given

Under Pressure

Restless Kings

Rise of the King

Broken King

Fallen King

The Risks We Take Duet

Worth the Risk

Worth the Fight

Made in the USA
Las Vegas, NV
01 April 2024

88113773R00215